The Euclidian: The Unforeseen Alliance

Jay Cannon

The Euclidian: The Unforeseen Alliance

Copyright © 2012 Jay Cannon (JC)

For more information contact the author at EuclidianBook@gmail.com.
First edition: December 2012
Cover illustration by Igor Kieryluk
Editing by Joel David Palmer
Book design and formatting by Cheryl Perez

For my sons Davon Joharri and Dakar Jorré and all those who dare to chase their dreams.

PROLOGUE

The Euclidians arrive on Earth and begin stripping it of its resources. Earth's defenses have been rendered ineffective with the removal of all military vehicles, ships, nuclear weapons, and personnel. The XO of the *Andrea* in his greed decides to overthrow the captain, while Morgan and Pico gain unexpected allies.

CHAPTER I

The Awakening

"Somebody stop the pain…the pain. I can't stand it anymore. Where am I? HELLO! Can anybody hear me? Please help me," she cried out, to no avail. She was in the midst of an overwhelming darkness. *Am I blind or have they shoved me into some dark pit?* "Oh, the pain," she cried again. *I know I'm not dead because the pain is too intense. But how can I be alive when my body is in so much pain?* She whimpered uncontrollably, not understanding her condition or her fate. She let out a low groan and passed out. Hours passed before she came to. She attempted to take an inventory of her surroundings, but her senses were fractured. She couldn't see anything and didn't know why. The only sound that shared the darkness with her was that of her own breathing. *There is that familiar smell again, something recent, but what is its origin?*

She felt around but there was only the damp floor. She tried to get up, but the pain prevented her and she passed out again.

She awoke. How long had she been lying there? She felt hungry, but this was not her focus. Her pain was the distraction she could not ignore. She tried to wipe her face, embarrassed by her beslobbered state.

I've soiled myself, I've wet myself, my nose is running and I can't stop crying. I must be bleeding as well, considering how badly I hurt. I can't possibly live much longer with all this loss of fluid. Is this how I die? Is this how it ends? In the dark. A million light years from home. My fate unknown by anyone I know. I wanted my life to make a difference. I wanted to make life better for my people, but now I'm moribund and my life will probably end. A career of insignificance. She whimpered uncontrollably then once more passed out.

She came to again. The pain had subsided a bit, partially due to the numbness that had engulfed the left side of her body. She looked around and again tried to see something, anything. But there was nothing to see except the darkness. She tried to remember how she had got there, but didn't have a clue.

The last thing I remember was being with asshole, Cobalt. Wang ba dan! Once again I give myself to a man and he screws me over. Obviously even alien men enjoy abusing me.

Li Xiao thought back to happier times during her childhood. She would spend all day in the rice fields with her parents on her father's farm outside of Nanjing. In the beginning she would ride in a pouch on her mother's back. As she grew older she worked beside her mother to tend the fields. Her mother's mother also lived with them. Her mother's father and father's parents had been killed during the Eight Years' War of Resistance. Her parents did not want the farming life for their daughter. They felt she was a bright child with a future and when Li Xiao became a teenager they sent her to her aunt and uncle's house in Beijing to go to a private school with her cousins, Ema and Maya.

At school, Li Xiao excelled in languages. She liked the new sounds she could make with her mouth. She wanted to find a job where she could use this talent. Maybe she could even prevent another occupation of their land. She decided she would be a diplomat and see the world, possibly help change the world. Evenings and weekends she practiced her language skills by working as a guide at the Forbidden City and by giving private tours of the Great Wall and sites around it. Upon graduating from college, she joined the military as a way to give back to her country and to learn self-defense skills. After basic training, she spent every day continuing to learn small arms, sniper, and martial arts techniques.

Li Xiao was assigned to a general who worked with the American military. She worked as his translator and assistant bodyguard, and spent a great deal of time learning how to protect him, though there was little danger of him being attacked. She was more in danger from the foreign officers and diplomats the general met with. They would often get drunk after all-day meetings and then come on to her. When going to the bathroom, Li Xiao found herself using the Adrien stall maneuver, with one foot on the floor and the other against the stall door to keep the drunks from bursting in on her. She had learned that maneuver from Adrien, an American friend who worked for the American military as a translator. She had met Adrien in a bar in Amsterdam where the women's restrooms were less than ideal. Adrien warned Li Xiao about men bursting into the stalls and taught Li Xiao her technique.

Li Xiao was resigned to the fact that fending off drunken diplomats was probably going to be her destiny, until one fateful evening while she was guarding the general and a Chinese diplomat by herself. They were leaving a bar in the Soi Cowboy district of Bangkok when three men approached, looking to rob them. The men saw that the general and diplomat were drunk and viewed Li Xiao, as a woman, to be of little consequence. They pulled knives on the three and demanded money. When Li Xiao protested, one of the men swung his knife at her and laughed. Li Xiao backed away and took a karate stance.

"You want to dance, little lady?" laughed the assailant. "How about I put a dog collar around your neck and make you my bitch for the rest of the night? I'm sure my friends would enjoy partying with you."

"How about you leave before I make you my bitch?" Li Xiao replied. "Otherwise, the only party you three will be attending tonight will be in a hospital emergency room."

"Just let them have our money so they go away," the diplomat protested.

"Too late for that," one of the assailants replied. "Cutesy here wants to dance and I'm going to make her dance on the end of my knife."

The man smirked and then jabbed his knife at Li Xiao. She shifted to the left, thrust out to break his right elbow, and shoved his knife into his thigh. She then spun to her right to engage one of the other men coming toward her. She grabbed him by the wrist, pulled him forward, and chopped him across the throat. He went down gasping for air, and the third man ran off. The general and diplomat stood there looking at her, stunned.

The next day during breakfast, the general asked Li Xiao if she would be interested in leaving the army to become the diplomat's bodyguard.

"What about my military obligation?" she asked.

Don't worry about that," replied the general. "The army will gladly accept your resignation. After all, being a translator and bodyguard to the Chinese ambassador to the United States is still serving your country."

Li Xiao was surprised, excited, and honored at the offer. "How can I possibly say no?"

"Then it's done. I'll start the paperwork once we return to Beijing."

"Li Xiao," said the ambassador, "I am delighted you have accepted this position. When you saved my life last night I knew you were someone I wanted to add to my team." He extended his hand to her. "Welcome aboard."

Her assignment was in Washington D.C., where she could perfect her English. She loved living there. She had a beautiful little apartment with a view of the capital building. She got to attend diplomatic balls, stay in nice hotels during trips across America, and to meet the president of the United States. She spent most mornings jogging around the National Mall and practicing her martial arts skills.

Her assignment, though, soon took a negative turn when she found it required her to be a pawn in diplomatic negotiations, which included being more than friendly to foreign diplomats. When she protested, the ambassador lectured her about the obligations of her position and her patriotic duty. If she refused to support her boss, she risked being sent back to Beijing in disgrace.

She reluctantly agreed to entertain foreign diplomats as ordered. In return she was showered with lavish gifts, to which she quickly became accustomed. A few months later, after helping to complete a negotiation to the benefit of China, she was introduced to the countryman she had helped in the negotiation, the Chinese ambassador to the United Nations. He was slated to become the Secretary General of the U.N. and wanted her to be his attaché and part-time lover during times when his wife was away. He assured her she would not have to sleep with anyone else.

"Miss Li Xiao, this will be a very important position," the U.N. ambassador stated. "You will assist me with all of my foreign negotiations, attend diplomatic social events, and travel with me across the globe. I know you have a passion for languages. At the U.N. you will have the opportunity to learn and practice almost any language you desire."

"Sounds appealing, but New York can be an expensive place to live," she replied.

"Very true, but don't worry. I have an extremely generous budget and I assure you that you won't want for anything while under my care."

Li Xiao smiled. "Then how can I possibly say no?"

A few weeks later she was staying in a beautiful apartment on the upper eastside of Manhattan. The number of diplomatic events she attended, her foreign travel, and introductions to foreign dignitaries increased enormously. She couldn't believe her luck, to finally get the dream job she had always hoped for. She didn't like sleeping with her boss, but felt it was part of her diplomatic duty. Anyway, she never had time for a real relationship.

A year and a half later, that all changed when she was replaced by a younger, prettier version of herself and given a menial job with a lot fewer perks. She could no longer afford her posh apartment.

But before moving out, she was contacted out of the blue by a man she thought was a Chinese agent. He offered to get her job back in return for information about any nuclear weapons that might be a threat to China.

"In addition to getting your job back," the agent stated, "I can make sure that new floozy is made to scrub toilets while you become a very wealthy woman."

"Well, how can I possible say no to that offer?" replied Li Xiao with a smile.

Li Xiao later found out her benefactor was Cobalt, an alien from another planet who recruited spies to gather intelligence on planets before they were to be attacked. That's when she decided to see if she could hitch a ride on Cobalt's spaceship. *Learning Earth languages is one thing, but to learn intergalactic languages would be truly wonderful.*

However, just when she thought things were going well, Cobalt shot her with some sort of beam from a handgun and the next thing she knew she was waking up in impenetrable darkness.

Her painful left arm was now numb. Her right arm, while still sore, she could move. She pushed along the floor to see what she could feel. The floor was sticky as if some fluid had dried on it. She thought it might be her own blood, but she smelled it and recognized the Laldexian Mind Bender cocktail that Cobalt had given her. She could also feel bits of glass.

Cobalt must have come to visit me, seen my condition, and dropped the beverage glass. She began to whimper again, but soon composed herself.

I've got to try to move. Try to get up. Maybe I can get out of here somehow.

She twisted her body around to see if she could feel a wall or furniture she could use to pull herself up. She stretched her arm behind her and it hit a wall that moved slightly. The wall had a familiar feel and sound to it. *It couldn't be!* She reached under the wall and grabbed the edge of a door. Recognizing where she must be, she started to cry. She was in her shower stall at home. She had no idea what that meant, but knew she had to get to a phone before she died in there.

Li Xiao grabbed the edge of the shower with her right arm and pulled herself out of the shower toward the bathroom door. It seemed to take an eternity to reach the door. She reached for the handle, twisted it down, and pulled the door open. Peering into the adjoining room, she confirmed it was indeed her bedroom by the familiar clock on the nightstand. The only thing left to do was reach her phone and call 911. Slowly Li Xiao dragged herself across her floor, feeling pain in every movement. Her muscles ached, breathing was difficult, and she struggled to keep her senses about her. There were moments when she wasn't sure where she was anymore. Maybe her disorientation was due to a drug-induced delirium.

She found herself losing consciousness, but fought through it. After what seemed like hours of clawing and crying she yanked the phone from the nightstand, poked at the keypad, and rambled incoherently at the voice that answered. In a daze, she went from darkness to looking up at flickers of light. She was on a gurney, being pushed down the hallway of an emergency ward as doctors worked on her. In her stupor she saw Cobalt smiling down at her.

"Don't worry, Xiao, you're going to pull through this," he said.

"Yeah, and when I do I'm going to pull your heart from your chest," she responded.

A doctor leaned close to Li Xiao's mouth. "Did you say something?" But she had drifted into unconsciousness.

A thorough examination determined that Li Xiao had suffered a dislocated left shoulder, cracked ribs, a bruised hip, two twisted ankles, lacerated lips, and a concussion. She lay medicated in her hospital bed for several weeks, healing from her injuries. *I've been given a second chance here and I don't want to waste it. Once I'm out of this hospital I'm going to focus on making a positive difference for my people.*

When Li Xiao was finally released, a nurse wheeled her to the front door of the hospital where she caught a cab for home. She arrived limping, but alive. The first thing on her mind was investigating her shower. With the lights on she noticed the remains of a broken glass and a Jimmy Choo handbag with Euro bills spilling out of it.

She sat on her bed and dumped out the money to count it: 20 million Euros. Among the bundles of bills she found some sort of device. It was like a Windows phone, but square and about 13 centimeters on a side. There was a blank display window in the middle, buttons on the corners and along the sides, and bars centered at the top and bottom of the device. There was a glowing line on one edge that she decided was the bottom of the device. She turned it over and looked it up and down. She figured that it must have come from Cobalt's ship. He had left her a gift.

She finally decided to see what it would do. One by one, she pushed each of the buttons until something happened. Pushing the top right button turned the device on. The screen showed the room where she was sitting. She slid her finger across the screen and the image moved across her apartment and then out the building. She used her finger to slide the display back into her room. She pinched the screen with her fingers and the image moved above her. When she spread her fingers across the screen she saw into the apartment below hers. Twisting her fingers around the screen turned the image around, but the view only looked down.

Li Xiao wanted the display to pan around the room. She tried moving her fingers around the screen in different ways with no results. She rested her hands on the screen to think and idly spun her fingers around: the viewing angle changed. *How clever!*

She played around with different viewing angles until she had the operation perfected. She was amazed she could see the back of her own head. She even looked inside her head, which she found a little creepy. Somehow the device could show images even where there was no light.

She tried to find her parents' house outside Nanjing, China, pinching the screen until the image showed Earth from space, then sliding her finger sideways and down until she was over her hometown. She then spread her fingers across the screen until she was over her parents' house and then inside. Her family was preparing for evening tea. She adjusted the display so she could see the entire room. Her father was sitting at the table while her mother and grandmother set the table.

She watched for a while, amazed that she could see them. She then started pressing the device's other buttons to see what they would do. She pressed the bar at the top and now she could hear them speaking. She tried to speak to them but they didn't hear her. She pressed the top left button and the screen displayed a list of items using characters she did not recognize. She pressed the button again and the list was cleared.

Li Xiao pressed a button on the left and a glowing outline appeared around her mother. Then the screen did something strange. It started following her mother around as she moved. She moved the screen and it stopped following her. Her grandmother walked by and she pressed the button again and her grandmother was outlined and the screen followed her. She pressed a button on the right that was similar to the button on the left and the screen switched to her mother. Pressing the button again toggled between the two women. Pressing the button on the left removed the outline from the person at the center of the screen and the screen stopped following her.

She pressed the bottom-left button and it didn't seem to do anything. She pressed the lower bar and suddenly fell onto her parents' table, knocking the teapot, cups, and plates to the floor. Her parents and grandmother looked at her in amazement.

"Where did you come from, Li Xiao?" asked her father. "You seemed to fall from the ceiling."

"I just jumped into the room to surprise you and lost my footing," she lied, hoping they would believe her.

They did not quite understand her explanation, but took her at her word. She apologized for the distraction, put the device in her pocket, and helped them clean up. While her sudden appearance was disturbing, they were happy to see her and Li Xiao was happy to visit home after being away for such a long while. For a long time she spoke with her parents, trying to understand how life was for them. For the most part her family was happy. The government provided the security and health care they needed. They had plenty of money to sustain them. They were concerned at the way some people were arrested or even killed for speaking out against the government. Her parents felt governments should embrace criticism as a way to improve themselves.

Li Xiao had a final cup of tea with her family, hugged them all, walked out the door, and beamed back to her apartment. She adjusted the location so she would fall gently upon her bed. She spent the next couple of days playing with the device, but there were still some features she did not understand.

CHAPTER 2

The Tammarians

Tammaria was a planet in the Storm planetary system. It was used as an outpost for the Euclidian military, which had several bases there. The planet had one well-known humanoid species. The Tammarians were primitive hunter-gatherers that lived in tribes. They had yet to advance beyond using stone tools. They lived in small huts made from the surrounding vegetation.

For the most part, the Euclidians left the planet intact. The only thing they harvested was the famous abbig fruit, from which Tammarian grog was made. The grog was an alcoholic beverage that the Tammarians had learned to make eons ago, and they taught the Euclidians how to make it. In return, the Euclidians taught the Tammarians how to grow abbig more efficiently and increase its yield. In that way they felt they had compensated the Tammarians for the fruit that they took every year.

Abbig was not very tasty on its own, but the grog was quite a delicacy. A person drinking this elixir experienced an immediate euphoria, which lasted about 30 minutes and produced no ill side effects. The feeling the grog gave individuals was not inebriation or lethargy, but exhilaration. It was also an aphrodisiac. It cured depression, pessimism, and sadness. Importantly, it worked on all species, which made it very valuable.

The Euclidians held exclusive rights to the planet and therefore the fruit. They kept all others away from the planet. Chaell was the captain of the Euclidian resource ship *Andrea* that was visiting Tammaria in between missions. Chaell was surprised when one of his scouts captured an Alpha male wandering around Tammaria while his ship was there to pick up several tons of recently harvested abbig.

"So what are you doing here?" Chaell asked the Alpha.

"I was left behind when my ship left in haste," he replied. "I was on my own in a remote region and when I returned to our encampment everyone was gone. I can only assume they were trying to avoid being seen by your ship."

"That sounds a bit flimsy. You couldn't use your communicator to call your ship?"

"We don't have the fancy ones you Euclidians use. The ship was out of range by the time I realized I was left behind."

"Is anyone else from your ship on the planet?"

"Not that I have seen."

"Why don't I believe you? How about I let my guys work you over a bit until you are ready to tell me everything you know?"

"How about you shove a Tammarian beetle up your nose?"

"You can be insolent if you want, but we have ways of getting the truth out of you."

"Go ahead. I'm sure your government would be happy to hear how you treated me."

The Euclidian treaty with the Alphas forbade their mistreatment. Though Captain Shisal did not care for the Alphas, he did not want to risk crossing the government over one supposedly lost individual.

"Relax, we're just having a friendly conversation. No reason to start making threats. Just make yourself comfortable here in this cabin and I'll have my crew bring you some food. For security reasons I can't have you wandering around the ship. We have Deltas onboard and they might not treat you very kindly."

"So transport me back to Euclidia."

"No reason to waste valuable energy. We'll be back on Euclidia before you know it. I'll hand you over to the authorities once we return. I'm sure they will want to hear your story."

"There's no reason to make me wait."

"There's no reason to accommodate you either." Captain Shisal stood and left the Alpha in his quarters.

Initially, Tammaria had been occupied by the Alphas, who used the planet as a launching point for a raid on Euclidia. After the Euclidians repelled the Alpha attack, they systematically cleansed each planet in their system of any Alpha presence and claimed those planets for themselves.

The Euclidians were only recently aware that there was a second race of humanoid creatures on Tammaria, the Magi. They lived in caves in a sparsely populated region, and used their persuasive powers over the other Tammarian species to prevent knowledge of their presence from spreading.

The Magi were short people, only about 160 centimeters. Living in the dark had caused their eyes to evolve to permit them to see well in low light conditions. This ability was augmented by their phosphorescent blue eyes, which emitted light and permitted them to see in the darkest parts of their caves.

The radiation from their eyes had a strange effect when directed at the eyes of other humanoid creatures. It increased their susceptibility to suggestion. The Alphas discovered the Magi when hiding in their caves to avoid the Euclidians, and noticed their ability to influence people while watching the Magi interact with Tammarians and Euclidians. The Magi could convince Tammarians to share their fruit and cloth with them.

The Alphas decided to exploit the Magi's power for their own benefit. Kenyon Filo, an Alpha commander, devised a plan to use the Magi for revenge on the Euclidians for destroying the Alpha's home planet. Filo used a cloaked ship to visit the Magi undetected to start the execution of his plan. He placed his ship in orbit around Tammaria and beamed down with a contingent to converse with the Magi. Unfortunately, one of his crewmembers got captured.

Commander Filo had never been to the Magi caves so he took his aide, Lieutenant Lephi Swantik. Swantik had made several visits to the caves and he prepped Filo about what to expect based on his experiences.

"Commander," Lephi began, "the Magi caves are an enormous labyrinth. They are dark and have numerous, difficult to navigate pathways that can only be learned by traversing them, as there are no maps. Each cave, path, cavern, even large stones, has a name, which the Magi use to navigate. They have no written language, so there are no signs. They just memorize the name for everything."

"So how are we supposed to find our way around once we get inside?" asked Commander Filo.

"I found a guide to take us through the exterior caves and into the central cavern, which hosts the seat of their government. She speaks Euclidian from conversing with the ones that are based here. She is one of those I saw charming the Euclidian soldiers with their eyes."

"How do we protect ourselves against their charms?"

"The lenses I placed in our goggles should help protect us. Just in case, we must also be careful not to simultaneously look into a Magi's eyes."

"I hope you're right, Lephi. A lot is riding on this. So where do we meet our guide?"

"Inside the cave entrance ahead of us. We just need to climb a few more meters and we will be there."

"I don't see anything."

"The entrance is situated at an angle. The Magi modified all of the entrances to obscure them from view unless you are right on top of one. We're almost there. Let me just catch my breath."

"Me too. I'm not used to this kind of exercise. How will we convince them to help us?"

"We have to let them think that we are looking to improve relations with our Euclidian friends. They are not likely to help us do anything that might hurt the Euclidians. Since they don't need money and have plenty of resources, we'll just have to converse with them to understand what might interest them."

"Doesn't sound very hopeful, but considering the enormous potential we had better pursue this possibility."

"Let's get going. She's probably waiting for us."

"If they don't have technology, how do they tell what time it is?"

"They use the level of a water pool which reacts to the position of their sun to determine the start of the day. They then split the day into one hundred equal periods using water clocks. At the beginning of each period they send a signal throughout the caves to synchronize the time. It's not real precise, but it works well enough for their culture."

"Yeah, that is a bit crude. Are we there yet? I may need another break."

"As a matter of fact we are. Just look to your left behind this boulder." Lephi pointed to the cave entrance.

"My goodness. I never would have noticed that."

"Let's go in and see if she is there."

***

"Lephi, how am I supposed to see in here?" asked Commander Filo after entering a few meters into the cave.

"Put on your goggles. They will permit you to see in the dark. They project an invisible wave that reflects off of objects and back into the goggles as images. We can't use light in here as it would hurt the eyes of the Magi and keep them from interacting with us. The goggles also have those special lenses I told you about."

"This is marvelous! Look at all the activity. It's as if we walked into some fairytale world."

Commander Filo took a moment to soak it all in. There were flying creatures of all sizes soaring throughout the cave. Lizard-like creatures climbed the walls. Luminescent water bubbled up from odd places to add a bit of light to dark areas. Water ran through the cavern carrying food that was eaten by the Magi. Some Magi were tending small plots of different types of moss that were distributed and eaten by villagers throughout the cave system.

"Are the Magi the large creatures darting about, with the blue glowing eyes?"

"Yes."

"How do we possibly find your contact in this mass of similar bodies?"

"She said to wait near the entrance of the cave by this blue gurgling water."

A Magi appeared out of the darkness. "Hello, Lephi, who is your friend?"

"Hi, Yoyo, this is Commander Filo."

"Hello, Commander Filo, I am Yoyo Snarky. I will be your guide during your visit."

"Pleased to meet you, Yoyo. I'm surprised you speak Euclidian."

"I learned it from meeting with Euclidians from time to time."

"You are obviously pretty smart. I'm looking forward to visiting this home of yours," replied Filo, looking at her in amazement. She was a few centimeters shorter than him and wore dark clothing that clung to her body. She had long, light hair tied behind her back. He could not see much of her face except her glowing eyes.

"It can be very difficult to navigate this place. These glowing yellow rings on my sleeves will make it easier for you to keep track of me. If for some reason you lose sight of me, just yell out my name and I will be sure to stop and find you."

"That's a great idea, Yoyo," replied Lephi. "The last time I was here you promised to introduce me to your chief so I could get her input on a business venture."

"And so I shall," responded Yoyo. "Follow me and I will take you there now. Watch your heads. Some of the passageways may be a little low for you two."

The three started off on their journey, which turned out to be a long one. They went through several kilometers of passageways, caves, and huge caverns. Other Magi darted in and out between them as the two Alphas struggled to keep up with Yoyo.

"Yoyo, can we stop for a moment?" asked Commander Filo.

"Certainly," she responded. "There are some flat rocks over there where we can rest."

"Thanks. I certainly needed this," said Filo as he sat down.

"Where can we relieve ourselves?" asked Lephi.

"Each cave has an area with a discharge pool. There is one just over there," Yoyo said, pointing to a corner of the cave they had entered. "You relieve yourself in the pool and the enzymes in the water neutralize the waste. The pools are continually replenished to maintain their effectiveness. You can clean your hands and other body parts in the pool as well."

"Thanks, Yoyo. I'll be right back."

"I think I'll join you, Lephi," said Filo.

"I'll wait here," said Yoyo.

"Lephi," said Filo, "do you think she is giving us the run around? We've been walking for over an hour."

"I don't see why she would. She has nothing to gain by doing so and nothing to fear from us."

"Okay, I'll be a bit more patient. It's not like we could find our way out if she decided to abandon us. I certainly don't remember the way and our communicators don't seem to be working inside these caves."

The two finished relieving themselves and returned to the flat rocks.

"Yoyo," said Lephi, "I had no idea this place was so enormous and beautiful. It would be interesting to be able to see it with your eyes."

"I have to say, I enjoy all of the different lights, colors, and sounds in the midst of the darkness," replied Yoyo. "Outside the caves one can certainly see everything more easily, but it doesn't have the same magic as this place."

"Yoyo, what is your main job here?" asked Commander Filo.

"I mainly work as a liaison between my people and the Tammarians and Euclidians, managing the exchange of goods. I also work with the food producers to make variations of our grog. I enjoy the drink well enough, but I enjoy the effect it has on others much more. So I spend a lot of time trying to perfect my version of the grog recipe."

"Very interesting," said Filo. "Tell me, what do you know about the Euclidians?"

"They are an extraterrestrial species that visits our planet from a planet far from here."

"How does a cave dweller know so much?"

"I'm curious, and when they arrived I spent time getting to know them."

"How would you like to see the planet where they come from, and many other places?"

"I like the idea, but you will have to speak to our chieftain about that."

"So let's go see her."

"No problem. I'll take you to her. We're just a few minutes away."

The three left their seats and proceeded through another series of caves and passageways until they entered an enormous cavern that was illuminated by colorful phosphorescent material that covered its walls. In the center was a large crystal palace. A large arched entryway at the front of the building was full of traffic from visitors entering and leaving the facility.

"This is where our chieftain lives," said Yoyo. "I will introduce you to her and you can negotiate what you need."

"Does she speak Euclidian?" asked Commander Filo.

"No, she doesn't."

"How about Tammarian?"

"Of course."

"Good. Why are so many people going in and out of the place?"

"Our chieftain has collected artifacts over the years and the palace has become a museum of sorts that attracts lots of visitors. Come with me and I'll take you inside."

They walked into the palace, amazed by its grandeur. Commander Filo and Lephi were enthralled to see all the items in the interior. There were wide walkways on both sides of the entrance, separated by display areas in the middle and along each wall. Yoyo gave a brief description of the items as they passed.

"On this side are skeletons from various cave animals. On the other side are early tools that were found inside and outside the caves. Here we have early pottery and clothing made from various animal skins. I don't know the words the Euclidians use to name them. Here we have the various kinds of vegetation that are found in our caves. Those are luminescent minerals and liquids that we use to light some of the areas in our caves, including this palace."

"Why isn't the pool at the end lit up? Has the chemical worn out?" asked Lephi.

"Not at all. The water contains a mineral that sparkles when you run your hands through it. Go ahead, try it," urged Yoyo.

The Alphas ran their hands through the water and watched as sparkles appeared around their fingers.

"This is quite clever," said Commander Filo.

"Watch this," said Yoyo. She threw a handful of water into the air and against the nearby wall where it lit up like miniature fireworks. The water sparkled all along the wall and down to the floor where it soon evaporated.

"My kids would have loved to play with this," said Commander Filo.

"You can take some home if you like," replied Yoyo.

"That won't be necessary. My children died when the Euclidians attacked my planet."

"That's unfortunate. The Euclidians don't seem like violent people to me, but I've had little interaction with them."

"Trust me, they are very violent people."

"I'll have to take your word for it. Let's continue on," suggested Yoyo.

They moved along a corridor and into another open area that was less dimly lit.

"Here, along the entire length of the wall on both sides, are the robes, sandals, orbs, necklaces, and headgear of our chieftains, dating back thousands of years. You can see how our culture and artistry has changed over the years."

"I'm surprised that nothing has been destroyed or stolen," said Lephi.

"Somehow I think we have just been lucky. No one has ever tried to steal anything that I'm aware of. In general, our people are very honest. Just in case, the Magi in the blue robes help to guard the place. To help preserve the items, we keep it dry in this chamber and coat the clothing with a preservative. After all that, the older items have still become a bit ragged. Let's continue up the stairs to the receiving area."

"How is this place so big when it seems so small from the outside?" asked Commander Filo.

"It's built into the cave wall," responded Yoyo. "It goes on for a ways inside the cave wall and comes out the other side into another large cavern."

"How clever!" said Commander Filo.

"Clever indeed!" agreed Lephi.

They reached the top of the stairs where there was a small reception area with chairs along the walls. Several Magi carrying spears guarded a door.

"I believe this is the first time I have seen weapons here," said Commander Filo.

"Yes, this is the entry to the chieftain's quarters. While we have never had attacks here in the past, we don't take any chances. No one else here carries weapons. We don't war with each other and outsiders would have a difficult time navigating the caves to get here, so weapons aren't really necessary. In addition, we have so many deterrents made from the minerals and liquids in the caves that invaders would find it too costly to attack us to get what little we have in here. Hold on, I need to let the guards know that you are here to see the chieftain. I'll be right with you."

Yoyo spoke to one of the guards in her language and then disappeared through the door, returning a few minutes later.

"Our chieftain can meet with you in two periods. In the meantime I can take you through the rest of the palace on the lower floor and then out for some food. By the time we return our chieftain should be ready to meet with you."

"That sounds like a grand idea," replied Lephi. "Go ahead and lead the way."

Yoyo headed down the stairs and Commander Filo and Lephi followed after her.

***

The Alphans were surprised at how much they enjoyed the food and drink that Yoyo found for them. She even treated them to her own brand of Tammarian grog, which they thoroughly enjoyed.

"Yoyo, you make the most amazing Tammarian grog that I have ever tasted, and I have tasted many. I could drink yours all day," said Lephi.

"Then you would be in no shape to see our chieftain," replied Yoyo. "We should probably be heading back."

Yoyo led them back to the reception area then disappeared through the door to the chieftain's chambers.

Yoyo stuck her head back through the door. "She'll see us now."

The Alphas entered the door and were surprised to see the ornate nature of the hall. The floor was covered in tapestry. Chandeliers lit by luminescent balls hung from the ceiling. The walls were covered in various types of art. The baseboards were made of a shimmering, gold-colored material. At the end of the hall were large doors with more guards.

They passed through the door into a large room full of activity. There were people everywhere, chatting with each other. These were village chiefs, elders, and dignitaries carrying on their business. The three stood for a moment to take it all in. Yoyo described the people waiting to speak to the chieftain.

"The three people in the blue gowns are chiefs from the Wochowo region discussing distribution of their new fungus crops to the other regions. The two in loincloths are Tammarians looking to barter for some of our Keegon fish. We served them some at a state dinner and now they can't get enough of it. Behind them is a group of construction planners, working on an extension of our cave system."

"It sounds like they are arguing," said Lephi.

"Yes, there are concerns that the extensions will make it more difficult to communicate across the many villages we have today. There are also concerns that there may be problems removing rock from the construction over the long distances to cave entrances. The interior minister is worried that the expansion will cause an increase in population that will place a strain on our resources. It takes time to develop additional sources of food and waste services, and to educate people about the new areas."

Commander Filo rubbed his chin. "Interesting problems."

"Let's continue on. The chieftain's throne room is through those doors," said Yoyo, pointing just ahead.

They stood at the door and waited to be announced. A Magi village chief was finishing up with the chieftain. He walked out and the chieftain's yeoman escorted them in.

The chieftain rose from her throne and smiled. "Yoyo! How have you been?"

"Chieftain Hilma, I am just fine," replied Yoyo, clasping her hands and bowing. "I have brought these two Alphas who wish to discuss a business proposition with you. This is Commander Filo and his aide, Lieutenant Swantik."

The two clasped their hands and bowed as Yoyo had done.

"Greetings, Chieftain Hilma," said Filo as he removed his goggles. "I represent an Alpha delegation that is interested in having formal relations with the Magi people."

"To what end? You are free to communicate with us as you wish," replied Hilma.

"We would like to set up more formal relations with your people by exchanging dignitaries. Our representative could stay here in your caves and some of your people could spend time with us, on our ship and on our planet. There is so much we could learn from each other."

"We are generally against mingling with outsiders. I certainly would not wish for you to take our people away from this planet, which I believe is what you are proposing," she stated with a stern voice.

"You are quite right," Commander Filo said with a bow. "We feel there is much we could share with your people to their benefit. It would be much easier to express opportunities with someone who had spent time with our people. And likewise, your use of chemicals and minerals could be of great value to our people. Having your people embedded with ours would be very productive for our engineers."

"This sounds interesting, but I'm concerned about the possible exploitation of our people and the negative influence that your culture could have on our culture. Yours is an advanced civilization. I understand the corruptive forces of technology and the greed that comes with that. Modernization does not come without a cost."

"I understand your hesitation, Chieftain Hilma. If I could have a second audience with you, I believe I can demonstrate my sincerity and provide specific examples of how the Alphas might be able to assist your people without disrupting the harmony of your culture."

"I am skeptical of your claim, but I am willing to hear you out. Yoyo, why don't you bring them back in two days and let's see what they have to present."

"Yes, chieftain. Be well." Yoyo bowed and the three walked out.

Yoyo escorted Commander Filo and Lephi to the cave entrance where she had met them. "I'll see you here at the same time two days from now."

"Yoyo," said Filo, "I appreciate your assistance in getting us an audience with Chieftain Hilma. I feel it was a productive meeting, and I look forward to seeing you again. Is there anything I can bring you the next time we meet?"

"I am happy to help out. I don't require anything at this time. I am merely doing my job," replied Yoyo. "I'll see you in two days. Goodbye." She disappeared through the cave entrance.

"Commander, what do you have planned?" asked Lephi as they started down the mountain.

"I'm not sure yet. Let me make a few calls and we will discuss it in the morning. I see the Magi as a great opportunity for us to enact our revenge on the Euclidians and I refuse to let it slip through our fingers without an effort. Let's get back to our ship and put some distance between us and this planet."

That place is wondrous, thought Commander Filo. *I didn't realize there was so much going on there. Those people have a formal society with villages full of huts, and roads and communications, though primitive. But what don't they have? They don't seem to need money, food, or other resources. Their desire to expand could be the key to gaining their cooperation. I need to find a way to show them that the Alphas can assist them with their plans without interfering.*

***

Two days later Commander Filo and Lieutenant Lephi were back in the cave waiting for Yoyo.

"So, where is Yoyo?" asked Commander Filo impatiently.

"I don't know," responded Lephi. "This is where we met her before. Unfortunately, the Magi are very liberal with meeting times. They only have a crude way of tracking time inside their caves."

"So how do we know if she will show up? The chieftain could have changed her mind, or Yoyo could be sick or dead, or maybe she came earlier and decided we stood *her* up! I don't like the casualness of these meetings."

"If she doesn't show up within an hour, I will contact one of their other emissaries and try to set up another meeting. In the meantime, have a seat on one of the boulders and try to relax."

"It's bad enough I have to wear these goggles, I'm not going to sit on a hard rock. Anyway, that would be unprofessional. I will stand here until she arrives. If she doesn't arrive, we will try to contact her or someone else."

Another few moments passed and Yoyo appeared in front of them.

"Hello, Commander Filo and Lieutenant Swantik."

Filo clasped his hands and bowed. "Hello, Yoyo."

"No need to be so formal. I'm not the chieftain."

"Still, I am happy to show you a little respect after the assistance you have given us. We have been here quite a while. You are late today."

"No, that is not possible. I came when I was ready. To have come earlier would be a waste of our time."

"Forgive me, I expected you about the same time as before."

"And that is when I arrived. Shall we go?"

Commander Filo, not wanting to belabor the point, nodded and gestured for Yoyo to lead the way. Lephi simply looked at the commander and shrugged his shoulders. Filo smirked back at him.

Yoyo led the Alphas to Hilma's chamber where Filo presented his case.

"Chieftain Hilma, thanks for meeting with us again. We continue to feel that there is much to be gained by an exchange of diplomats. As I mentioned previously, your use of chemicals, minerals, and cave technology is of great interest to us. In return for sharing these, I believe that we can assist with your expansion plans. You have a huge cave system that is difficult to navigate and communicate across. You also don't have precise timing devices. We could provide a wealth of technology to address those difficulties."

"Commander, we are not interested in bringing your technology into our caves. We have survived thousands of years without it and I have no desire for my people to learn the use of your devices and cripple them with reliance on foreign technology, thereby extinguishing years of our culture."

"Point well taken, Chieftain. I would not want to disrupt your way of life for the sake of diplomacy. But in the matter of expanding your cave systems, we have technology to carve out the rock and remove it in no time. We could then transfer any items you need into the new space. The Alphas could manage all of the work so your people would not have to deal with our technology."

"Those proposals sound a bit more acceptable, but I don't want life to become too easy for my people. Maybe we could look at a mixture of Alpha technology and Magi manpower. One thing we do not have is metal reinforcement to shore up our cave structures."

"That is something we would be glad to assist you with. We also have the means to stimulate the growth of plants and animals. That could help you start providing additional food for your expanding population. Once we have increased the size of your food sources, they should be able to sustain continued growth by your people. As a sign of good faith, I have brought a device that can stimulate the egg laying capabilities of your sea life. I would be happy to demonstrate it on two isolated animals and you can verify that it does not harm the creatures in any way."

"That would be a worthwhile experiment. Yoyo, will you be so kind as to have one of our marine biologists set up an experiment before Commander Filo ends his visit with us?"

"Yes, chieftain."

"I believe we have enough information to start working out an agreement between our peoples. Commander, what are your thoughts about an exchange of representatives?"

"Because Lieutenant Swantik already has a relationship with your people, I was hoping that he could be the Alpha Ambassador to the Magi people. There would be some additional people in his delegation to assist him with administrative work and the exchange of information. Likewise, Chieftain Hilma, I propose that Yoyo be appointed Magi Ambassador to the Alpha people. I would also like to see others in her delegation, to further improve our ability to exchange ideas."

Yoyo's mouth sprang open in surprise. She had never seen herself becoming the ambassador to another planet, and now her dream of traveling to the stars would be realized. *But can I be successful while still having fun?*

"Are you still with us, Yoyo?" asked Chieftain Hilma.

"Forgive me, chieftain. I was momentarily lost in my thoughts."

"What do you think of the idea of being an ambassador?"

"I would be honored and delighted," replied Yoyo with a bow to her chieftain.

"You've done an excellent job working with the Tammarians and Euclidians. I think you are the perfect choice for the position. Do you think you can find some of our specialists that would like to join you?"

"Of course, chieftain."

"How do you feel about the choice of Lieutenant Swantik as their ambassador?"

"I have had agreeable exchanges with him. He is patient and respectful, unlike Commander Filo." The commander looked away in embarrassment. "I feel he will be a welcome partner for our people."

"Commander Filo, as you know we don't use money, so we will be unable to fund Yoyo's position."

"We would be happy to take care of her basic needs. She should be able to find part-time work if she wishes to earn money.

"Then it's settled. Yoyo, have our foreign minister meet with his Alpha counterpart to iron out an agreement between our peoples."

"Right away, Chieftain Hilma. I appreciate your sponsorship."

***

A few days later, the two sides completed their agreement. Yoyo and several of the Magi boarded the cloaked Alpha ship for a trip to Euclidia.

CHAPTER 3

Betty Gets Kidnapped

Betty had a thrilling B&D session with Uan and was basking in its afterglow as she finished freshening up in her bathroom. She walked into her bedroom and was surprised to find that Uan had gone. *I risk my life to save that jerk in a bar fight, bring him back to my place for a little B&D as a reward to myself for saving him, and he disappears on me. He could have been kicked to death. The least he could do was indulge my fantasy. During the entire session he kept screaming about how he was going to kill me, all the way up to his orgasm.*

After all that tough talk I can't believe he just vanished without saying a word. What happened to all that "I'm going to kill you" talk? I guess the sex was just too much for him. I should stop procrastinating and get to work.

Betty got dressed, jumped into her squad car, and headed to her police precinct. She walked into the squad room to find everyone else was in the briefing room.

"Betty, what are you doing out there?" the captain shouted from the briefing room door. "The briefing has already started. Didn't you get my email?"

"Sorry, captain, I was just getting some coffee. What's going on?"

"Just grab your coffee and get in here."

The chief was already finishing his remarks. "I'm not going to take up any more of your time. I believe you all understand how gruesome these murders have been and the importance of finding the person or persons responsible for this mess. Now I want to introduce you to Special Agent Trent McKee from the FBI forensics team."

"Hello, everyone," said Agent McKee. "Let me give you a little of my background. I began my career as a Navy submariner, then spent four years in Nam with special forces. After that I joined the FBI and worked in the D.C. Gang Violence Division. I earned a doctorate and then transferred to forensics. In all that time I never saw anything quite like this. Over the past few weeks we've had several bodies come in with deep stab wounds to the chest, body parts missing, and a couple were even decapitated. One of the bodies was chopped up like a butcher had made steaks from a cow carcass."

"At first we thought it was just random gang violence," Agent McKee continued. "However, some of the victims weren't gang members and the locations where the bodies were found were too spread out. Initially we were unable to pinpoint any patterns that we could use to tie the killings together. The wounds were wide and deep, indicating a spear-like weapon. It would be difficult to make that type of wound with a knife. The angle of penetration leads us to believe that the perpetrator was short, between five foot five and five foot seven."

"We have only one lead that I'm aware of. Over at Louie's building, where a couple of these guys were killed, witnesses claim a man jumped to the ground from a third-story window, carrying another man over his shoulder, and then ran off."

There was snickering from the officers in the room.

"This isn't a joke, gentlemen," the chief interrupted. "The third-floor window in Louie's building was broken out and there was glass on the ground below. The witnesses were not junkies or drunks, but members of the neighborhood watch. They said that the suspect wore a hood, dark wrap-around shades, and had some sort of tiger markings on his face."

Betty gasped and began to feel faint. *That's the guy I just slept with!*

"Please continue, Agent McKee," said the captain.

"We tested the wounds of the murder victims for metal fragments to see if anything could be deduced about the weapon that was used. Let me tell you, I was caught totally off guard when we determined that the minute fragments from the wound were unidentifiable. They were certainly metal, but like nothing anyone had ever seen before. We sent the fragments to several other labs and they came to the same conclusion. It's as if our perpetrator is using a weapon that was not made on this planet."

"Are you saying that the murderer is an alien?" shouted one of the officers.

"I'm saying that the metal from the weapon cannot be identified. This person is the FBI's top priority and it should be yours as well. He's killed nine people so far that we know of and these unknown metal fragments were found in each one of them."

"Okay, that's it," the chief jumped in. "Get out there and chase down some leads for me, ladies and gentlemen."

Betty walked out of the briefing room holding her mouth and sat at her desk in a daze.

"Betty, you okay?" asked a passing officer.

"Yeah, Mack. I'm just distracted. Had a bad date last night that I can't get out of my head."

"It's probably due to those bad bars you hang out in."

"You're probably right, Mack," she said. *Little does he know how right.*

Betty reviewed her caseload, made a few calls, and set off to find Uan.

***

Li Xiao was fascinated with Cobalt's gift. She had finally forgiven him for causing her body to be banged up, figuring that the teleportation mechanism must have screwed up somehow and slammed her against the shower floor.

Visiting her family had been fun, but now she realized that it had also been dangerous. She could have killed herself or a family member. She spent the rest of the day practicing with the device, beaming herself around the apartment. She learned to set and remove waypoints. She learned to use the memory list to jump quickly from place to place. She knew she could take objects with her, and wondered if she could also take an animal or another human with her.

Li Xiao learned that when she carried an object that was tied down, the rope severed at a specific distance from her body. *What if it was a human chained to a wall, or a large human or two humans? How would the severing mechanism work?*

Li Xiao decided to test transporting animals, starting with something small. She knew her neighbors kept a few goldfish and used the transport device to locate their fishbowl. After verifying that the apartment was empty, she pressed the transport button and instantly was standing in front of the fishbowl. She picked up the bowl and transported back to her apartment. The fish were still alive in their bowl. Just then she heard a noise from next door and used her device to see that her neighbors had returned. The husband walked into the living room while his wife went into the kitchen to put away the groceries they had purchased.

"Honey," said the husband, "the fish are gone. Do you think one of the kids came by to get them? You would think they would tell us that they were going to pick them up. It's not likely that someone broke

into our place just to take the fish and leave our big flat-screen TV.
That would be strange."

The man left the room and Li Xiao quickly popped back over,
replaced the bowl, and popped back to her place. As she watched the
screen, the couple walked into the living room.

"Are those the fish that are missing, dear?" asked the wife.

The husband looked over in shock. "I swear to you, they were
gone."

"Go take your pills and lay down, honey. I think it's time for your
nap."

"I don't need a nap. Those fish were gone, I tell you!"

"You go get in your jammies and I'll get the Geritol."

Li Xiao laughed, happy that they did not suspect her.

***

Betty decided to chase down the only lead she knew, starting at
Louie's place. The usual guys were out front guarding the entrance.

"Hey fellas, how's it going?"

"Yo, Betty. You know, just getting some air," said one of the men.

"I heard you had a little excitement here the other day. Some tiger-
faced guy harassing Louie?"

"Yeah, that crazy fucker came over here with a friend of his,
looking for some kid."

"What kid?"

"Some kid that was outside Joey's Diner when that zombie
Bookhead showed up. I guess you heard about that?" the man said with
a chuckle.

"Sure, but I thought that was some sort of joke. What did he want
with the kid?"

"Who knows? Can't be no good. He wasn't a warm and fuzzy kind of guy, if you know what I mean. He cut up a few of our guys real bad."

"Yeah, I know what you mean. Where do you think I can find him?"

"Not sure. I heard he hangs out at Bo Sam's place. He might even be the one that offed him."

"I heard about that. I'll see what I can find out over there."

"Okay, but watch out for yourself. They like to rough up cops over there. We cool, right?"

"Sure. Just be subtle about your shit and I'll keep the squad off your back."

"For shizzle, Betty."

"Okay, later, fellas."

Betty got back in her black and white and drove to Bo Sam's place. She parked her car down the street then took a position behind a tree across from the building. A few minutes later, Calvin approached the building.

This must be where he's staying. There's his friend right there, heading in. Uan has to be inside somewhere. I'd better call for backup. Betty reached for her radio.

"The only backup you're gonna get is your back up against a wall," said Little Randy as he stepped in front of her. "You think 'cause you a cop you got juice around here? Think again. Ain't you that bitch the Italians are pissed at?"

"Those goombas are always pissed at somebody. Why do you give a damn?"

"'Cause I want to keep them off my ass and out of my territory. Plus, they'll probably toss me a little change to take you to them."

"How about you introduce me to the guy across the street and I give you a pass on this little operation you got going on here?"

"How about you shut the fuck up and I send you beddy-bye?" Little Randy nodded and someone behind her knocked her out.

When Betty regained consciousness she had a horrible headache. She was tied to a chair in a damp basement. A bare light bulb burned dimly overhead.

"Betty, you're still alive," said a man from the shadows. "Those knuckleheads brought you in a bit busted up. I thought we were going to have to bury you without the chance to let you know how much we appreciate all the attention you've given us in the past."

"Is that Antonio? I hope the pen wasn't too hard on you. If you can't do the time, don't do the crime, right?"

Antonio stepped into the light where Betty could see him.

"That's absolutely right, Officer Betty. And now it's your turn to do some time for the crime you perpetrated on me and my family."

"Antonio, before we get started, do you think I could get a bathroom break? They give you those even in prison, right?"

"Betty, don't expect any breaks tonight!" said a new voice as someone entered her room.

"Hello, Luciano, or should I just call you Lucy?" Betty replied with a quaver in her voice.

Luciano leaned toward Betty and slapped her across the face, knocking her and the chair to the floor.

"Pick her up!" Luciano yelled at Antonio. "Okay, Betty, I heard you like to make men your bitches. You better believe that won't be happening here. This time you're my bitch. This time you're the one getting slapped. How does it feel? Trust me, you're getting off a lot easier than a lot of my guys that you put in prison, spending years rotting in a cell, having to use the toilet in plain view. The only bathroom break you'll be getting is in your pants."

Luciano slapped her again to the floor. When Antonio lifted her up her chair was wet.

"That didn't take long, sweetheart. Did you enjoy pissing your pants?"

"Not as much as I would enjoy pissing on you," Betty sneered.

"Well, that's never going to happen, little lady. You recognize this?" Luciano showed her an old pocketknife.

"It looks like the knife I pulled off your brother."

"That's right. You pulled it off him when you arrested him a couple of years back for trafficking. They sent it to me with the rest of his stuff after he died in prison."

"Sorry to hear that."

"Not yet, you aren't. But you will be. He wanted you to have it so here it is," said Luciano. He opened the knife stabbed it into her thigh.

"Arghhh. You bastard!" Betty screamed.

She kicked and flailed in her chair, but the men ignored her.

"Antonio, I want you to take her to the Wendy's on Jewella, just south of I-20 in Shreveport. I'm going to let the Cajuns take care of her where no one will hear from her again. Tell them to take their time with her. I want her to suffer for 642 days, just like my brother did in prison."

"Sure, boss."

"Keep her in the chair. Put her in the back of the SUV and take her to the airfield. Our plane will be waiting to take you to Shreveport. There'll be another SUV waiting for you when you arrive. Use it to rendezvous with Pierre at the Wendy's. You can spend the night and gamble or whatever. The plane will bring you back in the morning. When you get back I'll have another job for you."

"Will do, boss. Let's go, little lady." Antonio dragged Betty into the garage and put her in the back of the SUV.

"I guess you're not going to give me a bathroom break either?" Betty asked.

"Sure. You can take as many as you like as long as you take them from that chair." Antonio closed the hatch and drove off to the airfield. Three hours later they were in a similar SUV in Shreveport, driving toward the Wendy's on Jewella. Behind the restaurant, a man waited in a delivery truck.

"You must be Pierre," said Antonio.

"Yes. I believe you have a package for me from Luciano."

"It's in the back of the SUV. She can be a bit feisty," Antonio said with a smile. "But I've assured her that if she screams again like she did at the airport, I'll fill her mouth with dirt and tape it shut."

The two men pulled Betty out of the SUV and into the back of Pierre's truck.

"Be sure to tell Luciano that Boudreau sends his regards," said Pierre.

"I certainly will. Is she going to be okay in the back of your truck?"

"Don't worry. I'll tie down her chair so she won't slide around and hurt her little head."

"Excuse me, sir," interrupted Betty. "Can I please get a bathroom break? I'll let you watch."

"Go ahead," said Pierre. "I'm watching."

"Really? You can't just let me drop my pants for five minutes?"

"Sounds like a good idea. Would you also like me to leave the light on back here and get you a CD player to listen to on the trip?"

"Why do all you hoodlums think you're comedians?"

"My goodness, I think I just got a promotion," laughed Pierre as he closed the door, leaving Betty in darkness.

Pierre jumped into the cab and drove to Natchitoches where he met Boudreau and his associate Kevin in the parking lot of a Piggly Wiggly.

"Hey, Pierre," said Boudreau, "what you got for me?"

"A pretty little cop lady to keep you warm at night. She's tied to a chair inside."

Along the way, however, Betty had managed to lean down in the chair and pull the knife from her leg with her mouth. She stretched her head back and to the side and dropped the knife into the darkness, luckily catching it in her hands. She managed to cut the rope that bound her then went to the front corner of the truck bed and took her long needed bathroom break. She put the knife in her back pocket, moved the chair to the rear of the truck, and waited.

Pierre unlatched the door to show off his gift. Betty slammed the door open and thrust the chair into Pierre's chest. Pierre fell backwards and hit his head on the pavement, knocking him out.

Betty leapt to the ground, twisted her body, and kicked at Kevin's ankles to topple him.

She jumped to her feet and attempted to run but was stopped in her tracks when Boudreau grabbed her ponytail. She turned to strike him, but curled up with pain and fell to the ground as Boudreau struck her in the abdomen with a Taser.

Boudreau kicked at Pierre and Kevin, saying, "Get up, you idiots. Tie her up and throw her in the back seat of my SUV. And try not to get beat up this time."

With Betty in the back of the SUV, Boudreau and Kevin drove off to Negreet where Boudreau lived in a big white-columned house on a small island in the middle of the bayou, just past Collier Memorial Park.

It was only accessible via a small makeshift bridge that led to Negreet's main road. The island was surrounded by a strong chain-link fence that kept gators from wandering around the property. Boudreau and Kevin dragged Betty into the house and threw her on the bed in one of the guest rooms.

"Why don't you lay there and relax, little lady," said Boudreau. "I'll send a few of my girls up in a bit to get you presentable for a late night visit. I'm going to enjoy having you around the place. Something about having a cop as my sex slave really turns me on. You must have pissed those Italians off something fierce for them to pay me to take you off their hands. I keep you alive for 642 days and then I get another stack of cash. Go figure!"

"Kevin, let's go get some grub and afterward we can come back and have some fun with our private little police force." Boudreau laughed as he closed and locked the door.

"You betcha," replied Kevin, slapping Boudreau on the back.

CHAPTER 4

Cobalt Returns

Li Xiao was perplexed about what had happened to her. Why did Cobalt shoot her? How did she arrive in her shower all broken up? What did Cobalt want her to do with the device? She had to see him, to get some answers, and because she truly missed him.

She theorized that if the device permitted her to see places across the planet, Cobalt must also be able to see her somehow. He must have been watching her to know so much about her life when he recruited her. Maybe she was being naïve, but she felt that Cobalt had feelings for her. Either way, she needed to hear from him. In case he was checking in on her, she placed signs all over the apartment that read, *Cobalt contact me!* She attached similar signs to the front and back of her shirt.

For two days she displayed the signs on her clothes, receiving odd stares from the people she met as she went about her business. At the end of the second day, as she sat in her living room watching the movie *Avatar* and wondering if a planet like that really existed, Cobalt appeared before her. She leapt to her feet and hugged him. Cobalt hugged her back, enjoying her warm embrace and the smell of her hair.

"Cobalt, you don't know what I've been through. I missed you so much. At first I thought you had imprisoned me and tried to kill me. I later realized it must have been a transporter malfunction. I guess even in advanced societies there must be bugs in equipment or inept operators. Then I started to wonder why you shot me and didn't just send me to your transporter room. Was I knocked out for a while and then sent home?"

Cobalt released Li Xiao from his embrace and laughed. "I thought that women talking a lot was just a Majorellen phenomenon. Xiao, try to calm down and let me know what's going on. I'm not sure what you're talking about, but I'm glad to see you. So tell me, what can I do for you? I have to apologize up front and let you know that I cannot stay with you very long."

Li Xiao took Cobalt's hand and led him to the couch. She sat down and put her feet up. She patted the spot next to her, signaling for Cobalt to sit next to her. He sat down and placed his arm around her neck. He placed his index finger under her chin, lifted her head, and kissed her softly on her lips.

"Now tell me what's on your mind, Xiao," Cobalt prompted.

"Be honest, Cobalt. What happened after you shot me?"

"I never shot you, darling. The device I was holding was not a weapon but a transport device. I used it to send you into the transportation system directly from my room. The operators were supposed to send you safely back to your room. They screwed up, forgot to compensate for the acceleration vector. Luckily the transport device I gave you wasn't broken."

"So that's why I got so banged up."

"I was really saddened by what happened to you. I wanted to come to your aid, but the captain is not sympathetic to emotional needs and does not like us leaving the ship except for planned leave."

"Have you been watching me the whole time?"

"Just now and again. I hoped to see you again and wanted to be sure you were safe. The invasion of Earth is eminent. The device can help keep you safe, and may help you save others. You can make a difference on this planet. Individuals often underestimate the impact they can have on the world around them."

"When is the invasion supposed to happen? How many people will be impacted? Why would you bother giving me money and this device if our world is going to be ripped apart soon?"

"Don't worry about the invasion. They won't destroy the planet and I promise to keep you safe. Focus on using the device to help make the next evolution of your planet a great one."

"I don't know why you have so much faith in me. I don't think I'm worthy of your praise or trust. However, I will listen to your counsel and learn to use the device. I know a lot about it but there is more I need to learn. Please teach me everything." Li Xiao fetched the device and gave it to Cobalt.

"Okay, we need to be quick. At the top right is the power button. You don't need to worry about the device ever running out of power. It has a fifty-year power source. You will want to turn it off when you are not using it to avoid accidentally activating a feature. A momentary push of the button disables all the controls. If you hold the power button and press this button sequence, the device shuts down. To get the device to come on again, you hold the power button down and press the same sequence. This will prevent someone else from using it. Are you with me so far?"

"Yes, keep going."

"You seem to have learned how to use your fingers on the screen, but you can perform the same actions and more by holding your fingers above the screen and moving your hand in the way you want the monitor to move. Hold your hand over the screen with your fingers pointing at it. Now move your hand in and out. Notice how the viewing position changes based on the direction you are viewing. To zoom in and out, spread your fingers and hold them or squeeze and hold them. Twisting your fingers to the left or right causes the viewing angle to spin left or right. As you know, positioning your hand sideways and spinning it will spin the camera angle based on the orientation of your hand to the viewing angle. Wiping your hand across the screen moves the viewing position in the same direction as your hand. Still with me?"

"Yes."

"The button at the top permits you to listen in on conversations. The top left button is a timer. Pressing it displays a list of times on the screen. The first one is blank, which disables the timer. The next entry represents about two seconds using Euclidian timing. Each entry after that is the double the previous. Once you select a time you will always return from a transport within that amount of time. For example, if you select the third entry and transport to your parents' house, you will return to your starting point after four seconds. If you press the timer button while the timer is counting down it will disable the countdown. The next time you transport somewhere the timer will countdown again."

"Why would I want to use the timer?"

"Say you want to go somewhere to pick up something then return, but your hands are full and you cannot operate the device, you can return without pushing any buttons."

"Got it."

"You use this button to target people or items that you want to track. You can track as many targets as you like. Pressing the button over the target selects it. Pressing the button again deselects it. Pressing this other button cycles through the targets. Use the button down here to select destinations, as many as you like, the one over here to cycle between stored destinations, this one to deselect a destination. As you know, pressing the bottom bar transports you to the destination on the screen. You need to be careful about heights because you can easily kill yourself. Pressing and holding the transport bar returns you to your last transport location."

"Wow, that's a lot to remember."

"I suggest you practice, a lot, before you attempt to use it on a mission. Now, I need to get back to the ship."

"What missions? What am I supposed to do?"

"You'll figure it out. You want to make a difference for your people? Now you can."

"No time for a little loving?"

"Not this time. But I should be back very soon."

And without warning, Cobalt vanished and she fell from his arms onto the couch.

***

On Sunday morning, Li Xiao was in her living room watching *Fareed Zakaria GPS* when a report caught her attention:

"Chinese basketball legend Yao Ming was arrested while giving a speech in his hometown of Shanghai. Yao Ming has long opposed the Chinese government's detention and imprisonment of dissidents and critics, and now he has become a victim of this practice. Due to public outrage at the arrest, Yao Ming has been hidden in an undisclosed location, leading to fears for his health and the possibility that he will not be freed any time soon."

Yao Ming's imprisonment outraged Li Xiao, too. Though she considered herself a patriot, she disagreed with the government's crackdown on protestors. It was because of her patriotism that she had agreed to work with the alien she believed to be a Chinese agent. She thought she was helping to protect China from being attacked by nuclear weapons, although the aliens were in fact trying to obtain all of Earth's nuclear material before invading the planet. But even if the world was about to end, Li Xiao now had a chance to help her people.

Li Xiao reflected back on her short reunion with Cobalt and his parting words. She thought of her personal commitment to make a difference for her people. Was it her mission to free Chinese dissidents? She didn't know, but she couldn't sit idly by and let her countrymen be abused. She decided to use Cobalt's device to start freeing dissidents, and to protect her identity by taking on the persona of the Chinese goddess Guan-Yin, disguising her face with a mask.

CHAPTER 5

Filo & Yoyo at Bordelle Bar

During the trip to Euclidia, Commander Filo indoctrinated Yoyo in Alpha culture and history. He showed her the systems on his ship, but indicated that his plan was to work on a Euclidian ship to improve relations between Alpha and Euclidia.

Instead of teaching her the Alpha language he focused on improving her Euclidian, which he thought would be more useful for what he had planned for her.

"Yoyo, let's speak Euclidian for the remainder of your trip, if that's okay with you?"

"Yes, Commander Filo. That would be very helpful for me if we are going to spend any time on Euclidia and its ships."

"Wonderful. I am proud that you are dedicating yourself to your new role. I will be sending all but one of your associates to other Alpha ships to meet with my counterparts. The other two will join us on Euclidia."

"When will we be visiting your home planet?"

"We will visit the new Alpha home planet later. The original Alpha was destroyed by the Euclidians as the result of a misunderstanding between our people. I hope to address that matter in the near future.

For now, I want you all to focus on learning Euclidian language and customs, and on Euclidia we will visit several places to immerse all you Magi in their culture."

"There won't be a problem with us being on their planet?"

"No, they get new people there all the time. We will need to get you registered and have UCDs assigned to you, which will cost a few credits but shouldn't take much time. I'm sure it will surprise the officials to find out that the Magi are starting to visit their planet."

"Why would they care?"

"They try to keep track of such things and will probably be surprised that they have been on your planet for several years and just ran across you."

"I hope that won't cause a problem for my people. We don't like a lot of attention."

"You should be fine. The Euclidians usually leave people to themselves once they determine that they are not a danger to them."

"That's comforting. I look forward to seeing what life is like on another planet."

"You will find out very soon, Yoyo. I promise you that you are in for quite an experience. I want you to understand that to be successful here I will need you to use your unique talents to help persuade the Euclidians to build a relationship with us."

"Okay, as long as we are doing it to make life better for our people.

"Of course we will Yoyo. Of course we will."

***

The Alpha ship entered into orbit above Euclidia. Yoyo Snarky, newly assigned ambassador from Tammaria, stood at Commander

Filo's side, wearing goggles and a long, light, hooded robe to protect her from the sun's bright light. Little did she know of Filo's sinister plans for her.

Jesmino, Yoyo's assistant, accompanied them to the surface. Jesmino was a mineral scientist; she had developed several of the Magi's mineral-based technologies. Commander Filo found three small apartments for them in a neighborhood in the Euclidian city of Occum that was more or less accepting of lodgers from Alpha. He got the Magi plugged into the government system and they were each assigned a UCD. Yoyo was thrilled.

"Don't you just love your UCD, Jesmino?"

"It's not a bad device. It is certainly better than anything we have in the cave."

"What do you mean, it's not bad? It's amazing. Everything I want to know is right here. It can tell me where I am, about the people around me, and show me video of faraway places. I can even talk to it as if it were human."

"Yes, it has abilities, but it has no intelligence."

"Whatever you say, Jesmino."

Yoyo and Jesmino walked through their neighborhood to get to know their surroundings and test out their new devices. Occum, Euclidia's capital, was an enormous city of more than seventy-five million inhabitants, eleven million of whom were from the dozens of other planets whose people had formed relationships with the Euclidian government.

The neighborhood had people from many planets, typically individuals with few resources. The streets were bordered on both sides by shops selling goods from Euclidia and other planets. There was a multitude of different music, smells, and clothing. On top of the shops were apartments like those where Commander Filo, Yoyo, and Jesmino lived. Visiting the shops, Yoyo learned that she needed credits to purchase things. She desperately wanted to learn how to earn credits to supplement the money that Commander Filo gave her.

"Jesmino, isn't this place the greatest?" asked Yoyo excitedly."

"It's not bad."

"Again with the 'not bad' comment. What do you mean, it's not bad? I've never seen so many people or things from so many faraway places. There are so many worlds with so many cultures that I've never heard of. So many ways of communicating and procreating. And so much technology that helps people travel from place to place."

"Why does that seem so strange?" said Jesmino. "Non-organic devices are capable of many things beyond the abilities of organic life forms. Think about having limitless memory or lifespan, or being able to connect to life anywhere at a subatomic level. Once you can connect with a quark you can be anywhere in the universe all at once, though you have to be careful to remember your origin. Infinite destinations can take infinite time to research."

"What the hell are you talking about? Where did you learn all of that stuff?"

"Oh, I was just reading up on subatomic theory on my UCD."

"Already? And because you have nothing else to learn, I guess? I want you to study the Euclidians, who are they, what are they passionate about, and how might they benefit from our mineral expertise. I want to see if we can leverage that to build a relationship with them and help improve relations between Alpha and Euclidia."

"Understood, ambassador."

"Just call me Yoyo for now. If we get into some formal meetings, maybe you should use my title. I want you to perfect their language and then make friends with someone in the government. That may take some time, but I'm sure we will have plenty of that. I'll have further information about what we need to do once I've spent more time with Commander Filo. Speaking of whom, I am supposed to meet him in a few minutes to go to some bar." She caught sight of a robed figure and pointed. "Who is that?"

Yoyo chased after the figure as it hurried up a cross street. She caught up and grabbed at the robe. The person stopped and turned around, and Yoyo was startled to be staring at the face of a male Magi.

"What are you doing here?" exclaimed Yoyo.

"I live here. Who are you?"

"I'm Yoyo. I work as a liaison for the chieftain. And you?"

"I'm Belo. I came here on a Euclidian ship about two months ago. I was meeting with some Tammarians on the east side of Mount Chupachy when the Euclidians just showed up. I gave them some grog in return for one of the snacks they were eating and the relationship sort of blossomed from there. I eventually convinced them to let me board their ship with them."

"I didn't know we had caves out that far. Are there other Magi here?"

"Yeah, the caves have been expanding like crazy. I can't keep up with them anymore. And I have seen a few of us around here."

"Do the Euclidians know about our persuasion abilities?"

"No, I don't think so. We seem to have kept that to ourselves so far."

"I'm so glad of that. How do I find the others?"

"Look, I gotta run. I'm a techno slinger at the Dance Club 271, a few blocks from here. Come by later and I'll tell you more." Belo ran off.

"How about that, Jesmino? There are more of us here."

"Yes, I don't find that so surprising. I've finished learning Euclidian, so now I'm going to try to make the appropriate government contacts, as you asked."

"Really? You are a strange one, Jesmino. I'll see you back at your place tonight. I'm going to go find Commander Filo."

"Tonight it is," replied Jesmino, and she disappeared into the crowd.

I've got to learn more about Belo, Yoyo thought. *Maybe he can teach me to be a techno slinger so I can earn some extra credits.*

***

Commander Filo walked into the Bordelle Bar on the outskirts of Occum. This bar was the favorite of resource ship officers, and Commander Filo was looking for one in particular, the XO of the *Andrea.* He was key to Filo's revenge plot against the Euclidian captain of one of the four ships that had destroyed his planet. Filo blamed this man for instigating the attack in the first place: Captain Chaell Shisal!

Yoyo arrived and she and Filo found a booth that gave them a full view of the bar. Filo wanted to make sure he saw everyone coming and going from the establishment.

"Two Tammarian grogs," Commander Filo demanded from the server. "And a bowl of Gordon creatures. Fresh ones. I don't want any that look like they're on their last leg."

"Right away, sir," the server said and hurried off.

"They serve Tammarian grog in an establishment like this, so far from my planet?" asked Yoyo.

"Yes, you can get it almost anywhere these days. The stuff is too good not to have plenty of it on hand."

"So, are any of your contacts here?"

"No, not yet, but it's still early. The place gets plenty of traffic this time of day and I wanted to make sure that we got a seat."

"What makes this place so popular?"

"The dancers! See that stage over there, with the poles?"

"Yes."

"It's going to be full of naked women, men, and hermaphrodites of every imaginable species. They dance and grind and wiggle around with sexy gyrations while customers throw money at them. They are very talented performers."

"You can see nudity all the time. Why is seeing nudity here so interesting?"

"There is a big difference between nudity and sensual performances. These dancers move their bodies in provocative ways, touching themselves and exposing their genitalia in all their glory. The clients love it for scientific and erotic reasons and are happy to pay money to the performers."

"Wow, that sounds bizarre. Why do they do that?"

"Who? The performers or the customers?"

"Both!"

"The performers dance for the money and the fame they sometimes obtain. The customers pay to see them dance because they get to learn about the anatomies of different species, or just to feed their sexual beast!"

"Would they let me perform here?"

"I would think not. You can't just go up there and walk around naked. You have to perform and look sexy while you are doing it. Living in a cave all your life, you probably don't have much experience dancing naked. Those goggles and big robe you wear all the time won't help your cause either. Of course, you could use your abilities to make the customers give you all their money without even dancing. But if the

Euclidian government learns about your abilities, you'll probably be imprisoned or killed."

"There is so much I don't know about this place."

"What do you expect? You've been living in a cave your whole life."

The server walked up with a tray. "Here are your drinks and food, gentlemen."

"If you don't mind, I'm a woman," piped up Yoyo.

"Forgive my mistake. I was unaware." The server departed.

"What are those creatures walking around in the bowl?" Yoyo asked Filo.

"Those are Gordon creatures. Take one out of the bowl and place it on the table then, when it tries to run, stun it with your fist and pop it in your mouth. When you bite into one it makes a high pitched squeaking sound then stiffens and secretes a fluid that is very exhilarating. That only happens if you eat them alive. You have to wonder why nature would do that to a creature. Being eaten alive has to be a horrible way to go."

"Thanks for the graphic explanation. I think I will pass on that delicacy. I don't need the bad karma. Maybe I'll just get a vegetarian dish."

"Sure, whatever you like. But that will have to wait. One of my possible business contacts has appeared. See the man with the uniform that just sat down by the stage?"

"Yes, I see him."

"That's one of those that I want to give me an audience. I'm going to pay one of the lady dancers to offer him a visit to the Laldexian Room and then you can do your thing. I'll be right back."

"It's all set up," said Commander Filo upon his return. "We'll just wait until he leaves and then join him in the Laldexian Room."

"What happens in there?" Yoyo asked.

"That's where people go to get special acts performed for them."

"Like what?"

"You know, private dances, massages, hand jobs and the like."

"Oh, those kind of acts."

"There he goes. Let's get in there before he orders anything extra from the menu."

Commander Filo and Yoyo followed the Euclidian officer into the Laldexian room, tipping the server on the way in and asking for privacy.

"Hello, captain. I am Commander Filo and this is my associate Yoyo from Tammaria. May we join you?"

"Beat it, Alpha. I'm here for a little fun, not to have my appetite spoiled by the looks of you."

"I'm only here to improve our relations. Tell him, Yoyo."

Yoyo took off her goggles and let her glowing eyes fall on the captain's. "Relax, captain, we are your friends. Don't I have friendly eyes?"

"Yes, you do," replied the captain.

"I want you to feel comfortable with us. We are your friends. You would like to be friends with us, right?"

"Yes, I would."

"Good. Commander Filo and I are here to ensure you have a good time with the hope that we can improve relations between the Alphas and Euclidians. Commander Filo has a proposal that he wants to present, if that's okay with you?"

"Yes, of course. I'd love to hear it," the captain replied.

"I'm going to leave you two to talk. Listen to everything Commander Filo has to say, and agree to everything he asks."

"I would be happy to, Yoyo."

"Great. I will wait for you in the booth, commander."

"I appreciate your help connecting us, Yoyo," said Filo. "I'll join you in a few minutes."

Commander Filo waited for Yoyo to leave the room and then focused his attention on the captain. "You are Captain Yondel from the Euclidian ship *Tez*, right?"

"Yes, I am."

"You participated in the attack on the Alpha home planet that led to its destruction, didn't you?"

"I can proudly say that I did."

"Wonderful. I want you to enjoy your time here in the Laldexian Room. Tonight when you return home I want you to get some rope and a container of lotion and then stand on a chair. Attach one end of the rope to something sturdy above your head and attach the other end around your neck in a knot that will not be easy to loosen once tightened. Are you with me so far, captain?" Commander Filo asked with a smile.

"Yes, I am."

"Next I want you to drop your pants and shorts around your ankles, place some of the lotion in your hand and rub it on your crotch. Drop the container to the floor and then kick the chair from underneath you. The noose will tighten around your neck, but don't fight it. Embrace the pain. Enjoy the moment as I will when I think of you tonight."

"I will do as you requested."

"Great. Now forget that you ever saw me, or Yoyo. The server will be in soon to take care of you."

Commander Filo walked out of the Laldexian Room smiling. He contacted the server to make sure the captain got all the attention he needed, and then joined Yoyo in their booth.

"How did everything go?" asked Yoyo.

"I think it went quite well. I'll know for sure in the morning. One down, three to go."

"What's that?"

"Engagements, Yoyo. Merely engagements," replied Commander Filo, rubbing his hands together and smiling wryly.

CHAPTER 6

Finding Betty

Betty rested on the bed for a few minutes, recovering from her horrible ordeal in transit to Boudreau's place. However, now was not the time to become complacent. With her hands still tied behind her, she took the knife from her back pocket and hid it under one of the pillows. She then laid her head on the pillow and tried to get some sleep. Exhausted after four hours in the SUVs, the plane, the truck, and the sedan, she was happy to get some needed shuteye.

As Betty slept she dreamt of better times, when she first became a police officer. She had been full of hope and the belief that she could make a difference in the city of DC. But although she took several bad guys off the street, many got away. Some criminals got off due to legal technicalities, some from bribes, and others due to witnesses that died before testifying.

The dream changed and Betty was in her grandmother's backyard, eating a bowl of strawberries with cream. She loved to tip the bowl above her head and let the cream drip into her mouth.

"Having fun, Betty?"

"Yes, grandma. I love the strawberries. And the cream is so creamy."

"What you going to do today, little girl?"

Betty smiled up at her grandmother. "I'm going to save the whirl."

Next, Betty was on a horse, riding fast after some bad guys. Then she was wearing armor and carrying a lance. The dreaded Blue Beard was coming at her. She leaned forward, aiming her lance at his chest. Just as the tip was about to hit her opponent she fell from her horse and out of an airplane behind several other parachutists. Their chutes opened to reveal brightly colored cloth that filled the sky. She floated down on top of the cloths into a field of brilliant flowers.

Betty's brother Tommy came over and kicked sand in her face.

"Take that, you mean old sister," yelled Tommy as he ran off.

Betty chased after him. "Tommy, come back here," she shouted. "I'm going to kick your butt."

Betty tackled Tommy to the ground and started punching him while screaming at him at the top of her lungs.

"I'm the dominatrix. I do all the hitting and you do all the getting."

Three women had entered the bedroom. One of them poked at Betty and said, "Okay, dominatrix, time to get up so we can clean you up. I can't believe they didn't let you go to the bathroom. You smell like shit."

Another woman said, "This is how it's going to go down. I'm going to cut you loose and you are going to follow me into the bathroom. My companions will watch while you get cleaned up and I'll be in the hall with a stun gun in case you try to escape. Once you're finished cleaning up, you will put on this gown and come back here where you'll get some food. After you finish eating we will tie you back up. If you resist in any way you will be stunned, stripped down, tied up and the men will deal with you. Let me know that you understand."

"Yes, I understand," said Betty. "I won't give you any trouble."

The last thing Betty wanted at that point was to be stunned again. She was starving and felt grimy. Even if she could get away from the women, the chance of getting out of the house and off the island was pretty slim, though the thought of spending the rest of her short life as a sex slave didn't appeal to her either. She would be patient and wait for an opportunity to escape.

Betty was cut loose and she followed the two women into the bathroom. The bathroom smelled wonderfully of lavender and Betty took a moment to breathe in the fragrance. Across from the entryway was a charming wooden vanity with intricate carvings and a marble countertop. On the counter was a vase full of white Calla lilies, and lotion, liquid soap, and an assortment of perfume bottles. Neatly folded plush towels lay on heated shelves next to the vanity.

"There are toothbrushes, toothpaste, and deodorant in the drawers," said one of the women. "You can take a shower or bath if you like."

"Is it okay if I take both? I'd first like to sit on the toilet, then rinse off in the shower and then take a nice, long, hot bath."

"Whatever suits your fancy. Throw your clothes in the trash bin. You won't be wearing those again. That jar by the tub has some pretty neat bath salts. Now, we're going to sit right here and keep an eye on you. Judy is right outside the door."

"Can I at least sit on the toilet in private? I won't give you any trouble."

"Tell that to Pierre," the woman replied. "I hear you knocked out one of his teeth."

"Yeah, well, he deserved it."

"Whatever, lady."

Betty removed her soiled clothes and placed them in the trash bin. She sat on the toilet to properly relieve herself. *It never felt so good to take a dump, even if I am being starred at.* It was a little embarrassing, making all her bathroom noises and wiping her butt under the scrutiny of two strange women, but what choice did she have?

Betty wiped herself with a moist towelette, which felt much better than regular toilet paper. She finished and flushed the toilet.

"I hope the smell wasn't too noxious for you ladies," Betty said with a smile.

"We been out in this bayou for many a year. Trust me, we have smelled a lot worse," one replied. "What the hell happened to your leg? It looks pretty bad. Let me have the doc take a look at that before you shower. I don't want you to get an infection."

"I'm sure the men folk would hate to see me lose my leg. That would really spoil the romance," Betty said sarcastically.

"Don't worry, they'd just give you to the guards, who would find lots of fun things to do to you over the next couple of years while we keep you alive. I'll be right back with the doctor. Just sit there on the toilet until I get back."

Soon afterward, a doctor showed up to look at Betty's wound.

"I can't believe they didn't call me sooner. It's already infected, but it should heal okay. I'll clean it out, sew it up, and give you a shot to help clear the infection. I suggest you do not have sex for a couple of days."

"Is it okay if I take a shower and bath?"

"Sure, just apply some of this ointment afterward and apply a clean bandage."

The doctor took care of Betty's leg and prepared to leave. Betty thanked him and stepped into the large shower stall made from Italian marble. It had multiple showerheads protruding from several locations. She felt clean just looking at them. Betty turned on every head full blast, all the way hot. She stood in the middle and let the hot streams of water wash the funk from her body. From a tube on the shelf she squeezed aromatic liquid soap all over her body and rubbed it in. She couldn't help but want to pleasure herself, but there were too many eyes on her. She dreaded the thought that the remainder of her sex life would be forced on her by men she didn't like and end with her death.

Oh, what the hell, what are they going to do to me? Kidnap me and lock me up in a house in some backwoods swamp? Betty took a handful of the liquid soap and rubbed herself into oblivion.

She finished her shower and dried off with one of the large, warm, fluffy towels. They were the color of gold. *At least I will live in style the few miserable months that I have left on this planet.*

Betty ran hot water into the sunken tub, bending over to sprinkle some of the fragrant bath salts from the jar on the tub under the watchful eyes of her guards.

One of the women giggled. "Nice ass," she said. "Did you enjoy touching yourself in the shower?"

"You can be assured that I wasn't thinking about either of you," Betty snapped. She hated being out of control. That was one of the reasons she had become a police officer. But she decided she'd better get used to it if she wanted to survive in captivity. As long as she was alive she might have a chance to escape. For years she had played the role of dominatrix in her off-hours, making men cry out in pain and grovel at her feet. Now, if she couldn't escape, she'd probably be the one groveling. And the heavily guarded bridge that led from the compound, with a swamp full of alligators surrounding it, made her chances of escape pretty slim.

Betty sank down into the tub, enjoying the warmth of the water against her skin and its fragrance in her nostrils. She let sleep overtake her and rested there until awakened by her guards.

"Time's up, sleeping beauty. Put on this gown and we'll take you back to the room for some food. Looks like you got out of sex for the night."

"Lucky me," replied Betty sarcastically. She placed some of the ointment on her wound as the doctor had instructed and covered it with a fresh bandage. She put on her gown and followed her escorts back to the room. No sooner had she lain down than a servant brought her some food.

"Good evening, miss," he said. "I brought you a large bowl of jambalaya with rice and a glass of red wine. I hope you enjoy it."

"I'm sure I will. Thank you for bringing it."

"You're welcome. Just place the tray by the door when you are done. There's bottled water on the dresser if you need it. Good night, miss."

"Goodnight, sir," replied Betty.

Betty ate her food and placed the tray by the door. A little later two of the women came in.

"Betty, I'm going to tie your hands together in front of you. Somebody will be outside your door all night. Stay away from the door and the window unless you want to be tied up to the bed. You don't bother us and we won't bother you."

After the wonderful bath and food, Betty was ready for sleep. She was out cold in no time, even with her hands tied. She dreamt of great battles, flying fantasies, and sitting with her grandmother. A few hours later she awoke in the dark room to the sound of gunfire. Thinking this could be an opportunity for her to sneak out, she retrieved her knife from under the pillow and cut herself loose. She sat on the floor with a wooden chair before her and worked away with the knife until she got one of the legs loose. With the chair leg in one hand and the knife in the other, she looked out the window to see if she could view the commotion but there was nothing to see except the bars that covered the window.

Betty moved to the door. She tried the knob, but the latch was locked. She looked for a way to get the hinges loose, to no avail. She heard footsteps approach the door, and took a position behind it, poised to attack.

***

Late that evening, Uan arrived at the huge condo he shared with Calvin, angry that he had been unable to find that pesky alien or his earthling companion.

"Hey, Uan," greeted Calvin, Uan's assistant since Uan killed Calvin's previous boss and took over the boss' apartment building. Uan was a crewmember on the Euclidian resource ship *Andrea* and had come to Earth on orders from the captain to kill an escaped alien. Uan came from the Ossuary System and had joined the *Andrea* crew as an assassin. The alien he was chasing had special powers that could possibly thwart the *Andrea*'s planned invasion of Earth. The alien had befriended an Earthling named Morgan; the ship's security team had tracked down Morgan by tapping into security cameras on Earth. Uan had teamed up with Calvin because he needed assistance getting around DC and communicating with people.

Uan didn't like Calvin much at first because he wasn't very tough. Even after Uan had spent a couple of hours teaching him some fighting techniques, Calvin was unable to defend himself. When faced with a couple local gang members who threatened his life, Calvin had been too afraid to use the moves Uan taught him. After that, Uan was concerned that he couldn't count on him in a fight. But when a fight did occur, Calvin had jumped in to protect Uan.

"Hello, Calvin," Uan said sourly.

"You won't have to worry about that cop bothering you anymore."

"What cop? What are you talking about?"

"The lady cop that saved you from the bar fight then tied you to her bed and beat the crap out of you."

"She didn't beat the crap out of me. She is just more physical in bed than most women. So what happened to her?"

"Little Randy turned her over to the Italians. They had some sort of beef with her. Anyway, she's out of your hair now."

"Why would he do that?" Uan said angrily.

"I guess for the money. I thought you didn't like her."

"I did not like her, but I do not want to see her harmed. I am going to get some food. Find out where she is."

Uan grabbed some raw steak from the fridge and Calvin went to talk to Little Randy. Little Randy was a gang member that inherited the surrounding neighborhood to carry out his illegal activities after Uan killed the previous gang leader, Bo Sam, and moved into his building.

When Calvin returned he said, "Hey, Uan, I got some information for you on Betty. According to Little Randy, a couple of Luciano's guys picked her up this morning and took her to his place. That's all he knows."

"Do you know how to get to Luciano's place?"

"Yes, of course. He lives in Little Italy. It's just a couple of miles from here."

"Good. Go get the car. I want you to take me there. I plan to get her back from Luciano."

"If you say so. But it won't be as easy as your previous encounters since you arrived. Luciano has lots of guys who carry big guns with lots of bullets."

"I am not a fan of easy. I want it to be hard. I want them to put up a good fight. It will make killing them all the more rewarding."

Calvin walked out the door shaking his head and pulled the SUV out in front of the apartment building. Uan jumped in and Calvin headed out to Little Italy, where Luciano had a large three-story, ten-bedroom mansion nestled in a cul-de-sac surrounded by family members' houses. Calvin parked down the street from the mansion to stay hidden from its cameras.

"Calvin, just stay her. I'll go in and get Betty and be right back."

"What about Luciano's men?"

"I'll get inside using my stealth ability. I'll take out anyone I need to and bring her back. Of course, if she's dead I'll make sure everyone else in the house is, too, before I return," said Uan with a snarl.

Uan cloaked himself and stepped out of the SUV. He jogged up to the large brick fence surrounding the mansion, past the guards at the gate, and then hopped over the seven-foot fence in a single stride.

What I wouldn't give to have those powers, Calvin thought. *The honeys I could sneak up on!*

Uan had bitten Calvin soon after they met so that Uan's enzymes would permit Calvin to see him while he was cloaked. As an Ossie, Uan could make himself invisible to non-Ossies. He also had incredible strength for someone only five-foot six inches tall.

Uan walked around the side of the house to look for a good entry point. He spied a large third-floor balcony overlooking the swimming pool and surmised that it must lead to Luciano's part of the house.

One of Luciano's guard dogs noticed Uan's scent and trotted toward him. The dog was perplexed that it couldn't see what was giving off the strong odor.

Uan looked down at the Rottweiler unperturbed and then thought of a way to introduce himself to Luciano. Uan attacked the dog and killed it with a single thrust of his spear. Uan leapt with the dog to the balcony where Luciano sat in a lounge chair, smoking a cigar and chatting with one of his lieutenants. The two men looked up in utter terror as they saw the massive dog hanging in midair and bleeding from a wound in its chest.

Uan uncloaked and hurled the huge dead beast at the two men. Luciano's lieutenant went for his gun but Uan sprang forward, jabbed his sword into the man's chest and twisted it, causing him to momentarily writhe in pain then fall forward dead. Luciano gasped as events unfolded before him, dropping the cigar from his mouth. Uan turned toward him, aiming his spear.

"Take me to Betty and I will let you live," he demanded.

Uan noticed movement behind him. He cloaked and shifted to the side, avoiding bullets from two men that had stepped onto the balcony and were firing automatic weapons.

"Where did he go?" shouted Luciano.

Uan leapt and cut off the hand of one of the men then drove his spear into the chest of the other, pushing him from the balcony into the room against two other men that had arrived with guns drawn. Luciano watched in horror as his men were chopped up by the invisible assailant. As soon as Uan finished with those four, however, four more showed up, firing around the room trying to hit him.

Uan ducked and rolled toward a wall. He darted behind the men and stabbed two of them as the other two turned their guns on him. He jumped over their heads and from behind watched them shoot into an empty room. Luciano, still on the balcony, was calling for backup.

"Send everybody up here now! There's some invisible guy making mincemeat of my people. I don't give a damn what it sounds like. You call as many people as you can and get them over here."

Once the shooting died down, Uan shoved his spear into the smaller man and yanked the gun from the taller man's hands. This guy was six-foot seven and weighed well over three hundred pounds: just the challenge Uan was looking for. Uan uncloaked and threw his spear to the ground.

"How about you show me how tough you are, big guy?" Uan snarled.

The man was frightened but took a swing at Uan just the same. "I don't know what you are, but I am going to crush your tiny body."

His swing missed, but his follow-up kick caught Uan in the gut and hurled him across the room. Uan sprang to his feet and ran at the large man, ducking another blow and landing one of his own to the man's midsection, knocking him to the floor. The man took it in stride, rolling to his feet and delivering a blow to Uan's chest that knocked him down. He grabbed Uan by the foot and belt and flung him against the far wall to crush a framed painting and crack the wall behind it.

"Finally, a worthy adversary," yelled Uan as he jumped to his feet and lunged at the man. They traded punches until Uan got a clear shot at his face and stunned him with a blow to his cheek. As he staggered, Uan lifted him over his head and threw him at the men that were coming up the stairs, taking them out. Luciano stood in the doorway with a gun trying to aim at Uan, who cloaked and retrieved his spear.

Uan knocked the gun from Luciano's hand and dragged him back onto the balcony, putting the spear point to his throat.

"Now tell me where Betty is or I will cut your head from your body."

"What the hell are you? And who is this Betty person?" Luciano stammered.

"What I am is not up for discussion. Betty is the policewoman you kidnapped today. Take me to her now or I will chop off your body parts until your memory improves. If you are not the right person to talk to, I will kill you quickly and find someone who can help me."

"Oh, that woman. What would you want with her? She's just a policewoman and she's trouble."

"Do not worry about why I want her. You should worry about telling me where she is and that she is still alive."

"She's not here. I sent her to Louisiana. I had my people hand her off to an associate who lives in Nagadish."

"What is his name?"

"Pierre. Pierre Thibodeaux."

"What is his address?"

"I don't know. We only connect by phone."

"I think it's best if you don't call him. I am going to this Nagadish place to find Pierre and take Betty from him." Uan bared his sharp teeth and leaned into Luciano. His stale breath hit Luciano in the face, while blood from his spear dripped onto Luciano's clothes. "If Pierre Thibodeaux has killed her I will come back here and cut up the rest of your crew before I slowly peel the skin from your body and watch you bleed to death. If you are smart you will tell no one you ever saw me. I do not want you warning Pierre or anyone else of my plans."

"I promise I won't say a word," said Luciano, visibly afraid for his life.

Several more of Luciano's men had entered the room and were approaching the balcony. Uan shoved Luciano to the floor then turned and jumped from the balcony, cloaking himself on the way over. Luciano and his men looked over the balcony and saw nothing. It was as if Uan was never there. However, there were too many dead bodies lying around for Luciano to believe that he was just having a bad dream. He stood there looking at the pile of corpses and pissed his pants.

***

Uan climbed into the SUV next to Calvin.

"They took Betty to some city in Louisiana. Take me home and then show me where Nagadish is on a map. I will have our reconnaissance ship take me there"

"You mean, take us there, don't you? I want to join you on this trip. It could be like our trip to Tajikistan."

"No, that is not a good idea. This trip is likely to include a lot more violence. In Tajikistan we were just contending with an arms dealer. I suspect this Boudreau that has Betty is a violent killer like Luciano. In addition, I am sure that Luciano will warn his friends that I am coming. That makes things too dangerous for you. I just want to get in and out with as little death and destruction as possible. I am still supposed to keep a low profile here on your planet, even though I have slipped up from time to time."

"Okay, you're the boss."

***

Calvin parked the SUV in front of the apartment building. Once inside, Calvin attempted to look up Nagadish using Bing Maps with no luck.

"Uan, I'm not having much success finding this place. Let me call my Cajun friend Keith to see if he can help us out."

"Fine. I am going to grab a steak from the refrigerator."

Calvin placed the call. "Keith, my man, I'm so glad you picked up. I'm trying to find Nagadish on the map."

"You mean the one in Louisiana?" Keith replied.

"Yeah, that's the one."

"It's just south of Shreveport on Highway 6."

"How come I don't see it?"

"Probably because you don't know how to spell it," said Keith with a laugh.

"How hard can it be? Something like, N a g a d i s h, right?"

"No, it's N a t c h i t o c h e s."

"You have got to be kidding me. Why would someone pronounce that word like that? Hold on, let me take another look. Oh, okay. I found it. Now I understand why I couldn't find it. You people don't know how to pronounce shit. You can't even pronounce a simple name like New Orleans."

"Whatever, Calvin. I got your 'you people' hangin'. And it's pronounced Norlins."

"That's exactly what I mean. It's like you guys live in another country."

"Did you get what you need? I got a woman waiting on me," Keith said impatiently.

"Sure, I got it, Keith. Thanks for the help."

"Yeah, anytime," replied Keith, hanging up.

"Uan, I found it," shouted Calvin.

Uan came back to the room finishing off the last bite of his steak. "Let me see where it is." Uan looked at Calvin's computer. "I see it. I will add the coordinates to my UCD and send them to my ship to set up a pick up and drop off. I should see you in a few hours if everything goes well."

No sooner had Uan finished speaking than he beamed away. Calvin shook his head in amazement. *This is almost like Star Trek. And to think that I get to be part of the show.*

CHAPTER 7

Turning the XO

Commander Filo and Yoyo sat in the Bordelle Bar, waiting for the XO of the *Andrea* to show up. One of the man's staff members had told Filo to expect him there today, but so far nothing. If he were very lucky, though, another captain of the Euclidian resource vessels that had assisted with the destruction of the Alpha home planet would appear while they waited. The chances of that were slim but Filo did not have any better leads.

"This person must be awfully special if you are waiting for him for so long in this place," said Yoyo.

"It's important for our ability to connect with the Euclidians. He is the executive officer of the *Andrea*, a very prominent Euclidian resource ship. He has a direct line to its captain, who is very influential in the Euclidian military. The captain's father also has great connections in political and social circles."

Another hour passed, and then two of the bar's dancers walked into the bar on the arms of the XO from the *Andrea*. Commander Filo tipped the server to invite the XO over for a drink of Tammarian grog.

The XO asked his escorts to wait for him in a booth and walked over to see who had made the generous offer.

"Hello, commander. Please let me speak before you voice any objections."

"Sure, go ahead and speak your piece," replied the XO, taking a seat in the booth.

Commander Filo motioned for the server to bring drinks of Tammarian grog for the table.

"I am Commander Filo of the Alpha ship *Adele*. This is Ambassador Yoyo, representing the Magi people from the planet Tammaria. She makes a mean grog, by the way." The XO only grunted.

"We sincerely would like to improve relations between the Alpha and Euclidian people. Yoyo is acting as a liaison to help facilitate negotiations. I would like her to say a few words if you don't mind. Hold on, here are our drinks." The server placed three steins of grog in front of them. Filo raised his stein in a toast: "To the Euclidian Empire and better relations." The XO shrugged and took a big swig of his grog. Yoyo slurped down some of hers.

"Yoyo, if you please," urged Commander Filo.

Yoyo removed her goggles to reveal her glowing eyes, careful to keep her hood up to prevent onlookers from noticing. The XO looked at her in shock.

"Don't look away," commanded Yoyo. "Look into my eyes and relax. I want you to throw away your inhibitions and submit yourself to my gaze."

The XO leaned forward as Yoyo continued to gaze into his eyes.

"Think of me as your best friend. You trust me and would do anything for me. Being around me makes you feel comfortable. Do you like my smile?"

"Yes, I do."

"I want you to forget any animosities that you have against the Alpha people. Commander Filo is your new best friend. He just bought you a Tammarian grog. You feel completely at ease with him and are happy to do whatever he wants. It will even please you to obey him, will it not?"

"Yes, it will."

"Thanks, Yoyo," said Filo. "Now why don't you go off and enjoy yourself? I'm sure there are still parts of the city that you haven't seen."

"I'd be glad to. There's a club I would like to visit. Let me know how your meeting with him goes."

"Oh, I will, Yoyo. I will."

Yoyo walked out and Commander Filo turned to the XO.

"You're on the ship commanded by Captain Shisal, are you not?"

"Yes, I am."

"Did you know that he plans to cut you out of your portion of the revenues from your next mission?"

"He's mean, but he tends to be a fair person. I can't believe he would do that."

"Not only would he, but he has already told me that he will. He plans to frame you for stealing goods destined for the government and have you arrested. Doesn't that make you angry?"

"Of course it does."

"This is what I want you to do to protect your share of the bounty. When he is ashore during your next mission, away from the protection of the ship's systems, I want you to have him killed. That is the only way to protect what's yours. Don't you agree?"

The XO rubbed his chin in deep thought. "That's not an easy thing to do. I can certainly discuss it with him."

"That's not enough. You must kill Captain Shisal!"

"I will kill him!" said the XO with conviction.

"You can go rejoin your ladies now. Thanks for coming by. Please forget we ever talked."

"Sure thing. Goodbye."

Commander Filo clapped his hands together and let out a wicked laugh. *Two down, two to go!*

***

A few days later, Yoyo and Filo met again at the Bordelle Bar and watched as the captain of the Euclidian resource ship *Alvin* sat down at a table and hung his coat on the back of his chair. They walked across the room and struck up a conversation with him.

"Greetings, Captain Krashan. You probably don't know me. I'm Commander Filo of the Alpha ship *Adele*. I was in space en route to my home planet while you were busy destroying it."

"I hope you got to see the event. It was spectacular. I have a recording if you would like to get a look at it."

"No, I've seen other recordings, enough times to memorize them. Right now I want to see you get hacked up by that Ossie over there."

"Oh, because you're too much of a coward to attack me," said Captain Krashan, leaning into Filo with a finger in his chest, "you want me to attack someone who has done nothing to me. Is that right?"

"I'm not very good at explaining things. Perhaps my colleague can do a better job. Yoyo, this is Captain Krashan. Can you convince him that he and I should work together?"

Yoyo tapped the man on the arm. "Captain Krashan," she whispered, removing her goggles, "this Alpha is your friend and you want to do whatever he tells you. Do you understand?"

"Yes, little one," replied the captain.

"Thanks, Yoyo," said Filo. "I'll catch up with you later. I'm going to have a private chat with the captain." Yoyo departed and Filo took Krashan to a quiet corner of the bar.

"Captain Krashan, that Ossie over there is your mortal enemy. You hate him immensely. I want you to kill him, now, with your bare hands."

"With pleasure. Hey, Ossie, you're going down," screamed the captain, diving at the man.

The captain tackled the Ossie to the ground and started pounding on him, while the crew of the *Alvin* who had accompanied him to the bar looked on in disbelief. The Ossie kneed the captain over his head and jumped to his feet. He grabbed Krashan by the back of his pants and spun him backward, throwing him over his head to the floor five meters away. The captain rolled to a stop and looked back with disdain.

"Why are you attacking me?" shouted the Ossie.

"Because I hate your guts!"

"You don't even know me."

"I don't care. I'm still going to kill you." Captain Krashan got to his feet and rushed at the Ossie.

The Ossie cloaked himself and vanished as the captain's crew gathered around him.

"Captain, are you okay?"

"Yes, I'm fine." He pushed the crewmen away, grabbed his jacket, and walked out the door. A short distance down the street, his friend, Captain Witt of the resource ship *Bonni*, caught up to him.

"Krashan, are you okay? I walked into the bar just as you attacked the Ossie. What the hell happened to you in there?"

"I don't know, Witt. For some reason I felt compelled to attack him."

Commander Filo had followed Captain Krashan out of the bar and couldn't believe his luck when he saw the fourth captain on his list show up. He thought up a plan and waited in a nearby shop doorway to hatch it.

"Krashan, you need to get back to your ship and see a doctor," insisted Captain Witt.

"I will. I just need some time to clear my head."

"Okay, I'm going back to the bar. I'll see you later."

"Sure, Witt. Thanks for checking on me."

Captain Witt turned and walked away. Filo ran up to Krashan, whispered in his ear, and watched as the captain ran down the street after his friend. "Hey, Witt, wait up."

Captain Witt turned in time to see Captain Krashan stab him in the chest with a knife, killing him. Krashan then ran into the street, headlong into the grille of an oncoming military transport vehicle, killing himself.

CHAPTER 8

Retrieving Betty

Uan was irate to hear what had happened to Betty and he couldn't understand why. Somehow he felt an attachment to her. He deeply wanted to kill her for humiliating him the way she had, but he couldn't stand to think of anyone else harming her. He called up the Euclidian reconnaissance ship that was stationed on Earth on the floor of the Atlantic Ocean and requested transport to Louisiana.

The ship arrived in Natchitoches that evening and Uan went straight to a bar to begin looking for Pierre Thibodeaux. A few guys were drinking beer as they stood around a pool table and Uan decided to see what he could find out from them.

"Excuse me, I'm looking to score a kilo and I heard that I should look up Pierre Thibodeaux."

"He might be the guy," said one of the men, "but why should I tell you anything?"

"How about I slip you a fifty?"

"That would work. How do I know you're not a cop?"

"Really? A tiny guy with a Scottish accent and face tattoo. I don't think I would pass the entrance exam."

"Good point. Pass me the fifty."

Uan gave him a fifty and the man whispered in his ear. "He hangs out at JJ's Club, on Highway 1 just south of the airport."

"Thanks," said Uan. He walked out to the parking lot, jumped into the passenger side of a truck that a man had just started, and offered him fifty dollars to drop him off at JJ's.

"Get the hell out my truck, little fella, before I drag you out by your ear," said the man.

Uan placed the blade of his spear to the man's throat. "You take me to the club or I'll cut you from ear to ear. What do you think of that, big fella?"

"I think if you slide that blade back a bit I can put this truck in gear and git you to that bar you asked about," the man said nervously.

Uan obliged the man and ten minutes later he was standing in front of JJ's Club. Uan handed the man fifty dollars and stepped down from the truck, which immediately pulled away. The club was a long rectangular cinder block building in the middle of a dirt parking lot. Loud country music came from the open doors.

Uan approached the door where a bouncer blocked his path. "You don't look old enough to come in here, little fella. You got any ID?"

"Sure," responded Uan. He grabbed the man by the crotch and lifted him up and against the building. "It is in my hand. Would you like me to pull it out so you can see it?"

"No!" gasped the bouncer, astonished to be lifted up so high by such a small person.

"That is what I thought," replied Uan, releasing the man so he could drop to his feet.

Uan walked through the door and felt a hand on his chest that stopped his forward progress.

"Where you going, fella?" a stern firm voice asked. "It costs five dollars to get up in here."

Uan was being blocked by a petite woman. She was pretty, with piercing eyes and a tough demeanor that gave one the impression she was not the type of person to be ignored. Uan resisted the urge to simply snap her neck and throw her to the floor, concerned that this might draw too much attention now that he was inside the club. He didn't want to scare away the man he was looking for.

Uan handed her a twenty. "Here, just keep the change," he shouted over the loud music.

"Thanks. I'm Dominique. You look like you're new around here. I'm off in an hour, if you need a tour guide or anything else tonight."

"I'll keep that in mind. Can you point out Pierre Thibodaux?"

"Sure. He's the big guy with the beard in the blue three piece suit across from the dance floor."

"I see him. Thanks."

Uan walked into the crowded room toward Pierre, passed by him, and stood a few feet away, waiting for an opportunity to talk to him in private. Uan got a few strange looks from passersby, but ignored them. Pierre stood along the wall with some of his associates, admiring the women in tight short skirts on the dance floor. Forty-five minutes later, Pierre finally pushed away from the wall and headed to the men's room.

Uan followed. Another man was finishing up at the sink. Pierre went into a stall and closed the door. Uan grabbed the man at the sink and shoved him through Pierre's stall door, knocking Pierre onto the commode. Uan closed the door behind him and started chopping up the stranger with his spear.

"What the fuck!" exclaimed Pierre as he shoved his way to the back of the stall.

Uan dropped the stranger to the floor and looked at Pierre. "I have no idea who this man is. If I did not hesitate to cut him," Uan growled and leaned into Pierre with his spear at his throat, "what do you think I will do to a man who has hurt someone I care about?"

"What do you want?" asked Pierre in a trembling voice.

Uan just paused for a moment, staring at Pierre through his shades. "You brought a woman named Betty here. I want to know what happened to her. Tell me what I want to know and I will let you live. Hesitate and I will start slicing you up."

"I handed her off to Boudreau this afternoon. She was just fine when I left her."

"Where can I find this Boudreau?"

"He lives back up in the Negreet bayou on a compound in the middle of a swamp full of alligators."

"How do I find this compound?"

"Negreet isn't a big place. It only has one street. Two miles up the road is Collier Memorial Park. Just beyond that is the bridge to Boudreau's island. You should find her there."

"Good. If I do not find her there I will be back and you will lose some body parts."

"I can't say for sure, but she should be there."

Uan wiped his spear on Pierre's pants and walked out of the bathroom to the club entrance. He paused in front of Dominique and tried to think what to say.

"I'm on my way out" said Dominique. "You want me to show you around town?"

"Do you know where Negreet is?"

"Yes, but no one in their right mind would want to go up there. Especially this time of night."

"Who said I was in my right mind? I'll give you a thousand dollars if you drop me off at a bridge off the main road a couple miles beyond town."

"Oh, you're going to Boudreau's place. You definitely have a death wish. He owe you a bundle of money or something?"

"He has something of mine and I plan to get it back."

"Okay, but you better have an army of people meeting you there."

"I won't need an army. I just need you to take me there. I will do the rest. And I will pay you a thousand dollars if you take me there, wait for me to return, and then drive me to Shreveport."

"For a thousand dollars I'll carry you to Shreveport on my back!"

"That will not be necessary. Just get me to that bridge as soon as you can."

"Sure. Let's go."

Dominique led Uan to the black Lincoln she used as a limo to chauffeur people in her off-hours. She started the car and headed down Highway 6. Uan sat in the back and looked out the window into the darkness. All he could see were endless trees capped by a field of stars. He let himself get lost in the darkness as the anger welled up inside him. He wallowed in his anger. An anger that typically drove him to violence.

Uan had only known Betty for a brief time, but somehow she had gotten under his skin. He had been enraged at the fearless way she had tied him to that bed and had her way with him. Then she just untied him and walked away with her back to him when he could have so easily snapped her neck. Her confidence impressed him. Now he was afraid she might be dead.

The thought made him angry. Angry that someone would dare steal away a woman he cared about, despite not really understanding why he cared about her. If there was any good for Uan in the situation it was that pretty soon he would get to do some killing. Whether Betty was alive or dead, those that had taken her captive would pay.

Dominique drove through the small town of Many and continued down Highway 6 to the turnoff for Negreet. The paved road soon became a dirt road and the surrounding trees seem to swallow them up. After five minutes of jostling down the rutted road, Dominique pulled over and turned off her lights.

"The bridge to Boudreau's place is just around that bend in the road," said Dominique. "We should walk from here."

"There is no we," replied Uan. "You wait here for me to return."

"I didn't come this far to sit in the car and let you do all the work. He has a lot of men and you'll need my help. Anyway, he's a piece of shit lowlife that has more than once killed a friend of mine. I just want a little payback."

"Okay, but stay behind me. I want to make sure my friend is still alive before any shooting starts."

They slowly made their way to the bridge, which was blocked by a gate with guards on the other side. The water around the bridge was filled with alligators. At the other end of the bridge were more guards protecting the compound. The compound was surrounded by a fence to keep the alligators out.

"Let me tell you what is going to happen," whispered Uan. "I will jump the fence, take out the guards, and open the gate. If Betty is still alive I will free her and come running out with her. Shoot anyone that does not look like me."

"I got it. You're going to jump a seven foot fence, kill those guys without them seeing you, then run past the other guards, break your girlfriend out of a heavily guarded compound, and then come running back with her over your shoulder. Is that it?"

"Yes, something like that. I should be back in ten minutes. If I seem to disappear it is just a ninja trick I learned."

Dominique gave him a look of incredulity as he briskly walked away and cloaked himself.

What the hell? thought Dominique as Uan disappeared before her eyes. *That's some ninja trick.*

Uan hopped over the fence with ease and landed quietly on the other side. He quickly stabbed both guards in the chest with his spear and quietly laid them on the bridge. He ran toward the compound where four other guards were waiting, two on each side of the bridge. Uan approached the two on the left, sliced through their necks and threw one of them across the bridge at the other two guards. The guards stood there stunned as they watched their colleague suddenly take flight toward them. One of them lifted his automatic rifle and fired at the flying body. Uan ran over and quickly killed the two guards.

The noise caused a stir within the compound. Lights came on and more guards ran toward the bridge. Uan sneaked into the compound to find Betty. There were five buildings where she might be held. Uan spent fifteen minutes going through the first building with no luck. He was growing impatient and didn't want to waste any more time.

He found a guard patrolling the grounds, dragged him behind a building, and threw him to the ground. He put his hand over the man's mouth and stabbed him in the leg with his spear. The guard let out a muffled scream.

"Where is the policewoman that was kidnapped from DC? Tell me now or I will stab you in the other leg and then other body parts until you decide to talk."

"She's in there," whimpered the guard, pointing to one of the buildings. "Upstairs, in the back on the right-hand side."

"Thanks," said Uan. He tossed the man over the fence and into the bayou, where several alligators attacked him with much splashing and screaming. *I actually said thanks*, Uan thought with a snicker.

Uan entered the building and climbed the stairs. He found the door to the room the guard had described and eased it open, expecting more guards inside. He entered the dark room and from behind the door Betty hit him in the head with the chair leg.

"What the hell was that for?" screamed Uan as he uncloaked. "I came here to save you."

Betty flipped the light switch and was amazed to see Uan. "How was I supposed to know it was you? How did you find me? And why would you even want to save me?"

"No time for chit chat. We need to get out of here."

"If you'll notice my leg, you'll see I can't walk very well, let alone run."

"Not to worry. I will carry you."

"Really! You're just going to throw me over your shoulder and tip toe out of here? Is that right?"

"Yes!" Uan threw Betty over his shoulder, pulled out his pulse rifle and went down the stairs to the front door. As he exited the building he cloaked and headed for the bridge.

Betty screamed as Uan disappeared, drawing the attention of a group of guards near the bridge. Uan set the rifle for widespread stun and let them have it as he ran. They fell to the ground, looking in amazement as Betty jerked through the air toward them. Uan jumped over the bodies and ran across the bridge, followed by several more guards.

Dominique stood at the end of the bridge, watching the floating woman, which she figured was Uan's ninja trick again. She targeted the guards and took them out one by one with her 9mm pistol.

Uan shouted at Dominique to get the car. Someone screamed at them from behind. "You don't take what's mine and get away with it."

It was Boudreau. "I'm going to hunt you down like a dog and tear you limb from limb."

Uan turned and snarled, "She is my woman, you bastard." He fired his rifle and vaporized the man, leaving nothing but his shoes.

They ran to the car and headed back toward Many.

Betty was in shock. "How do you do that...do that invisible man thing?"

"I am an Ossie," said Uan. "I am from another planet. It is one of my abilities."

"An alien?" laughed Dominique. "Really? I thought you were a ninja."

At that moment a large truck came out of the trees and rammed their car to the side of the road. The truck backed up and Uan picked up his rifle but before he could fire the truck rammed them again, knocking the car into the bayou.

The car flipped over and quickly filled with water through the broken windows. As it sank to the bottom, Uan grabbed his universal connection device and started tapping away at it. An alligator poked its snout into the car and dragged Dominique out by her arm. Uan grabbed his spear, swam out of the car, and stabbed the alligator in the eye. The alligator loosened its grip on Dominique, but two more came after Uan and pulled him toward the bottom of the water.

Betty gasped for breath from an air pocket at the back of the car. She shivered with fear as an alligator came at her and opened its mouth around her head.

CHAPTER 9

Freeing Dissidents

Li Xiao did not know where Yao Ming was being held, but she knew that eight Red Wall dissidents, three women and five men, were being held in Qincheng Prison outside of Beijing. She used Cobalt's device to explore the prison and locate the dissidents. The women were in a comfortable cell, much like a college dorm room, drinking tea. The men were in a typical prison cell furnished with small bunk beds, playing cards. One of men was missing, perhaps in the infirmary or maybe even dead.

Li Xiao donned her warrior goddess outfit to protect her identity and transported to an isolated area of Xiao Tangshan Park near the prison. She assured herself that the area was free of people and security cameras. Setting her device to auto return in three seconds, she tucked it into her vest pocket and pressed the transport button.

Li Xiao appeared in the women's cell. "Stay calm. I'm here to free you," she said, putting her arms around two of the women. "I'll be back for you momentarily," she said to the third, and transported back to the park.

"Please stay here and wait for me to return," said Li Xiao. She pressed the transmit button on her device and reappeared in the prison as the cell door was opening. She tossed a concussion grenade from her vest at the guards entering the door and grabbed the remaining prisoner as the grenade exploded, stunning the guards into inaction. The two women rolled across the bed and then were rolling on the grass in the park where they knocked over one of the other women she had freed.

"Hello, everyone," said Li Xiao. "I am Guan Yin. I have come to free you and the other dissidents. There are five men that I still need to free. Once I have freed you all, I will take you wherever you wish to go. Please wait here for me to return."

Li Xiao set the coordinates to the men's cell, placed the device in her vest, and pushed the transmit button. "Remain calm," she said to the men. "I am here to free you."

She embraced the two men nearest her and transported out.

A hurried voice came over the intercom in the prison's security office. "The Red Wall women have been freed by the goddess Guan Yin. We are checking the status of the Red Wall men."

Three guards entered the men's cell just in time to see Li Xiao disappear with two of them. The sight of the ancient goddess gave them pause but they quickly reported, "Security, two of the Red Wall men have been taken by the goddess."

The prison warden pushed the security operator away from the microphone. "There is no goddess, you idiots!" he yelled. "Guard the other two. I will send reinforcements."

The guards placed the two remaining men on a cot with their backs to each other and pointed their guns around the room, waiting for Guan Yin to return. This time, however, Li Xiao dropped down from the ceiling on top of one of the guards, knocking him to the ground and kicking another in the head on the way down. The third guard spun around to face Li Xiao but she had already propelled a steel ball at his head. He fell backwards and dropped his gun. Li Xiao jumped up, grabbed the guard by his arm and spun him around hard against the metal doorframe, rendering him unconscious. Taking hold of the remaining prisoners, she transported back to the park.

"Director," said a guard into his radio, "they're gone. They're all gone. The other guards are all on the floor, unconscious."

"Get down to the interrogation cell now," shouted the warden. "I want Lee Ho Jong chained to his chair and surrounded on all sides. Do not let him get away. I don't want to have to send condolence letters to your families!"

In the park, all the former prisoners stood around Li Xiao, gaping in amazement. "Are you truly the goddess Guan Yin?" asked one.

"No, but I represent her. Is everyone safe? There seems to be one person missing."

"Lee Ho Jong was taken out of the cell this morning to be interrogated. He is probably being tortured in the interrogation cell on the top floor of the building at the north side. They typically only keep us there for about two hours."

"I understand. I will try to save him later. Right now I want to get all of you to safety. Let me know where you want to got and I will take you right away."

The prisoners spoke amongst themselves for a few minutes then responded to Li Xiao. "We all would like to go to the offices of the Free China Organization in New York, please."

"I know the place quite well," said Li Xiao. "Give me a moment and I will take you all there."

Li Xiao went off to the side and set up her device to transport the six dissidents to the Free China offices in Manhattan. She found an empty storeroom in the basement of the building that had light coming into it from a window near the ceiling. She set the device to send them and returned it to her vest pocket.

"Are you all ready to go?"

"Yes, we are ready, priestess. But first we would like to honor you and the work you do." They all cao taoed before Li Xiao, saying, "Xiexie nǚshén."

Li Xiao bowed to them and replied, "Bu ku qi. Now we must go. I need three of you on each side, holding my arms and one another's, and one person holding me around my waist from behind. Great. Now squeeze tight."

Li Xiao slid her hand into her vest and pressed the transport button. Before she could blink they were all inside the storage room in the basement of the Free China offices.

"Is everyone okay?" Li Xiao asked.

They all felt each other in disbelief. *From jail to park to Manhattan within minutes. It must be a dream.*

"I am fine," they all finally responded, one at a time.

"Great. I wish you well on your journey. Now I will attempt to free your colleague, if he is still alive. Peace be with you." Li Xiao vanished and the former prisoners all bowed and said a prayer for Guan Yin.

Li Xiao returned to her home, where she used her device to determine Lee Ho Jong's location. Guards completely surrounded him. He was chained to a chair and another guard was sitting on his lap with his arms around his waist. *This is going to be extremely challenging, but not impossible.*

Li Xiao set several coordinate points in her transport device, equipped herself with infrared goggles and a few other items, and transported to a crawl space above the interrogation room. She placed a concussion grenade on the light box and armed it to go off in eight seconds before transporting herself to an empty room adjoining the interrogation room. She set the transport timer for two seconds and then transported to the corner of the room where Lee Ho Jong was being held.

"Wei!" she screamed as she appeared. She ran along the wall toward the other corner and disappeared to the adjoining room just as the grenade went off, extinguishing the lights. The guards fired at the wall where they last saw Li Xiao.

Li Xiao lowered the infrared goggles over her eyes and transported to the other side of the interrogation room. The guards were still facing the other wall, staring into the darkness. She pulled out a tranquilizer gun and one by one took the guards out. The last guard, sitting on Lee Ho Jong, heard the other guards fall. He pulled out his gun and pointed it at the prisoner.

"If I feel as much as a pinprick I will shoot this man dead," the guard shouted into the dark.

Li Xiao decided to take the guard at his word and returned the tranquilizer gun to its holster. She quietly walked up to the chair, stooped and grabbed Lee Ho Jong by his ankle, and transported. The three of them were falling through the air. The guard screamed. He dropped his gun and held on to Lee Ho Jong. Li Xiao climbed up the guard's back, reached around and pried his arm away. She forced her way between the men, shoved the guard away, and transported away just as the three fell into the lake at Beijing's Summer Palace.

Tourists at the Summer Palace took pictures of the drenched guard as he swam to the edge of the lake. He was met by palace guards who were more than pleased to help pull him out and then arrest him.

Li Xiao and Lee Ho Jong appeared at the Free China offices in New York alongside his colleagues who had been discovered by an employee of the organization. They all cheered as the two appeared.

"Lee Ho Jong, please forgive me for getting you all wet. I have brought you here to join your colleagues. I'm sure they will take good care of you."

"Thank you, Guan Yin," Lee Ho Jong said with a bow.

Li Xiao bowed in return, and transported back to her apartment.

CHAPTER 10

The Gorman

The average life span of Ossie males was forty-five years. The females typically lived beyond sixty years. Most men died in tribal battles or war games. Some died hunting. These were the preferred ways to die. Dying of old age was not a death of honor for Ossie men.

Ossies enjoyed the challenge of hunting animals. Of all the animals they hunted, gormans were the most feared. They were ferocious fighters with sharp claws and teeth. Ossies usually hunted gormans in groups, the more assuredly to defeat them. Using their stealth abilities, a hunting party could usually defeat a gorman, but the Ossies had to be quick, strong, and above all extremely quiet. The gorman's sense of hearing and smell made it difficult to sneak up on one. Attacking one head-on and single-handed was suicide. On occasion, though, an elderly or sickly Ossie might attempt this, rather than die dishonorably from natural causes.

Gormans lived in impenetrable dens where they were basically undefeatable. The planet Ossuary had tiny, rainbow colored slime beetles that lived off of gorman secretions: their sweat, tears, urine, earwax, and feces. Gorman tears were a beetle delicacy, but these were only shed when gormans mated and at those times the gormans' eyes were covered with beetles, which caused mating to be agonizing. Only gormans that could withstand the pain were able to have offspring, which made them the toughest of the tough.

Because the slime beetles effectively cleaned the gormans, their dens were free of smells except that of the aromatic beetle slime trails. The trails were also phosphorescent, which caused the gorman dens to glow and kept predators from using the cover of darkness to sneak in and attack their young. This didn't stop the Ossies, though, who enjoyed gorman meat as a delicacy. Dangerous as they were, gorman flesh was comparably more delectable.

The slime beetle had another practice that made it dangerous for Ossies to venture inside the dens. Because the beetles could not see very well, they relied on heat to find their host animals, but couldn't tell the difference between a gorman and an Ossie so they would often land on Ossies as they attempted to sneak into a cave to kill a gorman. Even if the Ossie brushed them away, the beetles left a telltale phosphorescent secretion behind, making the Ossie visible to the gormans.

On rare occasions, an Ossie would be valiant enough to defeat a gorman in its den. When this happened, the other gormans would give the Ossie safe passage to drag the carcass home as a prize to be eaten by him and his chosen few.

Because of the difficulty in killing a gorman in its cave, a special tattoo was given to any Ossie that managed the feat. At this time, only two living Ossies carried the crescent moon tattoo, Uan and Malcolm. Out of respect and fear, no Ossie ever attacked another that wore the tattoo.

After the Ossuary system was discovered by extraterrestrials, the fighting between tribes ended. The Ossies felt it was more rewarding and practical to kill the outsiders.

The Ossies ignored all attempts by extraterrestrials to communicate with them. They saw no benefit in befriending outsiders, and felt that it would lead to misplaced trust and betrayal.

Several alien species attempted to tame the primitive Ossies, but their cloaking ability and relentless fighting style were too much for other species to cope with. They wouldn't surrender, or barter, and couldn't be threatened into submission. It was a badge of honor for an Ossie to sneak aboard an alien spaceship and kill the crew.

Transporting entire forts to the planet proved only a temporary solution. Any invading army eventually had to leave the fort to conduct its business, or the Ossies eventually found a weakness in the fort's perimeter and would throw bodies at it until the weakness was exploited and every inhabitant was killed. Any equipment or structure that was left behind the Ossies destroyed with fire or their primitive weapons.

The Euclidians were the only race able to form a relationship with the Ossies. They used their monitoring devices to listen in on the Ossies and thereby learn their language.

They studied what motivated the Ossies and when they thought they had a plan in place they sent a Majorellen down as a hologram to present an offer to the Ossie people.

"Hello, Chocto, chief of the eastern village," spoke the holographic image of Lanpilk the Majorellen. "I come in peace to make an offer to your people from the Euclidians."

Chocto swung at the image with his spear with no effect. "What manner of being are you and how do you know our tongue?"

"I am a projection of myself and I learned your language from afar."

"Speak your piece and then go."

"We respect your fighting culture and would like to give you the ability to fight many other species on planets far from here. We will give you the ability for your villages to view the battles and conquests by your warriors."

"And what is it you want in return?"

"We would like to build a base here to ensure that no unwanted species comes to your planet and causes harm to it. We do not desire to walk about your planet uninvited."

"That's it?"

"We would like to employ your tattooed warriors as special assassins and bodyguards for our people. They will be given special assignments that will take full advantage of their unique abilities."

"This offer sounds intriguing, but how can I trust your people?"

"To show our good faith we will prepare a feast of gorman and all your favorite food and drink. For entertainment at the feast, one of our people will challenge Malcolm to a fight using wooden staffs. The winner will earn this glowing golden crescent moon." Lanpilk held the emblem so the chief could see it.

"I like the idea, but wooden staffs are not much of a weapon. Can I see this fighter of yours?"

"I apologize for the crude weapons, but the fight is not meant to be to the death. I assure you, however, that our champion will be more than a match for Malcolm."

"Okay, I agree to a three month trial after the feast and we will see how it goes."

"Agreed. We will build a base seven kilometers south of here. Once the base is completed we will invite you to a christening ceremony at which the base will be named for the winner of the challenge."

"So be it," acknowledged Chief Chocto.

Three weeks later, Lanpilk appeared before Chief Chocto in person to invite him to a feast on the following night. The chief accepted and the next evening a large contingent of Ossies traveled to the new base to indulge in the feast, though most were more interested in the challenge match that would follow.

Two hours into the feast, Lanpilk signaled Chief Chocto who indicated that Malcolm was ready. The tables were cleared from the center of the camp and people gathered around to get a good view of the fight. Malcolm appeared, carrying his staff. He growled and cloaked in and out of view, taunting the crowd.

"Where is your champion?" screamed Malcolm.

Lanpilk came forward and announced: "Ossies, Euclidians, and other visiting species, I present our challenger, Phoebe from Delta."

Phoebe appeared, a tall muscular Delta who had been in many battles. She held her staff above her head and smiled and waved at the crowd. The Euclidians cheered and the Ossies laughed.

"She is tall, but she is a skinny woman," screamed Malcolm. "This is an insult."

Phoebe said, "I have not begun to insult you, little one. Wait until the gong sounds and you shall see the insults begin."

"Maybe so, but you will not see me."

"I will most certainly smell you."

The crowd laughed, but Malcolm just growled.

"I'm surprised that you speak Euclidian, Ossie," said Phoebe.

"I'm not just a pretty face. There have been enough of you here begging for a treaty with us that I learned a bit. Enough talk, though. We fight."

The two faced each other and Lanpilk struck the gong. Malcolm cloaked, made a flying leap behind Phoebe, and swung at her head with his staff. Phoebe turned, blocked his staff and shoved her staff into his chest, causing him to uncloak as he rolled across the ground in pain. Phoebe chased after him, swinging her staff as she went. Malcolm blocked her blows with his staff and jumped to his feet. He used his superior strength to force Phoebe into the middle of the ring where they traded blows back and forth.

Tiring of the back and forth, Phoebe vaulted over Malcolm and spun her staff against the side of his head to knock him down. She followed him to the ground, pinned his arms with her knees, and pummeled his face. With a grunt Malcolm flexed his knees and kicked her over his head. He grabbed one of her ankles as she passed over, rolled to his feet, spun her over his head and then face down into the ground, stunning her.

Malcolm grabbed her wrists, put his foot into her lower back, and pulled until she cried out in pain. "I'm going to show you what we do to women who don't know their place," Malcolm shouted. He grabbed both her wrists with one hand and with his free hand ripped the crotch from her shorts.

"It's going to be fun showing your people why the only staff you should be holding is right here," laughed Malcolm.

"If that's what you want, that's what you're going to get," responded Phoebe, giving him a scorpion kick to his back that flipped him over his head.

Malcolm quickly jumped to his feet and lashed out backward with his left arm, hoping to catch Phoebe coming at him. Phoebe ducked his blow, reached down to get a firm grip on his crotch, and lunged two meters into the air. On the way down, Phoebe grabbed Malcolm by the collar and drove his head to the ground, knocking him out.

"Having fun yet, asshole?" Phoebe snarled. She dragged Malcolm's limp body over to his chief and squatted over him.

"Chief, when he comes to, tell him this is how we treat men on our planet that mistreat women." Phoebe took a long piss on Malcolm's chest. "I expect to see him at the ceremony tomorrow as my name is raised over our camp."

The Euclidian crowd burst into loud roars of approval. Several ran from the sidelines to lift Phoebe over their heads and carry her around the camp to shouts of her name. "Phoebe! Phoebe! Phoebe!"

The next day, at the center of the camp, Phoebe and Malcolm stood on a podium with Chief Chocto representing the Ossie people and Captain Shisal representing the Euclidians. Chief Chocto presented Phoebe with the golden crescent medallion.

"Malcolm will now do the honor of raising the flag of this fort overhead for the first time," said Chief Chocto. "The flag bears the head of a gorman on a white background and the name of the Euclidian champion, Phoebe, in gold letters."

Malcolm raised the flag as the crowd cheered.

Captain Shisal spoke in the Ossie language: "Let this flag be a symbol of peace between our peoples." The captain and the chief clenched their hands and raised them high above their heads. Fireworks shot into the air as a band played music. Food and drink was served and the festivities continued well into the night.

Malcolm approached Phoebe and tapped her on the shoulder. "Phoebe," he said, "that was a great battle yesterday. You are a worthy opponent. I would like to offer this local drink as a peace offering." He handed her a mug.

"Thanks, Malcolm. You are quite the adversary yourself. I enjoyed the match." Phoebe clinked his mug with hers. "Here's to success in future battles."

"I really enjoyed our battle, but I think your act at the end was a little extreme, especially considering that I was unconscious."

"Considering what you were threatening, I feel you deserved it. Thanks for making that part easy for me. Though I had to walk around with my ass out the rest of the evening."

"It's unfortunate I missed that. Maybe we can have another battle in the not too distant future."

"Maybe so, Malcolm. Maybe so."

Malcolm gave Phoebe a nod, raised his mug, and walked away.

Captain Shisal appeared and said, "Great job, Phoebe. It's good that you two are on good terms after last night. It got a bit heated there for a moment. I was concerned that I was going to have to step in and stop the fight from going too far."

"Don't fight my battles for me, Chaell. I understand the risks I take when I agree to challenge someone. I don't want anyone marginalizing my abilities by giving me special treatment."

"Understood. Anyway, I feel your win last night secured our relationship with the Ossies. That's important because we need a base here."

"Glad I could be of service. I don't think they'll be pulling out of the agreement anytime soon. They would lose face."

"What would you think about us hiring one of their crescent tattooed warriors to help seal the deal? There are always opportunities to use someone who enjoys killing people."

"That sounds like a good idea. Let's hire Uan, though. I'm not comfortable with the idea of having Malcolm around all the time."

"Sure. I'll see what the chief thinks and if he has no strong objections we'll make it happen."

Chapter II

Yoyo Joins the Euclidians

The next day, Commander Filo and Yoyo were at the Bordelle Bar once again, waiting for other contacts from the Euclidian resource ship fleet.

"Have you and Jesmino been enjoying the city?" asked Filo.

"Very much so," replied Yoyo. "This is such a new experience for us. Tammaria is so primitive a planet in comparison, with no technology except what was brought by visitors. This place is more beautiful and exciting and even more dangerous than I could ever have imagined. Interacting with the different species has been eye-opening."

"Any luck connecting with the Euclidians?"

"Not by me, but Jesmino has learned the language and has connected with a few people. But no meaningful contacts yet."

"Just keep trying. I'm sure the two of you will make a breakthrough eventually. Jesmino impresses me with her progress. Or is she a he? I'm not really sure."

"To tell you the truth, neither am I. She appears to be a female, but I've never seen her in the bathroom or shower. Come to think of it, I've never seen her eat. She's a strange one. Pretty smart, though."

"Look, Yoyo. Another Euclidian captain just walked in the door and he's coming this way. Let me look him up on my UCD... It's Captain Lohmann, skipper of the resource ship *Aleecia*. I'm going to order a Tammarian grog for him."

A few minutes later, a server brought the drink to the captain's booth. "Excuse me, sir. This is from the gentleman in the booth next to yours."

"Really? I'll have to offer my thanks." Lohmann rose from his seat. "Oh, an Alpha." He spoke sharply to Filo, "What is it you want?"

"Please, just a moment of your time, sir and then I'll leave you to enjoy your drink in peace."

Captain Lohmann sat down next to Yoyo and Commander Filo began pleading his case for joining the captain's crew.

"Captain, I have served as navigator on three Alpha ships and a Delta freighter."

"You mean a Delta freighter that was commandeered by you Alphas," scoffed the captain.

"That's inconsequential. I had nothing to do with the acquisition of the ship. I was just there to plot its courses."

"You mean you were helping to steal the Delta technology. Thanks for the grog. I'll be moving to a booth where the air is less putrid."

"Yoyo, convince him that we would be good crewmembers," urged Commander Filo. "Think of life aboard a spaceship and all the places we would visit. Please wait just a moment, captain."

Yoyo thought for a moment then decided to help Filo. She pulled off her goggles and tugged at Captain Lohmann's sleeve to keep him in the booth. The captain looked over at Yoyo and couldn't stop staring at her glowing eyes.

"Please stay for a while," Yoyo said gently. "Commander Filo would make an excellent member of your crew. You should make him your navigator and I will be happy to work in one of the ship's entertainment areas."

"That sounds reasonable," replied Lohmann, "but I already have a navigator."

"I'm sure he would love to move to logistics or another department on your ship. Your ship will really benefit from having Commander Filo as your navigator."

"The crew is going to hate having an Alpha on the bridge," said Captain Lohmann, shaking his head. "I'm just not sure I can make that work."

"Be persuasive, captain. Be forceful. You are a strong supporter of inclusion and assimilation. Let it show."

"Okay, you've convinced me. Show me your UCDs."

The two presented their UCDs to Captain Lohmann and he used his UCD to encode theirs with a digital crewmember attribute that designated their new positions on his ship.

"You two are now members of my crew. Once our indoctrination office indicates that they are ready for you, get your gear and press your crewmember button and you will be beamed directly to the indoctrination center. Once your indoctrination is complete, Yoyo will be assigned to one of our bars and Filo will be assigned to the bridge. I suggest that you stay in your cabins until I arrive to introduce you. Now, if you don't mind, I'd like to enjoy some of this establishment's wares before heading back to the ship."

"Certainly, captain. We are honored to be members of your crew."

"Welcome aboard, gentlemen, and adieu."

The two stood as the captain walked off. Commander Filo startled Yoyo by giving her a huge hug.

"I'm excited too, commander," said Yoyo, "but I don't think hugging is necessary."

"Whatever you say, little lady. Let's get back to our apartments, collect our things, and get ready to board our new ship. In the meantime, we have to find a way to keep Jesmino busy while we are away."

"Don't worry. I'll take care of it."

Yoyo immediately left to meet with Jesmino.

"Jesmino, Commander Filo and I have taken positions aboard a Euclidian resource ship. I want you to stay here and continue forming relationships with the Euclidians. I will be in touch with you via our UCDs."

"Okay, Yoyo. I think I will be just fine here. If you don't mind, I'll stay connected to you at the subatomic level."

"Sure, Jesmino, whatever you say. Forgive me for asking, but are you male or female?"

"Which would you prefer?"

"A female, but it doesn't quite work like that."

"At some levels it can. I am most certainly a female."

"Okay, glad to hear it. Commander Filo and I are packed and ready to depart. We'll be leaving any minute and will hopefully be back in a few months. Just ping me if you need anything."

"I will, and you do the same."

"Goodbye, Jesmino I need to buy some clothes before I have to go to the ship." Yoyo walked out and Jesmino simply waved at the closing door.

Being a female Magi is not so bad, Jesmino said to herself. The sound of her voice changed. *But it would probably be more effective connecting with the Euclidians if I were a female Euclidian*, said Jesmino in perfect Euclidian as her body changed shape.

***

When Yoyo got back to her apartment with her purchases, Commander Filo was waiting for her.

"Yoyo, I have great news. I received a message from our new ship. They are ready to transfer us at any time. Our indoctrination starts in one hour. We should grab our bags and check out of here. I don't want to be late."

"Okay. Let me tell my boss that I won't be back."

"Sure, just make it quick."

Yoyo activated her UCD. "Call my boss," she requested. Moments later she saw his face on the screen.

"Hi, Yoyo, what do you need?"

"I'm about to ship out and I won't be back."

"Too bad. We are all going to miss you here. I'll send your last payment to your account and you should see it on your UCD tonight. Safe travels."

Yoyo joined Commander Filo in his apartment and they simultaneously pressed the crewmember buttons on their UCDs. An instant later they were sitting in chairs in the indoctrination center aboard the *Aleecia*, waiting for the next session to start. Yoyo almost exploded with delight.

"Hello, everyone, I'm Lieutenant Langford, your personnel officer. I'm here to indoctrinate you in the finer points of the resource ship *Aleecia*. Your UCDs have been updated to include the ship's layout, including your places of work and sleep. Command your UCD to 'map location' to display a layout of the current deck and then ask where you want to go. This ship is very large, over fifty kilometers in length, height, and breadth. You will use the personnel transports to get to most locations. Entrances to the transport areas are marked by mauve-colored lights. The transports move vertically and horizontally. Follow the rules and stay out of areas where you don't belong. Otherwise, you will get a warning and a fine. Do it again and you will be thrown off the ship, and I don't mean at the next port. You'll be thrown into space! This is not a joke. Transport by beaming is not allowed on the ship except by executive order. Now sit back and watch the video screen for a general explanation of shipboard life. When the video is over, go out this door and make a right down the hallway, which will take you to the ship's principal corridor. Turn left or right to the mauve-colored tubes for transport to your quarters."

The video started and a much more pleasant voice described the ship and its conveniences. It also provided a schedule for the upcoming mission, and another warning about following the rules. Once it was finished, most people filed out to find their living quarters and get settled. Filo and Yoyo stayed behind with a few others to ask additional questions.

"Excuse me, Lieutenant Langford," said Filo, "can you tell me how to access a flight simulator for the ship? I'm the new navigator and I'd like to brush up on the ship's controls."

"An Alpha navigator? That's awfully strange. I bet they're going to love you on the bridge."

"The simulator, lieutenant?" Filo asked with agitation.

"As navigator, your stateroom is equipped with a virtual command table that you can use to load any of the bridge systems. Just give it voice commands to enable the desired simulation."

"Thanks, lieutenant."

"So what do you want?" the lieutenant asked Yoyo.

"I've been assigned to a general crew lounge. May I be reassigned to an officer's lounge?"

"No, you may not. You just got here. Do what you're told."

Yoyo took off her goggles. "Please, sir," she begged. "Assign me to an officer's lounge. I so much want to show them my talents."

"Okay, you little cutie. I'll move you to our most happening officer's lounge."

"Yay," replied Yoyo, clapping her hands and smiling.

"Stop showing off," whispered Filo as they walked out. "We don't want to draw attention to ourselves. You might want to change out of that thick hooded robe and goggles. It looks odd on this ship."

"Don't worry. I got some comfortable fashion in Occum. I plan to try them out tonight in the lounge."

"Unfortunately, I won't be able to join you. I'll be busy learning about the Euclidian multi-dimensional drive. I'll probably stay out of sight until the captain introduces me. I think it's safer that way. Will you be okay in the lounge?"

"I'm adept at making Tammarian grog, which most people will be drinking. I'm sure I will learn how to mix the other drinks quite quickly."

They stepped into the corridor and were amazed by the size of the space and how full of life it was. The hall was thirty meters wide and so long that it disappeared into the distance in both directions. The walls and floor were bright white. The ceiling displayed an animation that simulated the Euclidian sky with its sun and its three moons as if day and night were passing on the surface of Euclidia. In the overhead space of the corridor, crewmembers flew by in elevated chairs with no visible means of suspension.

Passersby sneered and gawked at Commander Filo. Yoyo was looked upon as an oddity, which she found amusing, considering all the strange life forms walking, slithering, and floating by.

"Enjoy yourself, Yoyo. I'm heading for the transport and the privacy of my stateroom."

"Bye. I'm going to try out one of those transport chairs." Yoyo pointed as one whizzed by above their heads. "Excuse me," she asked a passerby, "how do I use one of those flying chairs?"

"You simply push one of the brown buttons on the wall over there by the pink light," he replied. "A chair will pop out. Aim the chair in the direction you want to go, sit down, and strap in. When you are ready, press the blue button to engage the chair and the yellow button to disengage it. Lean forward to speed up and lean back to slow down. Lean to the side to turn in that direction. Turning in your chair will take you down intersecting hallways or back the way you came."

"How do people keep from colliding into each other?"

"Not to worry. The system makes sure the chairs don't collide, no matter what you do."

"Thank you so kindly for the assistance."

"Your UCD has the same information. You only have to ask it."

"So I shall."

Yoyo walked to the far wall and pressed the brown button with trepidation, not knowing quite what to expect. A chair popped from the wall. She pointed it aft and took a seat. The chair was a bit large for her, but she didn't let that discourage her. She strapped herself in and pressed the blue button. For a moment nothing happened, but then the chair shot into the air and leapt forward alongside other travelers.

"Whee!" Yoyo exclaimed. The others around her smiled and nodded. She leaned forward to gain speed and found it simply exhilarating. The people below and the colored lighting tubes were a blur below her. On occasion the chair shifted from side to side to avoid other travelers. Yoyo sat back a bit to catch her breath and noticed a bunch of people in front of her turning down a hallway. She leaned and followed them around the corner into a narrow hallway dimly lit with large windows along each wall. Most of the chairs had slowed to a stop as their passengers observed what was going on inside the rooms beyond the windows: these were the ship's arenas. There were swimmers, acrobats, runners, and animal riders of all types. Yoyo was awed by the exotic animals from Euclidia and many other worlds. There were two, three, four, and six-legged beasts of all shapes and sizes.

Some rooms were reserved for sports and others for battle practice. Small armies in simulated jungles attacked each other with laser weapons. Not the toy kind, but the kind that cause real harm. The infirmary was able to put everyone back together but the injuries were still very painful.

Most of the sports activities involved a ball of some sort. There were several other sports that pitted teams and individuals against each other in feats of strength, speed, agility and teamwork. Some events were organized but many were ad hoc. There were even Olympic-type events where cities, nations, and planets competed against each other for money and trophies.

While the ship was docked in orbit around Euclidia the arenas were full of crewmembers. There wasn't a lot else to do, and the captain encouraged their use as it helped keep the crew out of trouble.

Yoyo lingered by the large windows, looking on in amazement. Growing up, she had never seen much in the way of sports. Even during her brief trips out of the caves, or while traveling with Commander Filo, she had not had access to many activities beyond bars, clubs, and restaurants.

Being short of stature and inexperienced, Yoyo felt there were not many sports that she could do well. Now, however, across one of the large fields, she saw a group of people engaged in an activity that she felt she was born to do.

Yoyo pushed the yellow button on the chair and it moved to the nearest chair transport station and settled slowly onto the floor. Yoyo descended from the chair and it immediately disappeared into the wall.

Yoyo walked along the corridor to an orange tube light, which indicated the entrance to a sports arena. She opened the door and a strong smell of sweat hit her in the face. She gagged but plowed forward and after a while her nose adjusted to the smell and her desire to puke subsided. She was in a corridor between playing fields that was made of a metal-based glass that protected visitors from athletes and their equipment. There were doors every few meters to access the fields. She walked to the end of the corridor where a group of people waited for their turn.

Yoyo stared through the window for a minute, a bit nervous about going in. She watched as each person took their turn and knew she could best any of them. Gritting her teeth, she pushed through the door and into the arena. She got in line with the rest of the participants to wait her turn.

"Hey, shorty," shouted someone with a laugh. "Are you going to climb the wall in that big robe?"

"He's probably going to ride someone's back up. How can he even see where he is with those goofy goggles?" said another.

"First of all, numbnuts," said Yoyo as she took off her robe and tossed it to the ground, "I'm a woman. Secondly, I'm wearing goggles because my eyes are sensitive to the light, but they also help protect me from your bullshit. Which takes me to my third point. I'm going to let you two get halfway up before I start and when you get to the top you will see my ass waiting for you."

The men who had jeered looked in amazement at Yoyo's strong wiry body. She had extra-long fingers and toes with which she had climbed cave walls back home all her life. Thick, shoulder-length, wavy white hair flowed from her head. She was wearing the tight brown leotards that she wore in the caves. Though she didn't have breasts, her body was curvaceous, and the two men noticed. She tightened her arms in a wrestling pose and growled at the men.

They were taken aback but then laughed, and Yoyo laughed, too. Perhaps, she thought, she might make some friends in this group. Since leaving Tammaria she had really only socialized with Commander Filo, and although she was suspicious of his intentions, he was one of the only friends she had.

"You have an impressive little body, but you are not going to beat us up this wall unless you use some magic or technology."

"I promise you, no tricks I'm going to beat you the old fashioned way. With my talent!"

"Okay, if we win, you do an exotic dance for us."

"Sure, and if I win, you two do one for me."

"Bet!"

"Okay, see where the person in the blue shorts is?" Yoyo pointed halfway up the face.

"Yeah."

"You can have until there before I start."

"You're nuts, lady. No way can you catch us after that."

"Then you have nothing to worry about, do you? It's your turn. Get going, suckers."

The three validated their bets with their UCDs and the two men started up the wall, which was made of a real rock face taken from Euclidia. The sport involved climbing without ropes. If a climber fell, and one occasionally did, a gravity system kept them from hitting the ground, though some scraped themselves up on the rock face on the way down, and sometimes others were taken out on the way down.

Yoyo watched with eagerness as the two men ascended. When they hit the halfway point she started her ascent. Now, though, she was a bit worried. Others she had watched seemed slow, but these two were pretty fast.

Yoyo used her long fingers and toes to grasp cracks and crevices in the rock and her strength to pull herself up. She created a rhythm with her body, swinging herself from side to side and up the face.

"Do you see her anywhere?" asked one of the men Yoyo was racing.

"No, I think we beat her. I'm looking forward to a sexy dance from that sweet little thing tonight," said the other.

Yoyo smiled at them from above. "I'm looking forward to a sexy dance myself, although I wouldn't call you two sweet little things. I should be at work around 7:50. Don't disappoint me, boys."

***

As a Lieutenant Commander on the ship, Filo was quartered in an area of the ship reserved for senior officers. There was a private lounge, club, kitchen, game room, and exercise area. His personal quarters consisted of a two-room suite with a receiving room for meetings and a large bedroom with an office area. He was most interested, however, in the virtual command table built into the desk.

Filo sat at the desk and placed his UCD on a spot marked for it. A graphical menu appeared on the desktop display. Now he could select commands from the menu with his hands or give verbal commands.

"Bring up the navigation console." The desktop converted to a simulation of the ship's navigation console.

"Chart a course to the Alpha system and put us in orbit around the fourth planet from the sun."

"Course plotted," responded the navigation system. It displayed the ship's current location and the path to its destination as a hologram projected above the desk.

"Initiate course on my command. Initiate!"

Filo executed the scenario several times, each time making changes to the various settings of the navigation system. Though it took him hours, he felt compelled to learn every nuance of the system. When he felt he was ready he performed the navigation manually several times, tweaking things here and there to learn the limits of the system and its fail-safes.

Exhausted by the effort, Filo eventually fell asleep with his face against the desk. He awoke with thoughts of revenge against the Euclidians. He stood up and wiped saliva from his mouth and sleep from his eyes. He dragged himself to his elegant bathroom, sat on the toilet, and relieved himself. As a warm spray rinsed his bottom, his thoughts again drifted to revenge against the people that he now served. He had to hit them hard in a way that would cause them to remember his name forever. A jet of warm air dried his bottom and then he stepped into the surround shower. Hot, tingling water hit every part of his body. He let his mind relax and drift to the memory of his sweet wife and three kids that were killed during the Euclidian attack. He touched himself as he had not been touched since her death. He climaxed and slid to the floor of the shower where he lay crying. *Soon, Euclidians! Soon you will feel the wrath of Kenyon Filo!*

***

At 7:30 that evening, Yoyo was putting the final touches on her hairdo. She had parted her silky white hair into quarters and tied the strands from each into a single knot. Her hair still hung ten centimeters from each knot. She dyed the tips of her hair pink to match the tight pink outfit that hugged her body. Her bare arms and midriff showed off her muscular physique. On her feet were sparkling, blue fifteen-centimeter pumps that glowed when she stomped them on the floor.

Yoyo had spent several nights at Belo the techno slinger's dance club in Occum after spending her days with Commander Filo. She loved the music, the lights, the dancing, the wild clothes, and the people from across the universe all having fun together. It certainly beat the dark Tammarian caves. Yoyo wasn't much of a dancer, but she enjoyed seeing people jump across the multiple levitating and revolving dance floors.

Yoyo eventually got the nerve up to ask Belo to let her operate the electronics and set the music mood. It was the one thing that could not be computerized. The music and ambience had to change with the audience, which consisted of people from many star systems and even more cultures. Deltas were different from Ossies who were nothing like Perjorans, who were unique from the Magi. Yoyo had to be especially attentive for Alphas walking into the club: no levitating floors or flashing lights when they were around, and nothing that might get people excited. Just low lights, mellow music, and the establishment's exotic dancers to keep everyone distracted from wanting to kill the Alphas. The only species the Alphas hadn't gone to war with was the Majorellens, whose planet was too far toward the end of the galaxy for the Alphas to bother going after.

The Ossies were the only species that had come out on top in a war with the Alphas. The Alphas sent few ships to the engagement and were unprepared for the Ossies ability to cloak and their relentless fighting style. An Ossie snuck aboard their command ship, killed everyone on the bridge, and then flew the ship into the ground while chanting a fighting song over the ship's PA system.

Yoyo enjoyed learning from Belo the subtleties of being a great techno slinger, and eventually developed her own style. On occasion she would use her powers of persuasion to get the pole dancers at the club to do group dances similar to the cave exercises Yoyo used to do, which brought a lot more customers to the club. The club manager noticed this and offered Yoyo a paid job.

"Yoyo," he told her, "you are fabulous on the electronic controls and getting people to dance. But you have got to find some hipper threads. I can't tell if you're a man or a woman under your robe."

"Thanks, I really appreciate the job. What do you think of these?" Yoyo took off her robe to expose the tight brown clothes that were her usual attire in the caves.

"Better. I like the tight fit, but the style is still a bit boring."

"Okay, with my first paycheck I'll get some new clothes."

In the meantime, Yoyo went to several other dance clubs in Occum to see what other techno slingers were rockin'. After a while she figured out what she wanted to wear.

Finally she got her first paycheck and ran out to buy clothes, makeup, and dye for her hair. She hadn't told Commander Filo about her new interests because she wanted to surprise him.

***

Yoyo took a deep breath and walked out of the door of her small cabin to take a transport to the officer's lounge where she was assigned. She stood in front of the door to the lounge, fretting. *You can do this, Yoyo. You're just wearing normal clothes for a techno slinger,* she told herself. *Though you've never worn anything but boring cave clothes, you can do this.*

A couple of crewmembers brushed past her and into the lounge. She followed them in, walked behind the bar, and introduced herself to the man standing there.

"Hello. I'm Yoyo, reporting for duty."

"Greetings, Yoyo, I'm Jorré. You don't have to be so formal. A simple 'I'm here' will suffice. I hope you're not going to wear that huge robe while you're working."

"I have an outfit underneath the robe, but I'm not used to being in public without it."

"If you want to keep working here, you have to be liked by the patrons. Otherwise, you'll be assigned to a less popular lounge where you'll make less money. And that would be a lot less fun, if you ask me."

"I would rather stay here. This place is spectacular." Yoyo looked around the huge room. There were digital lights, big video screens, pervasive music, game tables, and a levitating dance floor. The floor was empty, but Yoyo hoped to fix that.

"Where can I put my robe?" Yoyo asked as she removed the heavy garment and exposed her sexy outfit. She was wearing a tight pink top with a swirl design, tight pink shorts, glitter shades to protect her eyes, and the sparkling blue high-heeled shoes that glowed when she walked.

"Wow, you won't have any problems attracting attention with that outfit."

"You like it?" Yoyo asked shyly.

"Very much so. If we were more compatible species, I would be trying to get you out of those sexy clothes, except for the shoes of course."

Yoyo blushed. "I'm not sure if I should thank you or slap your face."

"Oh, I guess I was being a bit provocative, but not any more than your outfit. You can place your robe over there, and then get acquainted with the bar. Most people will order drinks and food with their UCDs, but others like the personal touch and you need to be ready for that."

"Got it," replied Yoyo. She hung up her robe and started touring through the bar area. *Dang, they have a lot of liquor and snacks back here.*

"Jorré, I tended bar on occasion back in Occum, but how do I figure out how to use all these different liquors in drinks?"

"Point your UCD at a container. It will describe the contents and the different drinks you can make with it, and how to make them. When you're here in the lounge you can use the room icon on your UCD to get information that's specific to the lounge. Press it to bring up the menu and then select the 'drinks' command. You can select a drink from the list or just say its name. Then you have the option of ordering the drink or obtaining the recipe for the drink. When you use the 'recipe' command, the containers holding the ingredients for the drink will light up. Don't worry about how much to pour of each ingredient, the container will automatically determine that."

"What if we are both making a drink at the same time?"

"The containers are smart enough to know that it's you reaching for it, and will extinguish the light or pour the right amount."

"Doesn't that make it easy for anyone to be a bartender?"

"Yes, but the way to be a great bartender is to understand the specific needs of your clients. Plus, adding your own flair to drinks will get you special attention."

That last statement lit a light bulb for Yoyo and she immediately knew how she could give Tammarian grog her own special flair. *The moss that grows in our caves is just the thing. I'll use it dried as a swizzle stick. The moss brings out the flavors in the grog in a way that excites people. I can't believe I*

only brought a small container with me. I hope the moss, plus my outfit and techno
slinger abilities, will secure my position here.

Yoyo contacted her Magi friend, Belo, to get her an additional supply of cave moss.

"Belo, this is Yoyo. I know you are going to Tammaria tomorrow. Get me a bushel of the cave moss."

"What cave moss?" asked Belo.

"The shooters that we use in the grog."

"Wow, I never thought of bringing any with me. I'll get some for you and have it transferred to you in a couple of days."

"Great. I'll transfer fifty credits to you as soon as I get them."

"No, you'll give me a private techno dance when you get back from your mission."

"What? I'd rather give you one hundred credits!"

"I'd rather get two private dances."

"Argh! You're worse than the men at the Bordelle Bar."

"I'll take that as a yes."

"Sure, but if you touch me I will crush your face."

Belo smirked. "I miss you too, and look forward to your return."

It was 7:70 and the two men that had lost the bet to Yoyo walked into the lounge. *This is going to be a fun evening,* Yoyo thought.

"Hello, gentlemen. I'm surprised you two showed up."

"We are not ones to welsh on a bet," one of the men responded. "Anyway, it was recorded in our UCDs so it would be difficult to ignore the obligation."

"Glad to hear it. Why don't you two put on these hot pink thongs under your clothes and come back at 7:90. I'll let everyone know you'll be dancing at 8:00."

"You must be kidding, lady. I'm not wearing that, or stripping."

"Me either, you little rip-off artist."

Yoyo raised her glitter glasses and addressed the two. "Gentlemen, do I look like someone who enjoys being ignored? You get dressed in those thongs like I asked you to, and be back by 7:90. Understood?"

"Yes, Yoyo," they replied in unison.

After the two left, Yoyo sent an announcement about the planned entertainment and finished familiarizing herself with her drink station. Once she was comfortable making drinks, she went online and awaited her first drink order. It took a while for the first one, but more soon followed.

"Hey, lady, I'll have a Marnician hinsar juice."

"Can I get a Pushan ball blaster?"

"Get me a Chasen brain stun."

"Hi, cutie. Can you make me a fresh Tammarian grog?"

"Yes! I'd be happy to, sir," said Yoyo with glee. *The moment I've been waiting for.* "Here you go, sir."

"What's this bit here?" asked the patron.

"It's a tam stick from the Tammarian caves. You stir the grog with it and then suck on it."

"Really? That sounds a bit odd. Why didn't you just give me a straw?" he said, walking off.

Yoyo crossed her arms in annoyance. "Hmph." But a few seconds later the man returned and raved about the extra flavor and sensation that the tam stick gave the drink.

"What is this thing, again? It's quite yummy."

"It's a tam stick from the caves of Tammaria. You can only get it from me and it only works with drinks made from Tammarian abbig fruit such as your grog. The stick should last you a couple of days depending on how much you drink."

"Can I get another one?"

"Sorry, only one per customer. It should last you a while, though. Next week I will be able to sell you as many as you like."

"Thanks, barmaid."

"The name's Yoyo."

"Yoyo it is then."

He spread the word about the tam sticks and thirty minutes later her supply was depleted, just in time for Yoyo to greet the two climbers in their sexy dancing outfits. Now Yoyo was going to liven up the place. She put on a headset microphone and addressed the lounge patrons.

"Hello, everyone. Can I have your attention up here on the floating dance floor? These two gentlemen in the sexy outfits lost a bet earlier today and are now going to demonstrate their version of a techno dance. Let's hear it for them." Yoyo applauded, and the patrons responded in kind, clapping and shouting, "Oye, oye, oye!"

Yoyo jumped to the music control center and turned up the volume of the Euclidian techno disco song. Quartz lights sparkled around the room, and as the men started to dance she levitated the dance floor up and down. The crowd hooted and hollered as the two men awkwardly stripped to their g-strings. When the music died down, Yoyo took to the stage.

"Let's hear it for these fabulous gentlemen! Next time they'll know better than to challenge a Tammarian to a climbing contest, because we rule! Now I'm going to show them how to do the techno dance right. Of course, it will be a clean version. I need six volunteers, women and men and hermaphrodites. If you have a tam stick, you are compelled to come up here."

The stage and surrounding dance floor quickly filled with people. Yoyo cranked up the music and levitated the dance floor. She popped up onto the stage with ease and addressed her dancers.

"Change of plans, everyone. There are so many of you that we'll do the Tammarian cave walk instead. Don't worry if you don't know it. You'll learn quickly. Everyone that finishes the dance with me gets a free tam stick when my shipment comes in."

More dancers rushed to the floor. *I'm definitely going to need more dance space!*

"Okay, everybody," instructed Yoyo, "line up and do what I do, in time with the beat. Lean forward and put your hands on your thighs. Take two steps forward and shake your hips from side to side. With your right foot forward, slide across the floor. Twist to the left, raise your left foot, and slide some more. Hop back once. Hop forward twice and spin around. Spin your hips to the left then to the right. Now drop it down. Now cave walk, everybody. Cave walk. Lean forward and put your hands on your thighs…"

Yoyo had the club bangin'. She completely forgot about her bartending duties, but Jorré didn't care.

CHAPTER 12

Saved from the Bayou

Uan, Betty, and Dominique lay face down on the floor of the Euclidian reconnaissance ship soaking wet and coughing up water. Grunting laughter could be heard in the background. The women looked around for the source of the noise and screamed when they saw the Euclidian crewmen. The screaming made the crewmen laugh all the harder, which made them seem even more menacing to the women.

"Ahhh! Who are those monsters and where the hell are we?" screamed Dominique, holding on to Betty in terror.

Betty said, "I think we've been abducted by Uan's people. I suspected he was an alien and this confirms it. Now he'll probably kill us with his spear."

Dominique took a closer look at Uan. "Oh, my goodness, you're right. How did I not recognize it? Does this mean I won't get my thousand dollars or my limousine replaced?"

"Stop it!" shouted Uan. "You'll get your money and you can have any car you like. Furthermore, if I wanted to kill you, why would I save you from the alligators?"

"Because you want to stab us yourself to make sure that we're dead," replied Betty. "Or maybe you want your friends to do it."

"I do not want to stab you and neither do my colleagues. They are here to help me find an escaped prisoner. I managed to call them with my universal connection device and they beamed us out of the bayou and away from the alligators."

"*Did you retrieve my UCD?*" Uan asked in Euclidian.

One of the crewmembers nodded to Uan and tossed the device to him. Uan caught it and nodded back.

"*Will you tend to their wounds?*"

One of them nodded and used a device to heal Dominique's arm and Betty's leg.

"*They're okay now, just wet,*" the crewman snickered.

Betty turned to face Uan. "You've been killing people all across DC with your spear, haven't you?"

"They were bad people that deserved to die," responded Uan.

"Really? What about the one you beheaded on the riverfront?"

"He littered."

"That is usually not a capital offense."

"He encountered me at the wrong moment. I had the escaped prisoner in my grasp and he used his powers to wrap me in cloth and throw me in the river. I hate being in water unless I am bathing. It stings my eyes and makes me feel helpless."

"If you want to call those slits you have eyes," said Dominique, staring at the Ossie.

"They are what I use to see with."

Uan didn't have eyeballs like most humanoid creatures, but slits that ran from the front of his head around along the sides, providing him with a greater than 180-degree view of his surroundings.

"Why," exclaimed Betty, "are you trying so hard to capture this prisoner? I bet he's not running around stabbing people in the chest with a spear."

"He has special powers, including telepathy and telekinesis. We don't want him to warn your planet about our presence."

"Why don't you just introduce yourselves to Earth?" asked Dominique. "You must have done that on other planets."

"This is not a friendly visit. We are here to extract minerals and take slaves. Introducing ourselves would be counterproductive."

"So why did you take time to save Betty?" asked Dominique. "Are you in love with Betty?"

Uan just growled in response.

"Of course not," said Betty. "He's an emotionless assassin. He probably just wants me to tie him to a bed again a few more times before he gets bored and kills me. Maybe he kept you alive because he wants a threesome."

"Now you are being absurd," said Uan. "I have feelings for you, Betty. That is why I risked my life to save you."

One of the crewmembers interjected, *"Uan, do you want us to drop you three off somewhere?"*

"Sure, just send us all to my place. I'll be in touch."

A moment later they were standing in Uan's living room with their clothes still soaked.

"My gosh, I wish you would stop doing that," said Dominique. "At least give us a warning before you beam us around."

"No kidding," added Betty.

"What happened to you three?" asked Calvin, getting up from the couch. "It looks like you were trying to find Nemo and got lost yourselves."

"Are you an alien too?" asked Dominique.

"No, that's Uan's valet," said Betty.

"Hold on. I'm no one's valet and I'm certainly not an alien. I'm Uan's associate. I help him get around."

"So you help him kill people," said Betty.

"Trust me, Uan doesn't need any help with that."

"What I do need help with," demanded Uan, "is getting these ladies some dry clothes. If you are finished with the chit chat. Then go tell Little Randy I want to see him."

"Got it!" said Calvin.

"Ladies, if you will come with me," said Uan, "there are a couple of bedrooms with bathrooms that you can use to clean up. They each have towels and toiletries. Calvin should be back soon with dry clothes. I will be in my room taking a shower."

Uan went into his room, showered, and put on fresh clothes. Soon there was a knock on his door.

"Uan!" Calvin shouted through the closed door. "Little Randy is out here with a few of his fellas."

"I will be right there."

Calvin returned to the living room where the group was waiting. Out of nowhere, Uan appeared without his shades or hoodie and brandishing his spear, startling everyone.

"Whose idea was it to turn my friend over to the Italians?" Uan bared his sharp teeth and the fear in Little Randy and his men was palpable.

Little Randy spoke up. "She was a cop that was sneaking around, spying on you. If she was your friend why did she hide behind a tree to watch your place instead of just knocking on your door?"

"Did you ask her?"

"She had a chance to speak up and said nothing," Little Randy pleaded.

"Fine. But from now on, people who visit me are protected. You figure out if they know me or not."

"No problem. So, we good?"

"Almost." Uan thrust his spear into the chest of the man on Little Randy's left. "Now we good."

"Uan, did you have to kill my boy?"

"If the loss of your friend causes you mental duress, I am happy to relieve you of that feeling," said Uan as he leaned into Little Randy, cocking his head to the side.

Little Randy threw his hands up. "No, I'm good."

"Good. Now take that bleeding corpse out of here. He is messing up my carpet. Next time I call for you, you come alone. Crowds make me nervous."

"No problem. That won't happen again."

Uan turned and vanished into thin air.

"Shit! What kind of crap is that?" said one of Little Randy's associates. "Is he some kind of ghost or something?"

"Oh no," said Calvin. "A ghost is just scary. Uan is terrifying to the point that he doesn't even have a shadow. They're afraid to be around him."

"Why aren't you afraid?"

"Oh, I am. Every minute of every day. So far he's been good to me so I'm going to be good to him. And one thing's for sure. None of you are ever going to mess with me as long as he's around. I suggest you get going before he comes back. He's not a patient kind of guy, if you know what I mean. And I think you do."

The three lifted up their dead friend and carried him out without uttering another word.

Uan reappeared. "Calvin, did you get the women some clothes?"

"Yes, I put them in their bedrooms."

"You know we still have that little alien and his Earthling friend to deal with."

"Yes, I remember. I just don't know why he continues to be important. He doesn't seem to want to cause any trouble."

"'Ours is not to reason why, ours is just to do or die.'" Uan quoted.

"Where did you learn that one?"

"They taught me a few English colloquialisms during my language training."

"But they didn't teach you contractions. That's a hoot."

"Just go start up the SUV. I will be down in a minute. I want to let the ladies know that they should stay put."

"Okay, I'll be waiting for you outside."

Uan found Betty and Dominique chatting in one of the bedrooms. "Calvin and I are going to look for the escaped prisoner," he told them. "The invasion of Earth is imminent. You will be safe as long as you stay here, so do not leave."

CHAPTER 13

Li Xiao Spots Uan

Li Xiao was using Cobalt's device to follow around the Chinese ambassador to the UN, trying to determine if his guest, the visiting Chinese defense secretary, would eventually discuss where Yao Ming was being imprisoned for speaking out against the government. She wasn't much of a basketball fan, but she knew who he was. The other people she had freed were Chinese dissidents who had never been to America. Yao Ming was a national hero and an American basketball legend.

There had been little media coverage following her freeing of the other dissidents. The Chinese government was being careful not to make a heroine of the woman who had spirited them away, and Li Xiao had few worries about being discovered. Helping Yao Ming to escape, though, would bring international attention, and endanger her ability to remain anonymous.

As she watched the pair ride around DC in a limousine, she listened carefully but they were only discussing the DC tourist sites and where to get great Szechuan food.

The limousine is stopping. Why would they be stopping here? Oh no, not the tourist bus. Now I guess I will spend the next two hours listening to you two rattle on about monuments and not Yao Ming.

The two men exited their limo, purchased tickets, and climbed aboard a double-decker bus and took seats on the top near the front. As the bus began its tour and Li Xiao was forced to endure more inane banter about the monuments they were passing. The Chinese ambassador took great pleasure in showing off his knowledge of DC.

But something odd happened as the bus went under an overpass. From out of nowhere a boy floated down into the bus. He landed in the back and no one seemed to notice.

Where did he come from? And why is he carrying that strange doll in a quiver? Wait a minute. That doll is moving! Li Xiao switched her focus from the two men she was following to this mysterious kid and his doll.

The two appeared to be communicating with each other, but their mouths weren't moving. As a matter of fact, the doll creature didn't even have a mouth. They looked over the back of the bus as if they were watching something. Li Xiao zoomed out the image on her device to see what they were looking at. It appeared that someone was chasing the bus. Not only that, the person was catching up to the bus, which must have been moving at thirty miles an hour.

The fastest human can barely run fifteen miles per hour. How is this person doing this? Li Xiao zoomed in on the person and determined that he couldn't be human, but what was this alien doing on Earth? *He must be chasing the little creature the kid is carrying, who must be an alien as well. They have to be from Cobalt's ship, which means this probably has something to do with the impending invasion. I would love to free Yao Ming, but this is probably more important right now.*

Dumbfounded, Li Xiao followed the trio through an incredible series of events. The chase continued onto a tourist boat. Then the kid and the small alien caught a hot air balloon and finally they escaped when the alien chasing them was dragged into a river and had to abandon his pursuit. Li Xiao set waypoints on Morgan and the pursuing alien so she could find them again whenever she wished. As they separated, she decided that following the alien would be more interesting.

The alien came out of the river near an entertainment area and beheaded a man, apparently for littering. She followed him back to his residence and saw that he was working with an American. Continuing to watch into the evening, she laughed when the alien apparently became drunk after drinking barely half a beer and then got beaten up at the bar. Later yet, the alien was tied to a bed and sexually dominated by a policewoman.

This is some strange stuff that you just can't make up. Li Xiao slept for a few hours then continued to follow Uan.

Li Xiao's eyes were glued to her device as she tracked Uan and Calvin as they went to Tajikistan to retrieve a package of plutonium from terrorists. She added another waypoint to the ship they used so she could track it as needed. She was surprised that her device could follow Uan even as he beamed to and from the ship.

I wonder why the American military or some foreign military can't spot this spaceship? I guess taking plutonium from terrorists is a good thing, but I just don't trust these aliens. I better get some sleep. I can check on them in the morning.

The following days, Li Xiao watched as the policewoman was captured by thugs and then freed by the alien, whom she now knew was named Uan. *I can't figure out if this Uan is a good guy or bad guy. He certainly has a mean temper. He seems to want to kill the little alien and his American friend so they won't warn Earth.*

Chapter 14

The Mining of Earth Begins

"Captain," said the navigation officer, "we are in position above the third planet."

"Logistics, give me your status," said Captain Shisal.

"All satellites have been disabled. The aviation intercept fleet has been deployed to intercept all aircraft. Ready to engage EMP," replied the logistics officer.

"Engage," ordered Captain Shisal.

A few minutes later, the logistics officer again reported. "Their aircraft have been shut down and transferred to our ship. They are being off-fueled and processed. Passengers are being placed in holding cells. The logistics team is transferring nuclear material to our special holding cells and we have engaged safety measures to prevent leakage and explosion, based on previously gathered intelligence. Transport into their sun of the planet's biochemical weapon material is now ninety percent complete." A short while later came the next report. "We have now fully completed the transportation of nuclear material and chemical-biological weapons, and all aircraft have been processed. All waste material has been transported to the sun."

Time passed and then the next reports. "Moving to military targets, captain. All aircraft carriers have been transported, stripped of personnel, and placed in holds for processing. Processing of submarines and all other military ships is sixty percent complete... Eighty percent now, captain... Processing of military ships has been completed. We have moved to land-based military personnel and equipment. Personal weapons and ammunitions not worth processing are being transported to the sun... Tanks and small armored vehicles are being processed to recover the metal, with ten percent kept intact for sale to collectors. The rest have been stripped of fuel and non-metallic waste... Waste has been transported to the sun while the rest has been compressed and stored."

"Good work so far, logistics," said Captain Shisal. "Give me an update on the collection of the civilian population."

"Captain," reported the officer assigned to civilian personnel collection, "we are making a pass across the planet now. Four columns of our flying vessels are making a sweep from east to west across their planet along its longitudinal axis. Crewmembers have employed the dimensional beacons to transport personnel from stadiums, malls, schools, high rises, highways, city centers, and resorts."

The crewmembers responsible for transporting civilians to the *Andrea* sat in front of large screens looking for people to beam to holding cells. They slipped seamlessly through walls, resisting the temptation to be voyeurs. This was a new planet with a new species of people and new cultures. The inclination of the Euclidian crew was to learn how this new species lived and how it had built its civilizations. But while they were on duty it was their job to quickly transport as many people as possible.

On the surface, most of the population was trying to understand what had happened to their electrical and motive power. Others were just making the best of the situation: eating dinner, taking a shower, having sex, sitting on the toilet, playing sports, or getting high. But it didn't matter. They were all swooped up en masse just as they were. They were all placed into similar holding cells, naked or not, finished peeing or not. This was very embarrassing for some, but of no interest to the logistics officers. When one cell filled the system automatically switched to filling the next.

The operators skipped hospitals and nursing homes and otherwise did not collect the old, the sick, the crippled, and the obese. Those who happened to be in basements, caves, or underwater at the time, and some who were just plain lucky escaped collection. The Euclidians' goal was not to get everyone, just a majority. And when their sweep of the planet was complete, more than ninety percent of Earth's population had been taken.

John had a maintenance job at the Cotton Bowl in Dallas, Texas. He was sitting in the basement, watching the Texas vs. OU football game when the power went off. He went up to the stadium stands to see what had happened. His jaw dropped as he looked around to see that there was no one in the stands, on the field, or in the booth. How could so many people have disappeared so quickly? He went outside and found the parking lot still full of cars. He eventually decided to go home, but his own car wouldn't start so he began walking. The streets were full of abandoned cars, and there was no one to be seen.

"Logistics," said Captain Shisal, "what luck are we having with the businesses that sell and store the minerals we're looking for?"

"We are having tremendous luck, sir. There are thousands of places that have gold, silver, platinum, and other precious metals. They also have precious stones. The banks are a treasure trove of minerals, and the national governments have warehouses and minting operations full of gold and silver and various other metals."

"That makes our job easy," said Shisal. "Keep the jewelry intact. It might be more valuable than the loose stones and metal. The marketers back on Euclidia will make that call."

"Captain, many of the individuals also have jewelry, coins, and other types of valuable metal, though it is tedious to find. We could spend ten minutes looking through a house and find nothing, or we might find a large collection of items."

"As long as we're here doing the mining, have our people focus on the larger homes. I don't want anyone sitting around doing nothing just because the hit rate is so low on houses."

"Aye, aye, captain."

"As we retrieve the atmosphere, water, animals, and processed minerals, remember our exit strategy. We're going to establish a base here so I don't want the planet left uninhabitable."

"Understood, captain."

"Once we near the end of mining operations, I'm going to celebrate with a ball on the planet's surface, and I want as many of our people as possible to attend. We'll have some people visit in waves to make sure we have coverage for important posts. Mining operations will cease during the ball so that those personnel can attend. I don't want people to think I'm a complete hard ass."

"No one would think that of you, sir."

"Plenty of the crewmembers probably think that," Captain Shisal laughed stridently. "They just better not say it out loud."

"Of course not, captain."

"Now, have all of the mining vehicles been deployed?"

"Aye, captain. What should we do if we run across additional people that were not captured during the initial sweep?"

"Unless they get in the way of operations, just ignore them. We need to leave enough people on this planet to perform manual labor and supply information as needed."

"Aye, aye, captain."

"I want you to find a warm place to establish our camp. Someplace on the water in a resort area. Ensure that there are no inhabitants remaining in the area and set up a security perimeter. Once the camp has been secured, have the area set up for shore leave."

"Right away, captain. I'm sure the crew will look forward to it."

"And so they should."

CHAPTER 15

Saving Morgan

The next morning, Li Xiao checked in on Uan and found him sitting in the passenger seat of a black SUV next to Calvin. They seem to be watching a hospital room and waiting for someone to show up. It has to be the kid and small alien that Uan was chasing. Somehow these two little guys are a threat to the aliens' plan to attack the Earth. Why are one human and a small alien of so much interest to a supposedly large attack force? She adjusted the device to listen in on Uan and Calvin's conversation.

"The invasion must have started," said Uan. "I can't believe it is happening already. We have to get that alien right away."

"What invasion? Who is starting what invasion?" asked Calvin.

Uan ignored him and checked his UCD to see what alerts he might have missed. He learned that Morgan had entered the room and that Denise later left with Pico, leaving Morgan inside, next to his mother's bed.

"They are back," snarled Uan. "This time they will not get away."

***

What the hell is going on? thought Li Xiao. Are the aliens invading now? What was that? The television in her living room shut down. She looked around and noticed that the clock, the DVR, and the stereo had lost power. She wondered if just her building had lost power, and looked out the window to see if anything else was impacted. Cars on the street weren't moving. She watched in horror as a helicopter fell from the sky and crashed into a tree nearby.

Li Xiao's transport device was still working. She looked around Uan and Calvin's SUV and noticed that the power was out around them as well. Upon returning to the SUV she saw that Uan was no longer there. In a panic, she switched the device to Morgan and Pico. They were in a hospital room and Morgan was talking to the patient. It appeared to be the boy's mother.

Is the alien inside the hospital? She switched the device back to Uan and saw him go into the hospital. She decided she had to act, so she quickly put on her Guan Yin mask and robe and beamed to the hospital room.

***

Uan reached for his pulse rifle and aimed it at Morgan to snuff out his life. At that moment a masked Earth woman appeared out of nowhere and hugged Morgan and his mother as if to protect them. No matter, thought Uan, I'll just kill all three. Before he could pull the trigger they all disappeared.

What the hell just happened? Uan looked around the hospital room, but it was empty. He had to find Morgan and that alien. He knew Pico was probably still in the hospital somewhere, because his UCD had recorded him leaving the room with the doctor. He followed her scent down the hallway but lost it at the elevator. He hit the stairway and ran onto each floor until he picked up the scent again.

He followed the scent into the rehabilitation center and there was Pico, sitting on a bed next to Jerome with Dr. Turner standing next to them. Then she appeared again, that strange Earthling. She grabbed Pico and Pico knew instantly what was happening. Take those two as well! a voice screamed in Li Xiao's head. She wasn't sure where the request came from, but obeyed the strange command. She got her arms around Dr. Turner but Uan aimed his rifle and she had to transport away. Uan fired through the space they had occupied a moment before, killing Jerome.

Uan screamed and shook his fist in the air. That damn alien has way too much luck. He left the room and rejoined Calvin at the SUV.

"Calvin, let's get back to our place. I need to get everyone into the basement before the ships appear and start gathering people up."

"What do you mean?"

"The invasion of your planet has started, which means that our ships will be collecting people for storage and later sale. Going to the basement might save you, because we usually don't bother to look for people below ground."

"Oh, that's generous. I guess the thousand people left behind can get together and repopulate the planet, maybe in a million years!" Calvin said sarcastically.

"Just drive!"

***

Morgan and Norma stared in amazement as Li Xiao returned with Pico and Denise in her arms. Denise screamed when she appeared in Li Xiao's living room. "Where the hell am I and how did I get here?"

Li Xiao released Denise and set Pico down on the floor. "I used a transportation device to get you out of the hospital and bring you to my apartment. An alien was about to kill you so I didn't have time to explain anything."

"You need to go back and get my brother," Denise said hysterically.

"I can't go back with that assassin in the room." Li Xiao took out the device. "Let me look at the viewer… Oh my goodness." Li Xiao covered her mouth and shook her head. "It looks like the assassin killed him."

Denise's eyes welled with tears. "No, no, no!" She fell to her knees. "I was supposed to take care of him. He was going to get better. Let me see him," she said, reaching for the device.

Li Xiao showed her the image of Jerome on the screen. Denise collapsed on the floor in tears. Norma hugged her and took her to the couch.

"Are you an alien?" Morgan asked Li Xiao.

"No. I'm Chinese. I'm just someone who wants to help. I followed that alien to the hospital and saw he was about to kill you, so I brought you here. My name is Li Xiao. I disguise myself as the goddess Guan Yin to protect my real identity."

"Wo hen gao xing kan jian ni," replied Morgan with a bow.

"That's pretty good. Did you learn Mandarin in school?"

"No, I learned it at home after school."

"When did you have time to learn Mandarin?" asked Norma with surprise.

"Pico modified my brain so I could concentrate better and I used the ability to learn Mandarin in one night."

"Very impressive, Morgan," said Li Xiao.

"I think I heard about you," he said. "Was it you that freed the Chinese dissidents?"

"I did."

"Li Xiao," asked Norma, "Do you have some clothes I can wear instead of this hospital gown?"

"Certainly. I'm sure I have something in my closet that will fit you," As Li Xiao left the room, her device chirped to indicate that she was getting a message.

"Xiao, this is Cobalt. You should be able to hear me though you won't be able to speak to me. The invasion of your planet has started. You must get below ground level as soon as possible. You should be safe after twenty-four hours. I will come for you after they have finished sweeping your planet. Go quickly, Xiao. I hope to see you soon."

Li Xiao touched the screen softly with her fingertips as Cobalt's image faded from view.

She returned to the living room with clothes for Norma. "Everyone listen up. We need to get food and water from the kitchen then move to the parking garage, as soon as possible. The power is out so we will have to take the stairs. Morgan, will your mother make it okay?"

"Yes, I'll help her."

"I can help too," said Denise.

"Pico," asked Morgan, "do you know what's going on?"

"The Euclidian invasion has started. Soon they will be beaming people off of your planet. Below ground is the safest place to be until they have finished."

"Mom, do you think you can make it down the stairs okay?"

"Sure. Thanks to Pico I feel like a teenager again. The way I feel right now, I bet I could take you in a game of tennis."

"Sure, mom. For now let's just see if you can beat me to the garage."

Li Xiao led them to the bottom level of the building's underground garage. Along the way, she attempted to convince her neighbors to join them, but they just thought she was crazy.

"Everyone, please stay here for at least twenty-four hours," said Li Xiao. "I know it may be uncomfortable, but it is the only way to stay safe from the aliens. You should have enough food and water. These buckets will have to suffice as toilets. Here are a couple of flashlights in case the emergency lights give out. I'm going to try to save my family. If I'm not back in an hour, I may not be back at all. Morgan has the keys to my place, so after the emergency, feel free to make yourselves at home there."

Li Xiao selected the coordinates to her parent's house and pushed the transport button. The four watched Li Xiao as she disappeared and wondered what their lives would be like after the alien's attacked Earth.

***

"There have been many movies about invading aliens," said Denise, "and in the movies we always find a way to defeat them. In retrospect it seems unrealistic to believe that a civilization advanced enough to travel millions of light years to Earth could be beaten by a civilization that can't even travel to Mars."

"Do you think they will destroy our planet?" asked Morgan.

"I don't know."

"When they came to my planet," said Pico, "their intent was not to destroy it. They only decided to do so after my people fought back. I believe that Earth will be left intact, but life won't be the same for the people who are left here."

"I hope that the people who are left can come together to build a better world," said Norma. "I would hate to see us turn on each other like we see in so many post-apocalyptic movies."

"Pico, can you sense what's going on above ground?" asked Morgan.

"No, I don't sense anything." Since Pico had made a mental connection with each of them, they could all hear his thoughts.

Morgan said, "To pass the time, why don't we all get to know each other? We can give a brief history of who we are and how we got here. I'll start by telling you that my name is Morgan Stewart. This is my mother, Norma Stewart. I never knew my father. I lived with mom until she got sick and I had to move in with a foster family. I went to private school until my move and then I went to public school. I really disliked my foster family and new school and I was considering running away when I met Pico.

"I was playing in an alley, hitting a tennis ball, when I saw a strange looking person with a gun who looked like he was going to kill another kid. I knocked the gun from his hand and then the police came and chased him away. That's when I met Pico. He was starving and I found a way to feed him. He told me about his shaman ball and his special powers, and he used them to help me think better and to heal my mother. An alien tried to kill us once and Pico used his powers to protect us. The alien came back today and this time Li Xiao showed up and brought us here. That's my story."

"I guess I should go next since I'm Morgan's mother. I'm Norma Stewart. I grew up in a decent family in D.C. When I was in high school I met a wonderful man. His name was Billy Davis. I was so in love and I thought we were going to get married and move to New York and sing together. Soon after I got pregnant, he disappeared and I never saw him again. My parents threw me out when I decided to keep the baby. I worked whatever jobs I could to keep Morgan in good schools. One day I had a fall at work. I was initially okay, but then the falls continued. I found out that I had a brain tumor and would probably not live much longer. I was in a coma until this morning. Somehow, Pico got rid of my tumor and I came out of the coma. I was just sitting in bed, talking to Morgan when Li Xiao showed up and here I am."

"I can go next," said Pico telepathically. "Can everyone hear me?" He had modified their brains to be able to focus without distraction. They all nodded. "I grew up on the planet Cerebran. It was a large gas planet millions of light years from here. People there communicate using telepathy. I breathe and eat through my skin. We use crystals like this one…" Pico pulled it from his abdomen and Denise and Norma gasped. Pico cocked his head to the side, confused by their reaction. "As I was saying, we use crystals like this to amplify our brain waves and thus our mental abilities. I'll show you."

Pico connected to the crystal and used his ability to lift a nearby car. "I can use the crystal to connect with people over long distances, to heal people, and to fly, among other things."

"Can you show us how you fly?" asked Norma.

"Sure," replied Pico. He levitated and made a quick tour of the parking garage. They all clapped when he returned. "On Earth," he continued, "I get nutrients from metal and citrus fruits."

"That's why you were carrying those nails and the lemon," said Denise.

"Yes. You were the only person to ever figure out that I was an alien and not an action figure."

"I am a doctor, you know, trained to be observant of people."

"I'm glad you noticed, because otherwise I would not have been able to help Morgan's mother properly."

"I never did get to thank you, Pico," said Norma. She walked over and gave him a hug. "Thanks for giving me more time with my son, even if it may be short."

"You're welcome," replied Pico.

"You know," said Norma, "it is really odd communicating with you like this. Is it a side effect of the treatments you gave me?"

"Yes, I modified your brain cells so you could focus better. That helped me communicate with you while you were in the coma. I was learning to become a shaman when the Euclidians attacked our planet. They were stealing our atmosphere and removing our minerals with their vehicles. The planet's shamans attacked their ship with their combined powers and tried to send it into our sun. The Euclidians somehow thwarted the attack and in revenge sent our planet into the sun."

"I hid in one of the Euclidian mining vehicles to keep from being killed by the aircraft that were flying around and firing on people. When the vehicle went back to their ship I was discovered and imprisoned. When I used my hands to get nutrients from the metal walls of the cell, I created holes large enough to escape through. I found my way to their transporter room and hitched a ride with a human that was on her way back to Earth. Soon after we arrived, a Euclidian security guard found her while she was walking outside and dragged her into an alley. When I tried to get away the guard came after me and that is when Morgan saved me. We became friends and I stayed with him because I didn't know what else to do. I was using my shaman stone to help heal his mother when Denise discovered that I was an alien. I was with Denise, helping to cure her sick brother, when the alien assassin showed up. Li Xiao suddenly appeared and saved me and Denise. Now I just want to help Morgan and others to survive the Euclidian attack."

"I guess it's my turn. I'm Doctor Denise Turner. I grew up in Grand Rapids, Michigan with my older brother, Jerome. We had a pretty good childhood and were lucky that our parents could pay for our college. After high school, Jerome went to medical school and a couple of years later I followed after him."

"I went to the University of Colorado in Boulder, Colorado, or CU as we called it, for my undergraduate degree. I simply loved Boulder. It was sunny about three hundred days out of the year. Even with the sun, though, it certainly got cold in the winter. I was enamored by how the people in Boulder embraced diversity. They didn't seem to mind where you came from or what your race was, they were just happy to engage you in stimulating conversation. They were less tolerant of smokers, though, or people who left their Christmas lights up after the beginning of the year. I miss the sense of community and focus on fitness in Boulder, and all the great places to eat and drink. I lived in a small apartment on a hill near the Fox Theatre. In the summer I would ride my bike to school and through the nearby neighborhoods. On the weekends I would ride my bike on the Boulder Creek Trail all the way across town without having to worry about traffic lights or cars. In winter I would catch the city bus and go skiing at the nearby Eldora Ski Resort. My favorite place to get a drink was the Rio Grande, or Rios as we all called it. They had the most amazing margaritas."

"What made you leave?" asked Morgan.

"I wanted to be closer to home in Michigan. I earned my doctorate from the University of Michigan and took time to go home once a month to visit my sick aunt. When I got married my husband and I moved to D.C. where I had a job at a hospital. We spent our honeymoon in Boulder. We stayed at the St. Julien Hotel and Spa. I got a massage there every morning and my husband and I spent the evenings holding hands and walking along Pearl Street Mall, eating dinner at a new place each night. I loved that man dearly. He was later killed in a traffic accident and I've never remarried. That last thing I said to him was 'goodbye, Max'.

"I decided to stay in D.C and one day Norma became my patient." Denise took Norma's hand in hers. "I got to know Morgan from his frequent visits, and one day he came in with what looked to be a doll." Morgan cringed. "Sorry, 'action figure'. I examined Pico and determined that he was alive. Pico revealed himself to me and showed me wondrous things that he could do with his mind while healing Norma. I asked him to help my brother, who was a heroin addict. We were in his hospital room when Li Xiao showed up and teleported us here. I have no idea what is in store for me next. I can only suppose that the world will always need a good doctor."

Norma said, "How do we know that the world that is left after the alien invasion will be a world worth living in?"

"It's too early to know," said Denise. "I hope that people such as Pico and Li Xiao can use their powers to help us build a new world that's better than this one."

***

"It's happening," said Pico.

"What's happening?" asked Morgan.

"They're taking people," said Pico. He pulled out his shaman stone.

"From this building?" asked Denise.

"From the city. They're all gone. I can sense waves of extinguished thought, all across the city. There are whispers from people that weren't taken, but they are few and far between. The Euclidians aren't taking people in ships. They're just vanishing."

"Is there anything we can do to save people? Can you teleport them down here?" asked Norma.

"It's already too late. I'm reaching out for hundreds of miles and there's almost no one out there to save."

***

In another part of D.C., Uan had returned to his apartment with Calvin. Betty and Dominique were with them in the living room, wondering what happened to the electricity.

"The invasion of your planet has started," said Uan. "One of the first things we do in an invasion is disrupt all the electronics. That is why you have no electricity."

"When will it come back on?" asked Dominique.

"Probably never."

"How are we supposed to survive without electricity?"

"You do not need electricity to survive. There is still plenty of food and water."

"The food is not going to last long once everyone starts stripping the stores bare."

"I'm sure we will be fine," said Uan, not revealing what else would happen during the invasion.

"What happens once it gets dark?" asked Betty.

"Don't worry," said Calvin. "I have flashlights and candles."

"The one thing you must do," said Uan, "is stay inside the apartment for the next day. I do not want any of you to be affected by the invasion."

"What does that mean?" asked Betty.

"Just do what I say," replied Uan.

CHAPTER 16

Saying Goodbye to Earth

Once the Euclidians had finished collecting people, cities across the globe became ghost towns. Cities once bustling with activity lay silent, and not just from the lack of people, but lack of electricity and vehicles.

Tokyo, Moscow, London, Beijing, Rome, Istanbul, Cairo, New York, and Mexico City were all empty except for the few people here and there that managed to escape the Euclidian teleport operators by being in basements or subways or simply by being lucky.

A day after the Euclidian ships had finished removing the Earth's citizenry, survivors were still afraid to move about, fearful that whatever took all the people would return and get them. Though it was dark at night, especially in windowless apartments, no one dared to light a candle or use a flashlight, light sources that escaped the effects of the EMP due to their simplicity. Julie sat in her apartment in downtown Austin, shaking with fear at every sound. She and her friend Patty, who was visiting from San Diego, had escaped the mass abduction and only now had they found one another.

"Patty, the past day has been horrible. It's been so hot I couldn't stand it, but I didn't dare open a window. I was just sitting on the fire escape, enjoying the sunset, when everyone started disappearing. A shadow passed over the city and everything went quiet. First the people were gone and then the cars disappeared. What could make that happen? When the electricity went out I thought it was just due to the summer heat. After the people disappeared I thought a government experiment had gone wrong. I got on my bike and rode to the water. I saw no one the entire way and when I got to the water I saw the most enormous ship floating over the water and I knew it had to be aliens. Then I saw a couple of aliens standing on the shore observing the ship. I just freaked out and rode my bike straight home. I was so afraid they had gotten you as well."

"I was at the museum, down in the basement where they keep the Indian artifacts. You know how I love that stuff. When the lights went off I was completely disoriented, but I wasn't afraid. It took me a while to find the stairs and make it to the ground floor. When I got there everyone was gone. I went outside and that's when I knew something was gravely wrong. No people, no cars, I felt like I was on some abandoned movie lot. It took so long to walk back to your apartment."

"I'm just glad you made it back. I was so afraid I was the only one left."

"I can't stay here. I know it sounds crazy, but I'm going to try to get back to San Diego. Maybe this incident is isolated, or my family was spared like we were. Either way, I have to try. You should come with me."

"My family is here and I need to try to find them. But I'm still very afraid."

Patty's gone, and now I'm alone in the dark, sweating, and waiting for aliens to come for me. During the day I feel safe, but at night my courage slips away and I'm just afraid. I'm certain that the aliens have been in my building. I could hear their quiet footsteps. I just sit here afraid to move. I've barely eaten, I can't sleep, and I haven't flushed my toilet since Patty left. I wish I could go back to just worrying about keeping my low-wage job or not getting herpes from some cute guy at the bar.

***

The next morning, Calvin looked out the window and said, "Uan, where is everybody? The streets are completely empty. I mean, there is no one anywhere. There aren't even any cars out there."

"They have all been taken to our ships for processing."

"What do you mean, processing?" said Betty. "Like for food?"

"No, we do not eat sentient beings. The people are being held in large rooms for transport aboard our ship. We will make an inventory of each person. Size, height, strength, looks, and so on."

"What happens next?"

"They will be sold to whoever will buy them. Some rich person might buy two as museum pieces, or a company may purchase a million or more to help clear or cultivate a new planet. Many will be used for mining. Just like in the early days on your planet, stronger civilizations conquer weaker ones. And to the victors go the spoils."

"So what happens to us?" asked Dominique.

"I go back to my ship, and you stay here to live out your lives."

"What kind of life is it going to be," said Calvin, "when we have no utilities, no means for creating goods, and all of our vehicles are gone? How many people are even left here to rebuild our planet?"

"Why are you complaining? There is plenty of food in your stores and in the meantime, learn to grow more. There are probably still a hundred million people left scattered across your planet. At least your overpopulation problem has been solved."

"I would rather have overpopulation than live on an empty planet with inoperable technology."

"I can help you all find a safe place to stay with plenty of food and water. I can even get you some special weapons to help you protect yourselves."

"I can't believe you risked your life to save me," said Betty, "and now you're going to abandon me. Why can't I go with you?"

"There is no room for you on my ship and the life is not as pleasant as you might think."

"You mean to tell me that there are six billion kidnapped people on your ship, but there isn't room for me?"

"You do not want to be in those crowded cells. They are smelly and uncomfortable. In the end you could end up as a slave on a hostile planet."

"For an advanced creature, you don't know much about love," piped up Dominique.

"What love?" said Uan.

"Betty, you dummy," said Calvin.

Uan pursed his lips and took a long look at Betty. Betty had tears in her eyes as she looked longingly at Uan. Her lips quivered and she shook her head as she began to plead. "Why can't I come with you? Is there someone else in your life or is it just shameful to be around a species from a conquered planet?"

"I can be with anyone I choose, but I have never had a mate."

"You're a virgin?" asked Calvin.

"No, you fool. I have taken several women and I probably have offspring. Ossies do not form relationships the way you do."

"You can say that again," said Calvin. "He almost killed me when I hugged him and thanked him for saving my life."

"I was not familiar with your customs at the time," Uan replied angrily.

"If you're so emotionless, why did you risk your life to save me?"

"I have taken many women, but I have never been taken by a woman before. It touched me. I did not want anyone to hurt you."

"But you're going to hurt me now by leaving me in this desolate place."

"I cannot take you with me."

"Then stay. Stay with me."

"I cannot. This is not my life."

"Then kill me. You're good at that. You might as well have left me with Boudreau. At least he treated me better than you."

"I could always send you back, but he is probably no longer there."

Betty lunged at Uan. "You bastard!" She knocked him on the floor and started swinging violently at his head. "Kill me, you bastard. Go ahead and kill me!"

Uan knocked her to the side like a rag doll and stood up. Betty got to her feet and came at him again. Uan grabbed her by the throat and lifted her up against the wall. He pulled out his spear and held it high, bracing to slit her throat.

"You cut her," said Dominique as she aimed her gun at Uan's head, "and I'll put a hole in your head big enough to fly your spaceship through. I'll bet these bullets still work, don't they? And if you try that camouflage crap I'll fill this room with lead until I hit you. This gun has an extended magazine and I'm one angry bitch about now, so don't test me."

"Don't do it, man," pleaded Calvin. "Just let her go and leave."

Uan looked up at Betty, who was whimpering uncontrollably under his grip. He slowly slid her back to the floor.

"Okay, I will take you with me. Just stop crying. It makes you look weak and you are anything but weak, dominatrix."

"Just weak for you," said Betty as she hugged Uan. "Give me one moment for happy tears and I promise you'll never see another one."

"You cry when you are happy and you cry when you are sad. I do not understand how humans have survived so long."

"They're coming, too," she said, pointing at Calvin and Dominique. "They can work as bodyguards."

"You will not need protection on the ship. It is quite safe."

"No, they will be your bodyguards, to protect you from me."

"Okay," laughed Uan, and the room erupted in cheers.

"Can we take anything with us?" asked Dominique.

"You can each take one bag," replied Uan. "Calvin, pack a bag and take a last look around, because we will not be coming back here. When you are ready I will have the ship pick us up."

A half an hour later, Calvin returned with a black Nike duffle bag filled to the point that it couldn't be closed.

"Okay, I'm ready for my next great adventure," he said.

Uan spoke into his UCD and moments later they were aboard the Euclidian reconnaissance ship. Uan had a few words with the crew and then turned to Betty. "I gave them the coordinates for your apartment. Are you ready to pick up your stuff?"

"Yes."

"You will have thirty minutes, after which you will be beamed back to this ship, ready or not."

"I understand."

Uan nodded at the crew and Betty disappeared.

"Your turn, Dominique," said Uan turning to Dominique. "Show me on my device where you live. This is the club where I met you." Uan indicated a point on the screen.

"Wow, how are you doing that? That looks like a live shot."

"We have monitoring devices all over your planet. I can tie into any of them with my device."

"Can I move the screen around by touching it?"

"Yes, just move your fingers across the surface to slide the image around."

"This is pretty cool. There's my building. My goodness, the camera is going right inside. I have got to get one of these devices."

"You will, after you have been indoctrinated aboard the resource ship."

"This is my apartment."

"I will have the crew send you down and you will have thirty minutes before they transport you back here."

"Trust me, I won't need fifteen. I assume I can get more clothes where we are going."

"Yes, of course. Just shout when you are ready and they will beam you back."

Uan nodded to the crew and Dominique was gone. Uan used his UCD to call Captain Shisal to update him on the events that had transpired.

"Captain Shisal, this is Uan. Are you free to talk?"

"Go ahead, Uan."

"I found the alien, but I was unable to kill him."

"Not to worry. You kept him out of our hair, which is all I cared about. We have set up a camp for shore leave in a beautiful place called Key West, Florida. We are on the west side of the island at the Westin Resort. There will be a formal ball there in a couple of days and I want you to be there. You deserve the recreation. I'm sure that living in the primitive conditions on this planet has been miserable."

"Yes, but I have had my moments of excitement."

"Come on down. We'll have a drink and chat. They've got some stuff here they call ganga that you've got to try."

"That might be a bit difficult. I have some Earthlings that will be sharing my cabin. They saved my life in recent days and I promised to find them a new place to make home since their own won't be habitable for a while."

"Why don't we just make them members of the crew? Get them formally loaded into the system, and assigned their own cabins on the junior crew deck. Have logistics schedule an indoctrination session for them."

"I am a bit worried about the discipline required for them to succeed as crewmembers. Earthlings are not experienced with intergalactic travel or being around aliens."

"If they can't handle it then they don't deserve to be on the ship. They are either captives or they are crew. The *Andrea* is not a cruise ship."

"Understood, captain."

"If they survive indoctrination, get them some formal clothing for the ball and bring them along. I want to meet them."

"They may feel a bit uncomfortable."

"Trust me, they won't be the only Earthlings. It's the same everywhere we go. Capture most of the inhabitants during the first wave of the invasion and befriend the ones that are left. It gives us a chance to understand a new species, and they can be great sources of conversation."

"I would like to shield them from the kind of scrutiny and abuse that can happen during those events. After all, they did save my life."

"All the more reason to bring them. So it's settled. The ball starts at 2:70 ship's time. Just as the sun sets here. Sunset is a big event for this planet's inhabitants. I expect to see you all are there."

"Not to worry. We will all be there."

Ten minutes after beaming to her apartment Dominique was ready to depart, having packed just a few belongings into a simple Coach bag. She left a note for anyone left who might come looking for her.

Dear family,

I've hitched a ride on a spaceship to the other side of the universe. I fear I will never return.

Much love,

Dominique

She paused for a moment before standing up to depart. *Now I guess I'm supposed to shout out, as if they'll hear me on the ship.* "I'm ready to return," she called. *As if that is supposed to work.* "Whoa!"

"Welcome back, Dominique," said Calvin. "You didn't bring much with you."

"I'm starting over. Louisiana was sort of a dead end for me. I'm happy to be gone, though I'm a bit apprehensive about my future. I didn't think I'd be leaving home on an alien spacecraft."

"Me either. But all in all, I'd rather be visiting a new place with Uan than taking my chances on a post-apocalyptic Earth. I've seen too many of those movies and none of them end well. Even when the good guys win, they're stuck in a life that isn't worth living."

"I've never seen one where the aliens have a successful invasion and some Earthlings get to start a new life on another planet."

"I admit I'm a bit nervous. But Uan says it will be like being on the Champs Elysees in Paris. There will be so many people from so many places you sort of get lost in the mélange."

"That's good. I hope he has a large cabin. I hate sharing, but it's better than being crowded into a cell with the captives."

"I hear that. I wonder what the bathrooms are like. They have to have at least fifteen kinds humanoid poop to deal with."

"Yep, and what are showers like, and can I get I get my hair done? I wonder if they've ever seen a 'fro before? Do you think he's just faking us out and will stick us in with the slaves once we're on the ship?"

"No, that's not going to happen. Uan doesn't lie. He has no reason to. He's not afraid of anyone or anything."

"He seems to be soft on Betty, though, if you can call it soft to almost cut her throat and then ask her to join him on the ship," Dominique said with a smile.

"One day I'll have to tell you about the whole dominatrix bit she pulled on him. That made him respect her. I think that's as close to love as he gets."

Suddenly Betty appeared, beamed aboard the ship with a trunk.

"Speak of the devil. Hey, girl," greeted Dominique.

"Hey, Dominique."

"I see you filled an entire Louis Vuitton trunk."

"I wish I could have brought more. We don't know if they have skillets, plates, or even silverware where we're going, so I got as much kitchen stuff as I could carry. Plus heirlooms, clothes, weapons, and my dominatrix gear. You know Uan would be pissed if I forgot that."

"You've got to turn me on to that dominatrix stuff when you get a chance."

"I'd love to."

"I spoke with the captain," Uan broke in, "and he is going to let you be members of the crew. You will get your own cabins and universal connection devices. You will also be assigned jobs on the ship and expected to perform."

"I think we can handle that, once we learn the language," said Calvin.

"They will teach you Euclidian once you are on the ship. It is a requirement for crewmembers. I will teach you something now. *Stowtan char* means 'greetings, captain'. You must say that when you meet the captain at the ball he has arranged."

"We're going to a ball?" Dominique said frantically. "I don't have anything to wear."

"That will be taken care of on the ship. It is more important that you learn the greeting. So say it," Uan said emphatically, "*stowtan char*, with your fists together and eyes looking down."

"*Stowtan char*," they all repeated.

"The captain is not one to be disrespected. That can easily get you killed," said Uan.

"Maybe we should skip the ball," Calvin said nervously.

"That would not be wise. He is expecting you. He did agree to let you on his ship as crewmembers."

"Boy, do I regret that decision," said Dominique.

"On the contrary," said Calvin. "This is one of the most life changing decisions that you have ever made. You will not regret this."

Betty took Uan's arm. "I'm game, honey," she said.

Uan pushed her away. "Please do not call me honey in public. I prefer to keep our amorous moments within the confines of private spaces, if you do not mind."

The ship's crew snickered in the background, which unnerved Uan.

"I think it is time we headed to the *Andrea* to start your indoctrination," he said. "Is everyone ready to go?"

They all nodded, Uan turned to the crew and within an instant they were in the indoctrination area of the *Andrea*.

CHAPTER 17

Failed Attack

"I seen 'em, I tell ya. Hanging out at the beach just like they's on vacation. If we had a bunch of guns we could take 'em out. None of them's carryin' weapons 'cept a couple of guards. Them flyin' things are off to the edge of the island, coverin' the beach an' the bridge."

"Fine Jeb, but won't their flying ships shoot us down before we can get off the bridge?" said Ezekiel.

"That's it though. We don't walk across the bridge, we row under it."

"Won't they still see us?"

"They didn't see me," chuckled Jeb. "It was night an' I went right up on the beach. I was starin' at 'em from one of their beach bungalows. Big fellas they were, along with the women. There was a bunch of different types of aliens."

"You mean like in that bar on *Star Wars*?"

"Yep, just like that. But ya know what the strangest thing was, Ezekiel?"

"What's that, Jeb?"

"They all had to go to the bathroom, just like we do. They were goin' in an' out of the restroom like nobody's business. They laugh an' kid around too. You'd almost think they was human. Makes you want to go up an' chat with 'em."

"All except for they took all the people off the planet and now they're stealing all our stuff."

"Do ya think they took the people for slaves or food?"

"Hard to say. They don't seem like the type to eat humans. I mean, they seem civilized and all. After they finished scooping people up they just ignored the rest of us. I've seen them fly overhead and not pay me no mind. It's like they got their quota and we're just not worth the extra effort."

Ezekiel laughed. "Maybe they worried about their game warden finin' 'em for havin' too big a catch."

"You just a dang fool, ain't you?"

"Come on, you know I'm just funin'. Let's get back to the militia an' hatch ourselves a plan."

Jeb commanded what was left of the Twenty-First Militia Regiment. His military experience consisted of two years in the army before getting a general discharge under honorable conditions because he was determined to be mentally unfit for duty. He still wanted to be a patriot so he joined a local militia group.

Ezekiel had met Jeb in the militia. They had grown up in nearby small towns in the southern tip of Florida. Ezekiel liked to shoot and joined the militia so he could learn to shoot a lot of different guns. Jeb taught Ezekiel what he had learned in the army and they soon became good friends. They had always thought they might have to defend their country from invaders, but not that the invaders would come from another planet.

Ezekiel found out about the alien abduction from a neighbor who saw his wife and son beamed away from the top of the fruit cellar stairs. He came up from the cellar to see what had happened and his backyard, which minutes before had full of family and friends, was empty. Jeb escaped being grabbed by the aliens because he was passed-out drunk in his uncle's basement at the time.

Pissed because so many of their relatives had been captured, Jeb and Ezekiel joined up with what remained of the militia to fight the aliens in any way that they could.

***

Later that night, two boatloads of gun-toting militiamen headed toward Key West using simple outboard motors that hadn't been destroyed by the Euclidian EMP weapon. To hide from the Euclidian aircraft, they traveled beneath the elevated causeway that bridged the mainland to the island. They could see the glowing edges of the Euclidian attack vehicles hovering overhead, but either they weren't seen or the Euclidians didn't care about them.

"Jeb," said Ezekiel, "why the heck did you bring those damn water balloons? You think they're going to want to play games with us?"

"They's balloons all right, but they ain't filled with water. It's my backup plan, in case our guns don't work."

"Whatever you say, Jeb. Lookie, we actually done made it to shore without being spotted."

"Listen up, everybody," Jeb announced, "Them aliens are about a mile up the beach, at that Westin resort. Once we get there, the Team One'll go around to the other side of the main building. The rest'll wait on this side of the resort 'til Team One is in position. Team One, when yer ready you start unloadin' on them alien bastards an' we'll join in from this side. Any questions? Good, then let's head out."

After fifteen minutes the two teams arrived at the resort where the aliens were partying. Team Two, led by Jeb, hid behind a beach house while Team One continued to the far side of the main building.

"We'll jus' wait here," said Jeb, "'til we hear shots from the other side. When I reconned last night, there was only three guards. Everybody make sure yer safety is off, you got a round in the chamber, and keep yer finger off the trigger 'til yer ready to shoot them aliens."

"And once we start off, spread out," added Ezekiel. "It'll be harder for them to pick us off, and we don't want to shoot each other in the back, neither."

Bang! Bang! The sound of gunfire came from the far side of the resort.

"That's them. Let's move out!" commanded Jeb.

Hearing the shots, one of the Euclidian guards ran up the beach to engage Team One. The other two held their ground and called for air support. Jeb's group attacked the remaining guards but were unable to injure them. They seemed to be protected by some sort of personal force field. The guards easily picked off a couple of Jeb's team and then the aircraft arrived to kill most of the others. Jeb retreated behind the beach hut where he had stashed his balloons.

I'm not gonna let them damn aliens kill us off without killin' at least one of 'em. Let's see how they like these alcohol balloons.

Jeb tossed two balloons at each of the guards who were now searching the beach and getting closer. The balloons were filled with methanol, which ignited on impact. The guards panicked and ran into the water to douse the flames. Jeb jumped up and down shouting with joy. "Take that, ya damn aliens. Think yer invincible, do ya?"

Before he could enjoy his triumph, though, Jeb was vaporized by one of the hovering attack ships. The only person left from the two teams was a woman who hid beneath the awning of a towel hut near the swimming pool.

***

After the festivities recommenced, one of the partygoers discovered the woman as she tried to slip away from the resort. Several of the aliens came over to get a closer look at the Earthling. As they drew near she became incredibly frightened. She fell to her knees, put her face to the ground, and held out her hands. "Please don't hurt me," she begged.

The onlookers laughed, not knowing what she was saying. A Majorellen that spoke English came forward to speak to her. "Hello, female. I am Dexin. What is your name?"

The woman looked up wide-eyed, surprised that the odd looking creature could speak English. "My name is Pura," she said shyly.

"Standup, Pura, and talk to us. We won't bite. Anyway, we've already eaten."

The others laughed as Dexin's words were translated. Pura could not resist a smile when she heard the laughter.

"Come and join us," offered Dexin. "You'll see that we can be a lot of fun."

"*She's clear,*" a guard said to Dexin.

"You're not going to kill or enslave me?" said Pura.

"Of course not. As long as you do not try to kill or enslave one of us." The aliens laughed again, which elicited another smile from Pura.

"No, why would I do that?"

"Your friends sure wanted to."

"I really didn't know them. We only met this morning. Everyone I knew had disappeared. I thought it would be safer to be with them than to be on my own. They attacked you because you kidnapped our people and you're stealing our resources."

"We are taking some of your resources, but there will be plenty left for you. As for the kidnapping, we have all the people we need. The rest we will leave here unharmed as long as they don't attack us. Take my arm and let me get you some food and drink."

Dexin offered his arm and Pura took it. They walked to a bar by the pool where a Euclidian was serving drinks. All the standard alcoholic beverages had been replaced with strange bottles containing even stranger liquids. Some glowed, some sparkled, some changed colors, and some moved on their own as if they were alive.

Let me have two Tammarian grogs, Dexin said to the bartender. Dexin took the two drinks and handed one to Pura.

"Are you sure this won't make me ill?"

"Yes, I'm sure. Some Earthlings have already tried it," replied Dexin.

"Oh really?"

Dexin raised his glass. "To your health, Pura."

"Cheers," she replied. "Wow, this is yummy. What is this?"

"It's Tammarian grog. Earthlings tend to like it."

"So you know other Earthlings?"

"I've met a few here and there."

"How is it you speak English and know about our culture?"

"I'm a Majorellen and our race has a natural ability for picking up languages. We work as translators and interrogators on the ship. When the Euclidians planned our mission here, I was required to learn your planet's major languages. Do you mind coming over to our table? Several of my shipmates are interested in meeting you. I'll translate for you."

"I guess. As long as it's safe."

Pura followed Dexin to his table, where he gestured to those seated, apparently introducing her to them. They nodded and smiled at her. Pura smiled and nodded back.

"Pura," said Dexin, "they would like to touch your skin and hair, if that is okay. I promise they won't hurt you. They are surprised that humans don't bleed to death more often when your delicate skin is wounded. Of course, you are free to reciprocate."

"Okay, I guess. As long as they're not going to hurt me."

"Don't worry, they have no intention of hurting you."

Dexin gestured and the aliens arose from their seats to approach and touch Pura. She was afraid at first, but quickly relaxed and eventually worked up her nerve to touch them in return. She was surprised at the variations in skin texture, stiff or scaly or bumpy or leathery.

Someone squeezed her breasts and said something to Dexin.

"She wants to know what purpose the lumps on your chest serve."

Pura pushed the hands away. "They are used to feed our newborn offspring."

"Where are your babies?"

"I don't have any. They are for when I do have them."

Dexin translated for the group.

"*Seems like a horrible waste,*" one said, and they all laughed.

"Are you all from the same planet?" asked Pura.

"Not at all," said Dexin. "We represent three species from three different planets, though our homes all happen to be on Euclidia."

"You all seem to get along so well. People here don't get along and we're all from the same planet."

"It takes time to learn that everyone benefits when you all get along. Our civilizations are thousands of years older than yours and we still have the occasional war with other planets, but not amongst ourselves," said Dexin.

"Where are your planets?"

"Many lights years from here, in another galaxy. We travel in inter-dimensional space. It is much faster than traveling in normal space and doesn't cause us to age."

"Wow, that must be nice. I guess your planets are a lot different from ours?"

"Yes indeed. Here, have a look." Dexin showed her his UCD. "This is what my planet looks like from space. Now I'll zoom in and you can see that our cities, vehicles, and people are much like Earth."

"Yeah, roads and traffic signs. How fascinating."

Dexin took a moment to translate their conversation to the others.

"Robin wants to know why Earthlings wear so much clothing all the time."

"Mostly to be comfortable, but it's also a legal requirement. You can be thrown in jail for walking around naked."

Dexin translated and they all laughed. One of them spoke to Dexin.

"He wonders," Dexin translated, "why it is that on Earth, participating in things that can cause joy, such as nudity and drugs, are illegal, while things that can destroy civilization, such as guns, pollution, and nuclear weapons, are okay. At some level, you Earthlings will be better off now that your nuclear weapons and overcrowding problems are gone. I think that everyone here will be too busy putting the planet back together to start a war anytime soon, though I suspect you will focus on rebuilding your militaries before addressing other infrastructure issues. Those with guns will take food from those without guns and never understand that when you work together, everyone can be fed."

"But isn't that what you're doing to us?" Pura snapped.

"Yes, with one small difference. You are an inferior race of beings on a remote planet and your existence or nonexistence has no bearing on our home planets. Trust me, if your planet attacked ours we wouldn't be screwing over each other for the remaining scraps."

"Is there such a thing as abortion on your planet?"

"Not in the way that you perform them. If a person doesn't want to carry a fetus to term, we remove it without harm and nurture it in an artificial womb until it is born."

"Then who are its parents?"

"No one, unless someone adopts the child. Orphans are placed in schools where they grow up alongside others like them. They have guidance counselors who take on the duties of parents."

"You mean they are placed in orphanages."

"Trust me, they are nothing like your orphanages. Now," said Dexin, "Pura, this is Goron. He is a Euclidian officer on our ship. He would like to escort you to the formal ball we will have here tomorrow and afterward spend the evening having sex with you."

"Why would I want to do that? Is it even possible between our species?"

"I'm sure your two species can manage sex somehow. Goron says if he enjoys his evening with you, you can be his companion for the rest of our current mission. Afterward, you can return here or go to any other planet that you like. And they all have to be better than returning here."

"How would I survive on another planet? What about the air, and germs?"

"Most of our planets have enough oxygen for Earthlings. If not, you can get implants placed in your nostrils that compensate for any atmospheric deficiencies. As for germs, once onboard our ship we will modify your genes so germs won't be an issue for you anymore."

"Can I bring my sister?"

"He hasn't agreed to take you yet."

"He will. Trust me. He will."

"If I can bring my sister, he has a deal."

Dexin translated then spoke again to Pura. "Goron has agreed to your terms, but your sister will have to work as a crewmember. When you are ready he will beam you aboard our ship and get you your own room where you can prepare for the ball. He will make sure that you have something appropriate to wear and get you assistance for your hair and makeup."

"I'm afraid. I'm afraid to leave, and I'm afraid that he might hurt me."

"There is no reason to be afraid. You will enjoy being at the ball. Goron will not force you to do anything you do not want to do. At any time you can say 'enough' and he will send you right back here."

"Okay, I'll do it."

CHAPTER 18

The Holding Cells

Each of the holding cells aboard the *Andrea* housed about a thousand people. The cells had water and food dispensers, and bathrooms with showers. Any disturbances between people were immediately quelled with ceiling-mounted weapons. Repeat offenders were sent into space, in full view of the other captives on monitors set into the cell walls. One moment a person might be fighting with a cellmate and the next he would be floating in space with a momentary look of terror on his face, and the next moment he would be dead, eyes bugged out, skin ripped apart, a frozen corpse. The images on the monitors encouraged cell inhabitants to behave.

As each cell had been filled, an announcement was made by an animated image of a human on the screens, spoken in ten major Earth languages.

Please remain calm. You will not be harmed. This is only a temporary holding area. You will be released in a matter of days. During that time we ask that the following rules be followed. No physical activity is allowed between each other. No loud or disruptive behavior. Only one person in a bathroom at a time. No switching of beds. Failure to follow these rules will result in punishment up to and including death.

In response, many of the captives yelled at the monitors and threw their shoes or other items, hoping to get a response from whoever might be watching, but none came. Some attempted to damage the monitors, but were immediately subdued by the weapons in the ceiling. The most trouble came from those rooms holding military personnel. The Euclidians used those incidents as opportunities to train Ossie crew in crowd control for assignments at planetary outposts. Their challenge was to keep the captives under control without resorting to the automated personnel control systems, and to minimize harm to the precious cargo of humans.

One of the Ossies, Rean, had learned English in preparation for the mission and was assigned to a cell that housed a platoon of U.S. Marines, several Military Police officers, and a group of convicts taken from a an American prison. He arrived at the cell cloaked and invisible, and eavesdropped to learn what the humans might be planning. Rean found several groups combing the walls, looking for an exit.

"There has to be an opening somewhere," said a marine. "How else do people and equipment get in and out?"

Another said, "They also have to enter to replenish the food and repair things that get broken."

"Marines," said Colonel Roberts, the senior officer in charge, "just keep pushing, pulling, and tapping on every surface. I'm betting there's a way out through the top, since we keep getting zapped when we try to climb the walls. We need to figure out a way to take out those devices. They seem to be protected by some sort of force field. Every time we throw something at it, the object gets blocked and we get zapped. Does anyone remember how you got in here?" No one responded.

Rean walked over to a group of the convicts to hear what they were planning. "If we stick together," said one, "we can get out of here.

As soon as a door opens or someone enters, we rush them. If one of those marines gets in our way, we just take them out."

"What do we use for weapons?" asked another convict.

"How about the night sticks from those MPs feeling up the wall over there?" He selected a group of nine others to join him. "First we'll ask nice then we'll punch their faces in if they say no. Let's go."

Rean uncloaked in front of the group, cutting them off from their targets. He held a two-meter long staff above his head.

"There will be no fighting. Now go back to your beds or I will use force."

The convicts froze in place at the sudden appearance of the strange-looking being.

"Let's get him," shouted one of the convicts, and the group charged at Rean.

Rean crouched down and thrust the tip of his staff into the chest of the first convict. He spun the staff to the side and clubbed another on the side of his head, knocking him to the floor. He spun the staff back and took out three more. Another came at Rean from the side. Rean dodged his punch, grabbed him in his chest and flung him overhead. Rean bared his sharp teeth and growled. "Go to your bunks or I'm going to start killing people." The convicts continued to come at him.

Rean vanished and a moment later was visible and he dropped from the ceiling and crushed a convict's skull with his staff. Before the man hit the floor he was transported into space, his agonies displayed on the monitor screens. The remaining convicts hesitated then again attacked Rean. He disappeared and once more fell from the ceiling to crush another man's skull. He, too, was instantly transported into space for all to watch him die. This time the prisoners did not hesitate, but ran for their bunks.

Rean appeared in the middle of the room, hanging from the six-meter high ceiling with one hand and holding his staff with the other. He yelled at the marines who had been scanning the walls for an opening.

"Listen to me! There are no doors or exits. Even if there were, you would be dead the moment you stepped outside this room. Just relax, remain orderly, and enjoy the ride. Though you won't see me, I will always be here. If you step out of line I will have the pleasure of disciplining you."

"Excuse me. I'm Colonel Roberts of the Seventeenth Fighting Infantry. I demand to know where you are taking us and what you plan to do with us once we arrive."

"I am not here to answer your questions and your demands mean nothing to me."

"Fine, then we marines will fight you to the last man. We refuse to sit idly by while you take us to God knows where to do who knows what to us!"

"Did you not learn anything from the others? Do you really find the accommodations and lack of information intolerable?"

"We are marines, not convicts. We are battle hardened and will not be as easy to defeat."

"That is of no consequence to me. You will die all the same. Go back to your bunks or attack me. I will be happy to kill you before your bodies are sent into space. You will find that I do not tire easily. Killing you will be an honor."

There was silence in the room. Then Colonel Roberts shouted, "Marines, attack!"

The marines pounced on Rean and pinned him to the floor. Rean pushed through the men, grabbed a marine by the throat and leapt up to crush the man's head against the ceiling. The marine fell to the floor dead and was transported into space.

Rean hung from the ceiling with two marines pulling on his staff. He flicked the staff and sent them flying against the wall. Rean twisted his body and fell from the ceiling, spinning his staff above his head like a helicopter rotor. The men below leaped to get out of his way. Those that didn't were crushed and broken. They attempted to crawl out of striking range of Rean's staff.

As the marine's continued their attack Rean swung his staff like a baseball bat, knocking marines left and right with bone-crushing blows until they finally stopped coming at him. Rean stood in the center of the carnage, panting through his sharp teeth. He gave a signal and the dead and maimed marines were sent into space en masse. The people in the room shuddered to see so many of their comrades become frozen relics, exploded in space before their eyes.

"Now get to your bunks unless you want to join your friends in space," Rean growled.

The crowd reluctantly broke up and headed to their bunks. The occasional marine made a run at Rean, only to be cut down and transported into space. They were unaware of the Ossie's amazing three hundred-degree field of vision. It was hard to sneak up on an Ossie.

Once the marines were back in their bunks, Rean approached Colonel Roberts. "Keep your men in line and you will keep them alive. Where you are going is not home, but it is a lot better than this place."

"I could do a lot better job of calming their fears," said Roberts, "if I knew more about where we are going and what happened to our homes and families."

"I am not here to calm fears. I am here to keep the peace. Your entire planet as you knew it is gone. If you're lucky, your family is on this ship somewhere and you may see them again in the future. Otherwise, consider them dead." Rean turned away and disappeared into nothingness.

***

In another part of the Euclidian ship, a holding cell full of regular civilians was in turmoil. The inhabitants were not nearly as disciplined as the marines.

"Why do those things keep zapping me?"

"Honey," said his wife, "I don't think it knows the difference between people hugging and attacking each other. It's probably best if we stayed apart."

"Why is this happening to us?" another man screamed. "Why would someone treat us like this?"

"Probably for the same reason it happened to the Indians and Africans," someone answered. "Now that it's you being locked up like an animal, you don't understand why."

"We should all kneel down and pray to the Lord for deliverance from this captivity," said a priest. "Fighting amongst ourselves is not the answer."

"If God is going to get us out," came a response, "why would He let us be put here in the first place? Maybe their God is stronger than ours."

"There is only one true God and He will deliver us if only we will pray."

A woman called out, "Okay, you pray and I'll light this joint in my pocket, and let's see who's the first to escape this hellhole." She lit the joint and took a long drag. "I can feel myself floating out of here already," she said with a smile.

"May God have mercy on your soul."

"And yours."

A man by the food dispenser shouted, "What kind of crap is this? Looks like simulated meat and fish and vegetables. I bet it tastes like chicken but I'm not eating any of it!"

"Qu'est-ce qu'il a dit?" asked a French woman.

"Il dit que le repas gouter comme poulet," replied her husband.

The man at the food dispenser grabbed a piece of fake meat and held it up to one of the devices in the ceiling. "You hear me?" he shouted. "I am not eating this swill! I want real food!" He tossed the fake steak across the room and was immediately stunned by a weapon in the ceiling. He fell to the floor in pain, breathing heavily and moaning, but no one came to his aid. His pain became anger as he considered his loss of control over circumstances, and he exploded to his feet, shaking his fist at the device.

"Do you know who I am? I'm CEO of one of the largest manufacturing companies in America. I'm worth billions of dollars. You can't lock me up like this, without a word of explanation. I demand to speak to someone in charge! Do you hear me?" he shouted, tears streaming down his face.

He grabbed a stack of the fake steaks and began slinging them at the device. A moment later he disappeared and then showed up on the monitors, floating in space.

"That guy lost it," a man said. "I mean, the food's not great, but it's not worth dying over. For now I'm going to sit back and enjoy the ride."

"I hear you, brother. I just wish our lady friend over there would share her joint with us."

"Me too, but we know that's not going to happen. We don't dare try taking it, either. If we so much as sit on her bed, we'll get zapped."

"Tell me about it. At least they let us enjoy ourselves in the bathroom."

"They're probably watching."

"Let them watch. It's not like they're going to post it on YouTube. Look, she's heading for the bathroom. I'm going to join her."

"Do you think that's smart?"

"The doors don't lock and I'll be out of the view of those damn zappers."

The man got up and went to the bathroom door that the woman had just entered. He reached for the handle but was zapped before he could get the door open. An announcement came over the monitors: "Only one person in the bathrooms at a time."

"Qu'est-ce qu'il a dit?" asked the French woman not willing to wait for the monitors to translate the message.

"Une seule personne dans la salle de bain à la fois."

"Tampis."

The zapped man slowly stumbled back to his rack where his friend gave him a flabbergasted look.

"Man, you got to tell me what that felt like," his friend asked. "I always wanted to know what that feels like."

"It feels like someone microwaved me with a lightning bolt. If you want to know so badly, why don't you grab that bathroom doorknob yourself?"

"I'd rather keep my strikes down to zero, if you don't mind. Two and you're out around here. Seriously out. And you never know what will cause you to be zapped."

"You keep yappin'. I'm going to lie down and try to sleep off this pain."

"I wish they would show us some movies on those monitors instead of just space. It would probably help to calm people down."

"Yeah, something like *Independence Day* or *War of the Worlds* or maybe *Cowboys and Aliens*."

"I was thinking about the *Star Wars* trilogy. The original one, not that crap with the Jar Jar Binks idiot."

"Now you're talking!"

At that moment, *Star Wars, Episode IV* started up on the monitors.

"Oh my goodness," the man whispered, holding his hand to his mouth. "Can you see this too?"

"Of course I can see it. I was zapped, not made delusional."

"Could you dim the lights and turn up the sound, please?" the man asked at the ceiling, as if he had his own private valet listening to him.

The room lights dimmed and the volume from the monitors increased.

"Thank you," the man said. "If it's not too much to ask, could you follow this movie with *Star Wars, Episode V* and *Episode VI*, and then play the *Star Trek* movie series?"

"I don't know what just happened man, but from now on I'm sticking with you. You think you could ask them to take that strike off of me so I don't get prematurely sent into space?"

"I don't want to press my luck. Just lean back and enjoy the movies."

Slowly, everyone in the holding cell moved toward the screens. Some stood to watch, some sat on the floor. As the screens were above everyone's heads, no one was blocked from viewing the movie. The restriction of sitting on someone else's bed was relaxed. The mood inside the room suddenly changed.

Back in the operations room, the Euclidians noticed the change. "Kristi," said one operator to another, "I thought you had lost your mind when you set up that video connection. Go ahead and duplicate that feed in each of the cells. If there are complaints, switch the video to something else. Get a Majorellen to help you translate as needed. This will certainly decrease our spoilage. I'll see that you get a bonus for this."

CHAPTER 19

Boarding the Andrea

Betty, Calvin, and Dominique looked around at their new surroundings in wonder and fear, not sure what would happen next or what their new adventure would bring.

"Here are three new crewmembers for you, approved by Captain Shisal," said Uan to one of the training personnel in the indoctrination area.

To the Earthlings she looked quite frightening, but in a kind voice she introduced herself to them in English. She directed them to seats in a room in front of a monitor screen.

"I have to go now," stated Uan. "You are in good hands. When you have finished here you will be assigned a guide to help you get acclimated to the ship and teach you what you need to know to participate in the ball."

"How do we find you when we're done?" asked Betty in a worried voice.

"When you are assigned your universal connection device, my contact information will be programmed into it. Just say '*gekola Uan*' into it and it will direct you to me."

"You're just going to leave us?" fretted Calvin. "This alien looks like it might eat us."

"So do I, but you're still here. Just relax. Everything will be fine. Once you have finished your indoctrination we will meet back up and tour the ship together."

Uan walked out and a training video began in English, giving the three an overview of the ship and UCD operations.

Your universal connection device will be assigned to you at the completion of this presentation. It will be tuned to your biological frequency and cannot be used by anyone else. If it is lost it will be returned to you. If it is destroyed a replacement will be provided with the same settings and content. You will be asked to indicate next of kin when it is assigned, as it will be turned over to them in case of your demise.

"I guess we are each other's next of kin," said Dominique.

"Uan is going to be mine," responded Betty.

"Are you sure about that? Back at the apartment, he didn't seem eager to jump into a relationship."

"I know. He'll probably never love me, but he won't abandon me either. That's the most I can hope for."

"I guess that's good enough."

"For now, yes."

"Do you smell ginger in the air?"

"Pay attention, you two," interjected Calvin.

The ship is vast and can easily be disorienting. Your UCD will help you by answering any questions you have. Use the internal transports to get to your cabin and other locations on other decks. Use the corridor transports to reach distant locations on the same deck.

"I'm having information overload," said Betty. "My head is about to explode. This is way too much to take in at one time."

"I know what you mean," said Calvin.

You will now be greeted by your guide, Cobalt. Enjoy your stay aboard the Andrea.

A Majorellen entered the room. "Hello, you three. I am Cobalt. I will be your guide over the next couple of weeks."

Cobalt held his hand out to greet them, but they were frozen in place to see the blue creature speaking to them in perfect English.

"Please take my hand. I promise I won't bite."

They reluctantly shook his hand.

"Come with me. I will get you your UCDs and then give you a quick tour of the ship. Afterward, I'll take you to your cabins so you can get settled. Later I will help you design and create clothing for the captain's ball. Greetings and salutations will be your first Euclidian language lesson."

Calvin held up his hands in protest. "I don't think I'm ready to learn a new language."

"You don't want to go to the ball and not be able to greet people. The captain wouldn't be happy about that. It would also set you back on your schedule to learn the language in two weeks."

"You want us to learn an entire alien language in two weeks?" exclaimed Dominique.

"Don't worry. After two weeks, you only have to speak enough to do your jobs. You won't have to read or write Euclidian until later."

Dominique was worried. "I don't think I can do it. I took French for two years in high school and I still can't speak a word of it."

"You'll do just fine. We have great teaching aids. Anyway, it's better than the alternative."

"Which is?" asked Betty hesitantly.

"The captain would probably put you in a holding cell with the other Earthling captives, or have you executed. Probably the latter."

"Why would he execute us?" said Calvin.

"Because you are crewmembers. Learning Euclidian is a requirement of the job. Crewmembers that refuse to do their assigned tasks usually die horrible deaths. I can show you some videos if you like."

"You film the executions?" said Betty.

"They are shown throughout the ship."

"That must be motivating for the crew."

"I wouldn't complain. The captain permitted you to board the ship instead of staying in the wasteland that is now your planet. He is giving you an adventure that most people would kill for, and he is going to pay you quite well by Euclidian standards. Furthermore, if you perform poorly it will reflect negatively on Uan. Understood?"

"Yes," they all responded.

"The proper response is *sah*! Understood?"

"*Sah*," they repeated.

Cobalt helped them initialize their UCDs and then took them into the ship's principal corridor where they were taken aback by its enormous dimensions.

"Ohhhh myyyyy goodness," exclaimed Dominique. "This ship is huge!"

"How large is this thing?" said Calvin.

"It's about ninety kilometers wide, one hundred fifty kilometers long, and fifty kilometers deep," replied Cobalt. "This corridor is about one hundred thirty kilometers long."

"Is that why all those people ride in flying chairs?" said Betty.

"*Sah*, and soon you'll be flying in them."

"No way," said Dominique.

"Say *ahs* for 'no', Dominique," said Cobalt. "The experience can be overwhelming at first, but you'll soon get used to it. The mauve lights point out the transport areas and the pink lights indicate where you can pick up one of the chairs. Go ahead and lead the way to one of the mauve lights."

"Those aliens won't mind us walking between them?" said Betty.

"*Ahs*, they see new aliens all the time. Now proceed to the transport area."

They navigated through the passing stream of people to a transport unit door. Cobalt explained the operation. "This display tells you how many seconds before the transport arrives. Our seconds are longer than yours. Ten of our hours is equal to one day, which is twenty-eight of your hours. We have one hundred minutes per hour and one hundred seconds per minute. I'm sure you can do the math."

"*Sah*," said Betty.

"*Sah*," said Dominique. "Too bad we can't read your numbers."

"Don't worry. Soon you will. Did you notice that the people walking by were pointing their UCDs at you?"

"*Ahs*, not really," said Calvin. "Hey, I'm sort of getting the hang of this."

"They are using them to get information on you," said Cobalt.

"Isn't that an invasion of privacy?" said Betty.

"You have to be able to know who people are on the ship. You also have to know how to communicate with them. Knowing where someone is from and their attributes makes it easier to interact with them. You wouldn't want to challenge a person to a game of Rashnan ball if they weren't physically capable of playing, or if the person would crush you in the match. The UCDs do hide your personal data from that kind of inquiry. Of course, security personnel have access to everything on your UCD."

"So what does the UCD record?" asked Betty.

"Almost everything!" said Cobalt. "It's an extension of you. It sees your environment. It knows who is around you. It tracks smells and sounds and on occasion takes an omni-directional recording that it can later play back directly into your mind. All of the things that we experience are basically electrical impulses in our brains. UCDs can record those impulses and then play them back to our brains, and give us the sensation that we are reliving those experiences. I'll show you. Hold my device and put your thumb here. Now close your eyes and take a deep breath."

"Oh my goodness," said Betty. "I'm somewhere else. I see a beach. I hear the waves crashing against blue rocks. I can smell the water. It's sort of a mint smell. How is that possible?"

"The UCD used a recording of my brain to simulate impulses in your brain." The transporter arrived and a door opened. "Now," said Cobalt, "to get to your cabins, step inside and say *trey*. Only one of you needs to say it, because your cabins are all next to each other."

Dominique stepped inside the transport, with the others close behind, and firmly said *trey*. The transport shifted sideways and then moved downward, which caught the passengers by surprise.

"That was startling," said Calvin. "How does it do that?"

"The transports move in three dimensions," said Cobalt. "Be sure to hold on while you are inside. Unlike what is shown in your science fiction movies and TV shows, you will be impacted by the movements of the transports, and by the ship's movements. When we start moving through space at high speeds, you will need to be strapped into a chair if you don't want to be hurt or killed by the sudden acceleration."

The transport stopped and the doors opened.

"Each of you face your UCD and say *trey*," said Cobalt. They did as he instructed. "You should each now see a blue arrow on the display that points to your cabin. The length of the arrow indicates your relative distance from the target or next waypoint. Go ahead and use your device to find and enter your cabins. Take thirty minutes to make yourselves at home and then say *gekola Cobalt* into your UCD and an arrow will lead you to me. Don't be alarmed by your neighbors, who are from other planets. They won't harm you. See you soon.'"

Their cabin doors automatically opened as they approached them. The cabins were quite large, about a hundred square meters. A digital wall gave the appearance of a window onto the universe. The cabins were full of electronic gadgets and comforts that the three were eager to investigate. They unpacked their bags and thirty minutes later met in the hallway to take their first trip alone on the ship to find Cobalt.

"Did you see that funky toilet?" said Calvin with excitement. "It squats down as you sit on it, making the process a lot more comfortable and efficient. It cleans you up and finishes off with a blast of warm air on your bottom. Then it helps you stand back up on your feet. Very cool!"

"I was checking out the makeup mirror that let me adjust the shade of my face in the mirror," said Dominique, "and when it had the shade I liked, I said *sah* and an arm came out and applied makeup in that shade. How do you beat that?

"All I can say is I loved the storage space and feel of the bed," said Betty.

They spoke to their UCDs, *gekola Cobalt*, and were led back to the transporter. They rode for a short while then the door opened and the blue arrows on their devices led them down the hall of a new deck to a door with a green light. The door opened and there stood Cobalt.

"*Stowtan bitar*," said Cobalt, holding his fist up to his shoulder. They all responded in kind. "That means "greetings, shipmate'."

"We also learned *stowtan char*," said Calvin.

"Good. But you only say that to the captain," warned Cobalt. "And when you do, be sure to have your fists touching and eyes downward, like so. Now, please enter."

It was a huge room with many stations, each with what looked like holograms of people sitting at them. "What is this place?" asked Dominique.

"This is where we will make your clothing for tomorrow's ball. Let's find a spot and I'll show you how to do that. Here are three stations next to each other," said Cobalt as he took them to the rear of the room. Place your UCD in the carriage to the right of the screen to activate the system. Since you have never used the system before, you need to initialize it with your image. Stand on the pedestal and let the system scan you. Hold your arms away from your body and place your feet slightly apart."

Dominique went first. After positioning herself, a ring of light came up from the pedestal and disappeared above her head. She stepped down and a pseudo nude image of her appeared on the pedestal where she had stood.

"You use the avatar to help you pick your clothing," said Cobalt.

"Why is it naked? I don't want people staring at my naked body," said Dominique.

"If you look around you will see that no one is staring. In any event, you will have to get used to being seen naked on the ship. There are plenty of activities that require you to be naked to participate. You also don't want to ignore a call from an officer just because you are naked. That could cost you a lot more than embarrassment." Cobalt gestured to Calvin and Betty. "Get up and create your avatars. Then we will view them on your screens."

Soon all three of them had their avatars standing on their pedestals and similar images on their screens.

"The icons across the top of the screen are categories of clothing – hats, shoes, shirts, pants, coats, underpants, undershirts, and so on. Select the shoes icon and now you have a new row of icons below the first, representing different shoe categories. The symbol at the top left of the icon is the category number. Our numbering system is so simple that anyone that hasn't learned it by the end of this exercise will be severely punished, because you are obviously too dumb to be a crewmember. Take a moment to acquaint yourselves with the numeric symbols."

They studied the symbols and their progression.

"Who would like to explain the numbers to me?" asked Cobalt.

Betty raised her hand. "Zero is the empty circle. One to six are indicated by short slashes around the circle. Adding three dots in the middle of the circle gets you to seven, eight and nine."

"Very good Betty. Did everyone understand that? The figure for number nine represents the Euclidian solar system: our sun, orbited by six planets, and the three moons of Euclidia. Now select category twelve for formal shoes, and notice the new column of shoe icons. The ball's color theme is maroon. Use the wheel at the top to select color thirty-two. Now select a pair of shoes that you like. They will appear on the feet of your avatar."

"Now select the socks and stockings category, select the style that you like. Now, Calvin, select your pants, and ladies, select bloomers. Select pant subcategory fifteen, and bloomer subcategory twenty-two. Pick the pair that you like.

"Cobalt, will you help me pick a pair of pants that would be most appropriate?" asked Calvin.

"Item number six is worn by most men on the ship."

Cobalt helped them finish selecting items for their outfits and then asked them to look at their fully dressed avatars.

"Amazing!" said Dominique. "These clothes look great on us."

"They sure do," said Calvin.

Cobalt said, "Move your hands around over your avatars to move them around so you can see each side of the image."

"This is very nice, Cobalt. Now how do we have these clothes made?" asked Betty.

"Just press this button and the clothes will be delivered to your room."

"These intricate designs are going to be ready before the ball tomorrow?" asked Betty.

"They will be ready tonight," said Cobalt. "Probably within the hour."

"You've got to be kidding!" said Dominique. "Can we make anything we want and get it that fast?"

"Yes, you can. Right now I need the three of you to face your screens and select the shirt category. Now select subcategory four, followed by seventy nine, and lastly one hundred eighteen."

Each of them complied.

"Excellent! You all passed with flying colors. Rean, you can go."

An Ossie uncloaked with a weapon in his hand, startling the women. He nodded at Cobalt and departed.

"Where did he come from?" asked Dominique.

"He's been here the whole time," said Calvin. "Didn't you smell the scent of cinnamon?"

"You knew he was here?" said Cobalt.

"I assisted an Ossie on Earth and he bit me so his enzymes would permit me to see him while he's cloaked."

"That's interesting," said Cobalt.

"So why was he here?" demanded Betty.

"To kill you if you failed to complete your task or to learn our numbering system."

"So are we going to be constantly subjected to the threat of death while we're on the ship?" said Dominique with disgust.

"Not at all," said Cobalt. "But we do need to instill trust and set expectations for new crewmembers. Make it through the ball tomorrow and you can consider yourselves through your probationary period."

"How about we just skip the ball?" said Betty. "I don't think I can enjoy myself if I'm constantly being tested."

"Skipping the ball is not an option. I know it sounds arduous, but you will enjoy yourself. Plus, it will be a good way to meet people and get indoctrinated into our society."

"I know they seem harsh," said Calvin, "but they also appear to be fair. At least that's what I've learned from Uan."

Cobalt said, "If you are all ready, I will help you get to the language center to learn greetings and salutations." He led them out to the principal corridor. Into your UCD state *gekola platum charmal.* That will navigate you to the language center. I will meet you there. Just think, you finally get to try the transport chairs."

Cobalt walked off and the three of them were left staring at their UCDs.

"Do you two have the directions listed as well?" asked Calvin.

"*Sah,*" they replied in unison and laughed.

"Let's go then. I don't want to get shot for being late."

"That creature's gone, right?" asked Dominique.

"*Ahs,* he's leaning against the wall just a few meters behind us."

"How is it you can see him and we can't again?"

"He's an Ossie, just like Uan. Uan wanted me to be able to see him when he was cloaked, so he bit me to inject his enzymes into my bloodstream. Those enzymes let me see Ossies when they're cloaked."

"Hey, you two, we better get going," insisted Betty. "My UCD says we should walk down the hall a short distance."

They walked for a few meters and their devices indicated for them to stop in front of a pink light.

Dominique was nervous. "Now what?" At that moment a chair popped out of the wall and stopped in front of her. "I was afraid of that. You all know I don't want to be getting into no flying chair."

"We don't have much of a choice," said Betty.

Two more chairs came out of the wall.

"Strap in, everyone," said Calvin. "It could be a rough ride."

Dominique strapped in and reluctantly pressed the blue light flashing on the arm of the chair. The chair took off for the high ceiling with Dominique screaming her lungs out.

"Ahhh, somebody help me!" she shouted as she disappeared into the distance. Other chair riders stared in incredulity as they passed Dominique, wondering why she was screaming.

"We'd better go after her," said Betty. She pressed on her chair's blue button, and Calvin followed after her. Betty instinctively leaned forward to gain speed and soon passed Dominique, then leaned back and slowed to match her speed. Dominique was holding the arms of her chair in panic, with tears streaming down her face.

"Dominique! Lean back!" Betty shouted.

Dominique leaned back and slowed down. "I don't understand what's keeping these chairs in the air," she said in exasperation.

"It must be safe," said Betty. "Look around. There are hundreds of people up here and everyone but us seems to be calm."

Calvin caught up to them. "Hey, you two. This isn't bad, once you get the hang of it."

"Dominique," said Betty, "take my hand. We'll ride this out together."

Dominique took Betty's hand. They leaned forward and finished their high-speed trip with Calvin close behind. They lowered to the floor near a chair receptacle, stepped to the floor, and the chairs disappeared into the wall.

Dominique hugged Betty. "Thanks so much for getting me through that."

"No problem, girlfriend."

"Wasn't that fun?" said Calvin.

"It'd be more fun if I kicked you in the balls," said Dominique.

"Okay, I guess some people might consider it scary to fly in a chair with no visible means of support. I'm more worried about the Ossie who was following us. We better get going."

The UCDs led them along the corridor in the direction they had come from. Dominique slowly followed, still shaken by the chair ride and the threat of execution. She looked back to see if there were any sign of the Ossie but saw nothing. She was scared just the same. "Wait up, you two," she shouted and ran to catch up.

Their UCDs pointed to a door with a green light just a few meters away. The door opened and there stood Cobalt. "*Stowtan bitar*," he said with his fist raised.

"*Stowtan bitar*," they all responded.

"Now it's time for the most important lesson of your indoctrination. This will help you communicate with your new shipmates and integrate into our culture."

"Is the Ossie going to kill us if we fail the final exam?" asked Betty.

"Of course not," said Cobalt.

"So why was he following us?"

"I assure you he is not here and will not be involved in your lessons during this session."

Dominique nudged Calvin, who looked around and then shook his head and shrugged to indicate that he saw nothing.

"Follow me to the language pods. You will step inside and the doors will close behind you. Once inside you will watch a couple of holographic images go through a dialog in English and then repeat it several times in Euclidian. One of the images will then disappear and the remaining one will have the same conversation with you. Once you feel you have perfected the conversation you will take a final test. I will meet you here when you are done."

They took their lessons and each passed the test with flying colors. "Good job everyone," Cobalt said with a smile. "Your UCDs have been set to remind you when you need to get ready for the ball tomorrow. You should put on your clothes and get ready at that time. Uan will come to your cabins when it is time to leave and escort you to the ball."

"That's it?" asked Dominique.

"Yes, that's it. You still need to get a medical checkup, learn the ship's systems, and be assigned a job. All of that, however, you can do another day. For now, wander around and enjoy yourselves. Get to know the ship and its people."

CHAPTER 20

Saving Family

Li Xiao's family did not have a basement or storm cellar that they could go to. There was no nearby underground garage, cave, or large body of water where they could hide. Li Xiao transported to her parents' home, hoping that she would arrive in time to save them.

"Grandmother, where is everyone?"

"Li Xiao, where did you come from? Why are you dressed like that?"

"Grandmother, I do not have time to explain. Please tell me, where are my parents?"

"They went to a friend's place to see if they could get the generator going. The power is out everywhere. Cars, generators, radios, lawn equipment, none of it works. Flashlights work. I don't know why they work."

"Grandmother, please, look at my map device and show me where they are."

"They are right down the road, in the village. I can't see your map thing without my glasses."

"Where are your glasses?"

"I don't know. I lost them in the dark."

"Forget it, grandmother. Let's take the bikes. If I didn't think it would give you a heart attack, I would just pop us to town."

"What are you talking about?"

"Nothing, grandmother. Let's focus on where to go."

"They're just down the road in the village. One of the shops has a generator. I think everyone in town is there. Nothing else to do with no electricity."

"I think I know the place. Get your bike and follow me. I'll ride ahead and see you when you catch up."

"You go. I'm slow, but I'll be there."

Li Xiao grabbed one of the bikes at the side of the house and rode quickly toward the village. *Why, today of all days, are they away from the house? I don't know why I'm worrying, the aliens are probably not anywhere near here. They probably won't even bother coming to this place with so few people. There they are! Wasting their time on that zapped generator...*

Li Xiao rode toward her parents amid a group of several townspeople that she recognized. As she approached they started to disappear.

"No! Stop! They're my people," Li Xiao screamed. She jumped off her bike and ran to the spot where her parents had been standing a moment before. "Grandmother!" Li Xiao shouted, and turned to see that she was gone. The riderless bike wobbled and fell in front of her.

My aunt and uncle! Li Xiao grabbed her transport device, set the coordinates and transported into an empty apartment. They were gone, along with her two young cousins, Ema and Maya. She fell to her knees and shook her head. *All these powers and I can't save my own family!*

Li Xiao lifted her device and clicked on the waypoint that she had set for her mother. She could see her parents and grandmother together in a holding cell. *They look and sound okay. I'll just go and get them.*

Li Xiao pressed the button over and over again, but failed to transport. The *Andrea's* defenses would not permit her aboard the ship. Somehow, having the device had spared her from being captured, but did not permit her to save her family.

Li Xiao took a moment to watch her family in captivity. *Just like them, to complain about no tea to drink after they've been captured by aliens.*

Li Xiao returned to her apartment just as Cobalt arrived. Giving her a hug, he said, "Hello, Xiao. I'm glad you're all right."

"Cobalt, they took my family. You have to help me get them back."

"I cannot, Xiao. They are beyond my ability to assist you."

"What good was it to free those dissidents from prison, just for them to be put in another one?"

"You knew this day would come and that it wasn't in my power to help you. Though many people are gone, there is still much you can do to help this world."

"There are not many left to help. And why would I want to stay here when everyone I care for is on your ship?"

"Then come with me. Spend the rest of your life with me. There is so much I could show you."

"I would just be a freak on a ship, in a world full of aliens unlike me."

"It wouldn't be as bad as you think. There are already Earthlings who have joined the crew. I promise that you will fit in aboard the *Andrea*. It could also give you a chance to rejoin your family."

"When do I need to decide?"

"You should decide right away. If you come, though, you will have to be indoctrinated and join the ship's crew."

"Okay, but I need to let the people in the basement know that I am leaving. After your ships have finished in this area, I'll come with you. Just signal me somehow."

"Our vessels have already cleared this area. We can leave whenever you are ready. Pack one bag, whatever you think you can't live without. Everything else you need to survive will be provided on the ship."

"I didn't expect to have to decide so soon. Xiao laid her head against Cobalt's chest. "I'm frightened."

"You've done a lot of brave things, Xiao. Trust me, this won't be anywhere near as dangerous as your prison-break escapades. Indoctrination can be a bit difficult, but I'm sure you will have no problem getting through it."

"Okay, give me an hour to get everyone situated and I'll be ready to go. Just meet me in my bedroom when you can."

"See you then." Cobalt kissed Xiao on the cheek and disappeared in a sparkle of lights.

Li Xiao transported down to the garage where she had left Denise, Pico, Morgan, and Norma.

"Hello, everyone," she said to the startled group. "We can go back to my apartment now."

"I thought we had to wait twenty-four hours," said Morgan.

"I assure you, it's safe now."

"What have the aliens done?" asked Denise.

"They are removing people from our planet and placing them in holding cells aboard their ship."

"What about us?"

"We are safe. The aliens have moved on to other regions. We can leave here, see who else is left, and get to work rebuilding our world."

"That's going to be easier said than done," said Norma.

"Mom, let's go to my foster family's place and see who is left there. I'm sure they wouldn't mind if you stayed with us."

Li Xiao said, "I'd prefer that you all stayed at my apartment tonight, and tomorrow morning I can take Morgan and Norma to Morgan's foster parents."

"She's right, Morgan," said Norma. "There's no reason to rush."

"Then it's settled. We'll climb the stairs back to my apartment."

"Why don't you just beam us up?" asked Morgan with a smile.

"I didn't want make anyone feel uncomfortable, but there are a lot of stairs. Everyone give me a hug." They held on to Li Xiao and in an instant were in her apartment.

"Norma, you can sleep in my spare bedroom. Denise, you can sleep on the couch or find an empty apartment somewhere on this floor. Morgan and Pico can find an empty apartment too, if you like."

"If it's okay with you," said Morgan, "I would rather sleep here than in a strange apartment."

"I second that," said Denise.

"Okay with me. I'll get blankets and pillows for everyone."

Li Xiao returned shortly to pass out the items. "You should have everything you need to make yourselves comfortable here. There are candles in the kitchen. Feel free to eat and drink whatever you can find in the kitchen. I'll see you all in the morning."

Li Xiao retired to her bedroom and found Cobalt waiting for her.

"Cobalt, I apologize, but I need until morning to make sure my guests get to safety before I leave. I will pack tonight and I should be ready by eleven o'clock in the morning. Why don't you spend the night here? I'll make it worth your while."

"Xiao, you are such a bad influence. I do have some down time, but I'll have to leave early. While I'm here I can teach you how to count in Euclidian."

"Great. We can count strokes."

"Strokes?"

"Yeah, strokes. Get your clothes off and I'll show you what I mean."

"Oh."

"Oh yeah," Xiao replied with a devilish grin.

They undressed and Xiao mounted Cobalt. "Okay, you count my strokes in Euclidian and I will repeat after you."

"Before we start, I want to draw out our number symbols. They are pretty simple."

"If they are that simple, just draw them below my breasts."

"I'll try, but it may be difficult for me to concentrate."

"Do your best, baby."

"Okay, first we start with zero, pronounced 'ooo'. It is drawn as a circle, which represents our sun. For one through six, you place six dots around the circle, which represent our six planets. Ahh! Could you pause for a moment to permit me to finish my drawing?"

"Of course. I'll just sit here and squeeze while you finish."

"Good. Now three dots inside the circle represent Euclidia's three moons."

"That's easy. I got it. Now let's start counting," Xiao said impatiently and she slid down on Cobalt.

"Ooo is zero."

"Ooo, I like that." Xiao slid down on Cobalt once more.

"Er is one."

"Errrr."

"Ah is two."

"Ahhhhh."

"Eu is three, because Euclidia is the third planet from the sun."

"Euuuu."

"Somehow it sounds better when you say it. Oh is four."

"Ohhhh."

"A is five."

"Aaaaaa," said Xiao, stroking Cobalt faster.

"E is six"

"Eeeee."

"Erba is seven."

"Erbaaa."

"Ahba is eight."

"Ahbaaa."

"Euba is nine."

"Eubaaa."

"That's zero through nine," gasped Cobalt.

"Let me see if I got it." Xiao increased the speed of her thrusts. "Ooo, er, ah, eu, oh, a, e, erba, ahba, euba. Did I get it right?" asked Xiao as she continued to grind away at Cobalt.

"Yes, yes, that was perfect," panted Cobalt.

"Okay, I'm going to count from zero to nine two more times real fast to make sure I've got it down, then I'm going to squeeze that special spot on your neck. Is that okay?"

"Yes, yes," said Cobalt, his voice cracking.

"Ooo, er, ah, eu, oh, a, e, erba, ahba, euba. Ooo, er, ah, eu, oh, a, e, erba, ahba, euba." Xiao squeezed Cobalt's neck. He screamed in ecstasy and held her tightly.

"Keep it down. I have guests. Did you enjoy that, Coby baby?"

"That was fabulous, Xiao."

Xiao took a shower and then lay down in Cobalt's arms. As she fell asleep she thought about the fact that she was sleeping in her bed for the very last time. She was awakened the next morning by a scream.

"Xiao," said Morgan excitedly, "who or what is that in your bed?"

"I can't believe you didn't knock."

"I did, but you didn't answer. I didn't think there would be an alien in here with you. I thought that was just you screaming last night because you stubbed your toe or something."

"This is my friend, Cobalt. Cobalt, this is Morgan. I saved him and his mother from being killed by an assassin from your ship."

"Hello, Morgan."

"So you're one of the aliens attacking our planet?"

"I wouldn't call it an attack. We are mining your planet."

At this point Denise and Norma joined Morgan and Pico at the door.

"Are you people still trying to kill my friend?" Morgan pointed to Pico, who crossed his arms and gave Cobalt a stern look.

"I would think not. His presence here doesn't matter anymore. We will be gone in a few days and you'll probably never hear from us again."

"I guess that's a bit of good news after a lot of bad."

"It won't bring my brother back though, will it?" said Dense sadly.

"He wasn't a target of ours." said Cobalt.

"But he's still dead!"

"Li Xiao, we're ready to go when you are," said Norma.

"Let me get dressed and I'll be right there."

The four left Xiao's room and closed the door behind them.

"Cobalt, I should be back in less than two hours. I'll meet you here."

"Okay. Be safe out there. I apologize for angering them and getting you in trouble."

"It's to be expected. Their lives have been turned upside down."

Xiao got dressed and went out to meet her guests.

"Is everyone ready to go?"

"Yes."

She held out her transport device for Morgan to see. "Show me where you live in D.C. on this map. Just use your fingers to move around the map."

"There it is. Can you take us to the corner? I'd like to get a look at our neighborhood before going into the house."

"Sure. If everyone's ready, hold on to me and we'll go."

They transported to the street corner a few houses from Morgan's foster parents' house.

"Where did you get that device?" Norma asked in amazement.

"Cobalt gave it to me. I can jump from place to place anywhere on the planet."

"That guy from the alien ship gave it to you?" said Morgan with disdain.

"Yes. When I first met Cobalt, he was disguised as a human. I didn't know he was an alien, and I certainly didn't know the Euclidians were going to invade us. He gave me the device so I could help people, before and during the invasion. Now let's take a look around your neighborhood to make sure everything is okay."

Their tour around Morgan's neighborhood was quite eerie. The day was sunny and warm, but no one could be seen anywhere. There were no cars on the street. Even the birds were missing from the morning sky. If there was anyone left in the neighborhood, they were staying hidden. When they arrived at the Johnson house there was no sign of life.

"Morgan," said Li Xiao, "let me do a quick scan of the place before you go in." She used her device to look through the house. "Everything looks okay. Unfortunately, there is no one inside."

"Thanks, Xiao. We should be fine for now," said Morgan. "The grocery store down the street should have plenty of canned food and water. Hopefully enough good people are left here to form a small, safe government."

"Then I guess this is where we say goodbye. I'm going to join Cobalt on his ship. If I'm lucky I'll be able to reunite with my family, who were captured and placed in a cell there. Best of luck to all of you." Xiao gave each of them a hug. She then pulled out her transport device and disappeared.

***

"Give me an update!" shouted Captain Shisal.

"Captain," replied the logistics officer, "the mining is progressing according to schedule. We have deployed thousands of mining vehicles across the planet. There is a wealth of minerals here, and we are focusing our efforts on those identified as most valuable by the Marketing Guild. Scanners are fully manned, and we are transporting processed goods as quickly as possible. These civilized societies make it a lot easier to collect what we need. They also have some simple things that we never thought of, Slinkys, hula hoops, pogo sticks, chewing gum, Velcro…"

"Marvelous stuff, logistics," said Shisal. "Set aside a sample of each for me."

"Aye, aye, captain."

"Tell me about the exotic animals."

"There are a lot to choose from, captain. Each part of the planet has its own variety. I suggest you visit one of their zoos to get an idea of what you might like from each area. We can then set aside as many as you need. Images from the major zoos are in the logistics inventory."

"Excellent. I'll get back to you with what I want. When do you estimate we will complete our mission here?"

"It will take a few more days to fill the stores, captain."

"You are leaving enough to keep the planet stable and livable?"

"Aye, captain, there will be little danger to the inhabitants who will be left behind."

"Okay, keep me posted." Shisal turned to his XO. "I assume the camp has been set up and that preparations are underway for the ball?"

"Aye, captain."

"Begin authorizing the crew's shore leave, in rotating shifts."

"Aye, aye, captain.

Shisal spoke to another officer. "Operations, what is the result of our sweep of the population?"

"We have just over six billion people onboard, captain. There are spots of unrest in some of the holding cells that have a lot of military personnel or convicts. We are using Ossies to resolve those issues. The general anxiety that is normally experienced by captives has largely been assuaged with video entertainment. So far we have only lost a few thousand people."

"Why don't we just anesthetize them?"

"Due to individual differences in tolerance to anesthetizing gases, we estimate that would take our losses to around sixty million, which amounts to a lot of credits."

"Okay, scratch that idea. Just do what is necessary to keep the captives pacified without losing too many of them."

"The video entertainment seems to be working the best. A brilliant idea by one of our operators."

"Fascinating."

"It seems that this civilization spends a lot of time watching video presentations."

"Who thought of this idea?"

"Officer Kristi, captain."

"See that she gets a bonus."

"Aye, aye, captain."

"That's all, Operations. Logistics, I'm going down to the planet to visit some of its zoos. What's the security situation?"

"At this point you will be in more danger from the animals than from the humans. The few that are left are staying out of sight. Your personal shield will protect you from projectile-based weapons, though there is little danger that anyone will attack you.

"Fine. Have Phoebe and a security detail meet me in Transporter Room One."

"Aye, aye, captain."

"XO, you have the bridge."

"I have the bridge," the XO replied. He and the other bridge officers stood as the captain walked off.

CHAPTER 21

Commander Filo Prepares to Attack

"Hi, Yoyo, this is Jesmino. I've been talking with some Euclidians down here, and I think there is something you should know about the Alphas."

"What do you mean?" said Yoyo.

"The Alphas are a pretty brutal species. They have a history of attacking and conquering other planets, typically killing or enslaving the inhabitants and taking all of their resources. When the Euclidians visited their planet to institute formal relations with them, the Alphas pretended to befriend them while learning their weaknesses. One day, while most of the Euclidian ships were out on missions, the Alphas attacked Euclidia and killed millions of people. Years later the Euclidians launched a counterattack and destroyed Alpha. The Alphas found a new home planet, and for now there is a tenuous peace between the two peoples."

***

Commander Filo decided that it was time to execute his plan to attack the Euclidians. He knew how to use the ship's controls to open a space portal. He convinced Yoyo to persuade Captain Lohmann to let him have a shuttle for a short mission. A cloaked Alpha ship would be waiting to beam him to safety at just the right moment. Poor Yoyo would be left behind as a casualty of war.

"Yoyo," said Filo, "let's climb onboard the shuttle. The captain said we could use it and I don't want to wait around for people to get suspicious."

"How long will we be gone?"

"Only a few hours." Commander Filo smiled to himself. He was about to fulfill his dream. With the four captains that had attacked his planet dead, now he could attack their planet. The Euclidians had used their dimensional space drive to destroy his home planet, now he would to use the same technology to damage theirs. The shuttle didn't have enough power to destroy Euclidia, but could do significant damage. Filo thought he might kill as many as several million people with his stunt.

"Exactly what are we doing out here, commander?"

"Just running some experiments."

Something wasn't right. Yoyo took off her goggles. "Commander, look at me. Where are we going?"

"Yoyo, in a moment you will witness the pinnacle of my revenge against the Euclidians. The four captains of the ships that attacked our planet have been killed. Well, almost four. The fourth will be dead soon. He's still on a mission somewhere, but that XO we met is going to take care of him for me. Now I'm going to open a space portal and rip through Euclidia."

A voice spoke from the communications console. "Commander Filo, this is Alpha ship *Lansing*, come in."

"This is Commander Filo. I am eighty thousand kilometers from Euclidia in the center of its orbital path."

"We have you on our sensors, commander, and will rendezvous with your ship in seven minutes."

"Roger that. Did you hear that, Yoyo? In a few minutes my ship will be here to cloak us. And in less than an hour, Euclidia in all its glory will be just in front of us. I will open a dimensional portal, we will be beamed away by my ship, and from a safe distance we will watch the portal tear through the planet. If we are lucky, it might be destroyed. The security measures on the *Aleecia* were just too extreme to bypass unnoticed. It is much easier on the shuttle, especially with your power of persuasion over the crew. And with the *Lansing*'s cloaking system we will be hidden from Euclidia's silly space monitors. The name Kenyon Filo will go down in history as the Alpha that carried out retribution against the Euclidians for their attack."

"That's why you are trying to kill millions of Euclidians?" asked Yoyo.

"Yes, because they destroyed our planet."

"They only did that because you attacked them after pretending to be friendly, right?"

"Alphas have a spiritual right to all lands. It has been prophesied that we will rule all lands and I mean to help fulfill that prophesy."

"Was the prophesy legitimized because it was made by some visionary, or because one of your rulers felt it would justify the killing of innocent people for gain?"

"Alphas are a mighty race. It is our right to rule. Why do you question that?"

"Being mighty doesn't make you righteous, or even right."

"But here I am, just moments from commencing a new wave of attacks that will bring the Euclidians to their knees. Several hundred cloaked ships are waiting nearby. Once the destruction of Euclidia starts, the government will be too distracted to defend itself from space. Our fleet will swoop in and destroy all the vessels, space stations, and colonies in the Euclidian system before the government knows what is happening. And I will forever be a hero to our people."

"Interesting theory. Too bad no one knows you're out here. Remember, we told the people in operations to forget who we are."

"Who cares what Euclidians think? The *Lansing* knows who I am and the plans I made with our war minister."

"I'm thinking that you will be remembered for another reason."

"Really?"

"Yes." Yoyo pointed at one of the shuttle control panels. "Tell me, commander, what is this for?"

CHAPTER 22

Chaell Learns to Chill

With the planet's military dismantled and most of its population held captive aboard the *Andrea*, Captain Shisal decided to take some leave to relax and see what Earth artifacts he could pick out for himself.

Phoebe, Shisal's bodyguard, was waiting outside the bridge door, a woman trained for combat in the war with the Alphas on the planet Delta. Shisal never left the ship without her. They headed down the corridor to the transport room.

"So, captain, are you ready to go ashore?"

"Indeed I am. My bag is already packed. I'll beam it down after we arrive at the resort. First, though, I want to check out a few of the museums and zoos. I hear they have some fabulous items."

"Captain, you can use a remote monitor to view them. There's no reason to visit each place in person. I'm worried about your safety."

"You can stop calling me 'captain' for a while, Phoebe. For the duration of my shore leave, we're just friends. As for my safety, we've got the planet on lockdown."

"It's not the planet's population I'm worried about. This is your last mission, right? Someone may be looking to relieve you of your command a little early."

"Now I think you are being a worrywart. I have seen no indication that anyone wants to take over the ship. Plus, we have all the upgraded security precautions in place. At the first hint of danger, our UCDs will beam us back to the ship."

"So you're not bothered by the fact that the other three ship's captains that were involved in the destruction of the Alpha home planet are now dead?"

"I didn't know you knew about that. There are no Alphas on our ship in any position of power. And none will be on the planet while we're there, so I feel pretty safe."

"Okay, you're the captain."

"For the next two days I'm just Chaell."

"You know, on this planet Chaell means 'to take it easy'."

"Great! Then we should both just 'chill'. That's an order, Phoebe!"

"Aye, captain."

"Transport officer, drop us off at the Tower of London. I want to get a close look at the jewels there. Of course they won't be there much longer. I have a friend who has a birthday coming up." Chaell winked at Phoebe, who turned her head to avoid his look.

Though they were friends, Phoebe tried to remain emotionally detached, knowing that Shisal was looking for a romantic relationship. Her only focus was returning to Delta to join the resistance against the Alpha occupation.

Shisal and Phoebe transported to the Jewel House at the Tower of London. The security team was already in place, and one of the guards escorted them to the most remarkable set of jewels.

"Will you look at the size of those stones, Phoebe? I bet that crown would fit your head just fine."

"I'm not interested in jewels and crowns, Chaell. You want to excite me? Get me some weapons."

"I'd love to, but there is nothing on this planet that I would consider a weapon worth using to go into battle. Their nuclear weapons are the most powerful thing they have, but they leave so much pollution in their wake that you would be insane to use them unless you just wanted to make a planet unlivable. That's why we got rid of them right away. You have to wonder what these people were thinking. They ought to pay us for saving them from a fate worse than death."

"I'm thinking the captives on the ship don't think that."

"They'll be fine. They're used to the whole slavery thing. But enough of that talk. Tell me what you like here."

"If I pick something out, will you stop harassing me about gifts for the rest of the mission?"

"Sure, Phoebe. Come on, whisper in my ear."

"I like the ring with the giant red stone."

"So be it."

Chaell reached over, lifted the ring from its open case, and handed it to her. She slipped the ring onto one of her large fingers.

"Fits like it was made for me."

"It might as well have been. It's yours now."

Chaell sent a couple of other pieces to his quarters and the rest were sent to storage with the other items taken from the planet to sell. Chaell and Phoebe then visited the Louvre, the Smithsonian, the Forbidden City, and several other museums before transporting to the London Zoo.

"Look at that gorgeous creature, Phoebe. That long neck and long legs. It moves so gracefully. I've got to have one."

"You might want to get two. Just in case you want to expand the herd or something."

"I get it. I know how the whole procreation thing works. Even though I haven't engaged in it for a while."

Phoebe walked off, pointing at some elephants. "Wow, look at those animals over there." Chaell sighed.

"Praetor," he said to the guard assisting him.

"Yes, captain."

"Place two of these animals in my private storage. Make sure they are different sexes."

"Aye, aye, captain."

"No, make it four. Better yet, just take them all," said Chaell, frustrated with the whole ordeal. He caught up with Phoebe and said, "So, you like those animals?"

"Yes, they are so powerful and gentle at the same time. They lumber around so slowly, but at any moment they could grab you and snap you in two."

"I'll add them to my collection for you."

"Chaell, if you take them, you need to do it for yourself. Realistically, I will probably never see them again once we've left this planet."

"That's fine. I'll have them to remind me of you." Chaell instructed the guard to store the elephants then turned back to Phoebe. "We should head back to the ship and get ready for the ball."

"I'm not much of a ball person. I'll see you when it's over."

"Remember, where I go you go and I'm going to the ball."

"As you wish captain. Just don't expect me to enjoy myself."

"Just try not to attack anyone who asks you for a dance."

Phoebe grimaced and they both returned to the ship.

CHAPTER 23

Li Xiao Boards the Andrea

Li Xiao appeared in her bedroom and Cobalt instantly hugged her. "I've missed you terribly," he said. "I was worried that you might be killed before returning to me. Or that you would change your mind, which probably would be best for you, but I would be desperately sad if you had."

"How can I stay on Earth in its present condition? And how can I stay away from you since you made me love you? I was so afraid and then I was so curious. And now I don't want to be without you even though I don't know what the future holds for us."

"Then let's get going. We should get started with your indoctrination. I'll take you to my quarters first so you can put your bag away."

"I'm ready," said Xiao with a heavy sigh.

Cobalt spoke into his UCD and moments later they were in his quarters.

"This technology is so wonderful," said Xiao, looking around Cobalt's quarters. "Be honest with me. Are you okay with us being together?"

"Of course I am. Otherwise I wouldn't have offered to have you join me."

"On Earth, it is a concern if one's mate is from a different race. What would your mother think if you brought me, an alien, home with you?"

"I don't have a mother, but if I did she would welcome you with open arms. She would understand the world I live in. Maybe you would like to see more of the world where I come from."

"Can we go there now?"

"So to speak. Put on this helmet. I'm going to dial in my home city on Majorelle."

Xiao instantly found herself in an alien city. "Oh my goodness, this is marvelous. Look at all the people. Can they see me?"

"No, you are only there in a virtual sense. You can see, hear, and smell things as if you were really there. You can look inside buildings, sit in a vehicle, or listen to music playing. Lean forward to move forward and twist your body to turn. One of the neat things you can do with this device is look at an area over time. Say you wanted to see a building being built, watch the change in traffic, or study the effect of a river on terrain. You can do that by adjusting the start time and programming increments."

"How far back can one go? Could I see the planet being formed?"

"Only in a theoretical sense. We obviously don't have recorded history that far back."

"I love this device. It's really like I am there."

"If you're done, I should probably get you to indoctrination."

"Okay, I'm ready to go. Will you stay there with me?"

"Unfortunately not. But don't worry. You will be in good hands. Just don't freak out at the other species you might see there."

"Okay, I'll try to stay calm."

When Xiao arrived for indoctrination, she was assigned a guide other than Cobalt. Xiao passed her indoctrination tests with high marks, including creation of her ball gown – an intricate burgundy and white dress with a white mask – and her first language lesson. At the language center she finished the initial lesson right away and stayed for additional lessons. She was hoping to learn enough of the language to become a diplomat for the Euclidians. She took lessons on greetings and salutations, food, travel, military, and mining operations. She even learned to write some of the language. When it came time for the ball she was ready to converse with the Euclidian guests.

"Li Xiao, what are you doing?" asked Cobalt. "You can't spend all day here. You are such an overachiever."

"Maybe you would prefer going back to my cabin to practice counting?" she said with a smile.

"No time for that. You need to have a medical exam, and a tour of the ship."

"I hate being examined by doctors."

"It's not the same as you may have experienced on Earth. There's no pain and we provide a lot of services that can improve your looks and the way you feel."

"I guess I can tolerate it."

"So let's go to the transport chair station. I'll show you around the principal corridor before dropping you off at the medical center."

"Okay, if we must."

Cobalt and Xiao spent the rest of the day exploring the ship and the rest of the evening exploring each other.

***

Cobalt and Xiao spent the next day practicing the Euclidian language, holding each other, and then getting ready for the ball.

"Xiao, I'll be back in thirty minutes. I need to work with the interrogation team on a new captive. Once that is done I will come back and take you to the ball."

"That's fine, Coby, I could use the extra time. Just don't be gone too long. I want to enjoy all the ball has to offer. And be prepared to mingle, because I want to meet as many people as possible, okay?"

"Certainly, Xiao, just don't call me Coby at the ball, okay?"

"Oh, I think it's such a cute pet name."

"Maybe so, but let's keep it to ourselves."

"Sure, Coby baby." She smiled and kissed Cobalt on the cheek.

CHAPTER 24

The Ryan Nebula

Calvin woke up in a deep sweat in the middle of the night. He was somewhat disoriented by the ship's unfamiliar surroundings. He sat on the edge of his bed and wiped the sleep from his eyes.

What have I done? He slapped his hands to his head. *Have I sentenced myself to a life in a freak show with me as the main freak? I enjoy Uan's company, but will this force me to serve him for the rest of my life? I may end up with him as my only friend and he's not much of a friend. Plus I have to learn this damn alien language.* He pounded his fist into his other palm.

I know! I'll get a Euclidian girlfriend. I'm sure one of the short ones could get into an urban legend like me. Dominique certainly doesn't seem to like me, and besides, she's so cute that everyone on the ship will be after her. I need to take my mind off my loneliness and get some sleep. On Earth I was the guy who could find things. Here I can't even find my way back to my cabin without my UCD... Let's see what's on my monitor.

Calvin turned on his monitor and searched through the options. The alien entertainment wasn't of much value to Calvin since he didn't understand it. He decided to take a view at alien civilizations. He lay on his bed watching, fascinated by the different cultures.

A voice came from the monitor. "Use the immersion helmet for better viewing." A light from the ceiling pointed to a head covering made from nylon straps. Calvin put it on and lay back on the bed to see what the difference would be.

Wow, this is fascinating and almost creepy. It's like I'm right in the midst of these aliens, close enough to touch them, but my hand passes right through them. I can't get any sleep like this. Maybe something more scenic...

Calvin flipped through the selections and found something that looked interesting. It was simply titled *Ryan Nebula - Stellar Creation*. Its image looked a lot like the pictures he'd seen of the Pillars of Creation formation in the Eagle Nebula. He laid back down to check it out and then there he was, floating in space.

This is just spectacular. I'm surrounded by clouds, dust, and what appears to be newly forming stars. These stars have to be millions of miles away and it's like they're right in front of me. I can't imagine how fast I must be moving.

Calvin dozed off as his mind continued to drift through the Ryan Nebula until he heard "Dominique *mat blani*". He was woozy from being asleep but eventually responded with "*sah*".

Calvin's door opened and Dominique walked in wearing a silky blue robe with an intricate design. "Wake up, sleepy head," she said.

"I was having the most amazing experience. I'm glad you're here, though, and I love what you're wearing."

"I just had this made for me. I adore the facilities here, though I still miss home. How are you doing?"

"I've been having some anxious moments about my decision to come on the ship... I didn't have a great childhood, and my life before Uan showed up was tenuous at best."

Dominique sat next to Calvin on his bed. "What do you mean? Tell me about your childhood."

"Growing up in the projects was brutal. My father killed my mother and went to prison when I was seven. I got stuck with his crazy drunken brother. I got tired of him hitting on me and left to live with a friend of mine. I learned to steal and fence things. In the hood, you could always find someone to buy what you had.

"Did you sell drugs?"

"Not exactly. I moved stuff around to people who might sell it on the street. The major suppliers like to stay off the radar. That's how I met Bo Sam. I was making a delivery of product to him and asked if I could get him some other stuff. I found what he wanted right away and then he made me an offer I couldn't refuse. He paid me well, gave me a great place to stay, and provided protection from people who wanted to attack me during deliveries. It was a scary job at times but I didn't see an easy way out."

"How did you hook up with Uan?"

"I was at Bo Sam's place, getting him a drink. I went back to the room where Bo Sam was waiting for me and everyone was dead. Uan was just standing there holding his bloody spear. I thought he was going to kill me next, but I convinced him that I could be of use to him and he let me live. So what's your story?"

"I don't have much of a story. I grew up in a hick town in the middle of Louisiana. Because I'm small and cute every guy in town wanted to have his way with me. I learned to fight and started carrying a gun. A club owner I knew thought I would be good at his door. Guys appreciated me greeting them and when they got out of hand I threw them out. When I wasn't bouncing, I chauffeured people around in my limousine and did some bodyguard work."

"Why didn't you get married or go to college?"

"I wasn't interested in the guys in my town because they were just tired. My grades weren't good enough to get me into college and I'm not much of a studier anyway. I was saving my money to move to Dallas, but then this thing happened. So now I'm in outer space."

"How do you feel about that?"

"I was scared at first, but I figure it's better than being on a post-apocalyptic Earth."

"You're right about that."

"I've been playing some of the sports games and practicing my Euclidian."

"So I guess some of the aliens have been coming on to you."

"Yeah and it's been getting me horny and that's why I'm here."

"Excuse me?"

"Why do you think I'm wearing this robe with nothing underneath it? You don't expect me to sleep with an alien when there is a perfectly good human just down the hall, do you?"

Calvin choked on his words. "You mean me?"

"Yes I do." Dominique leaned into him. "So go take a shower or throw me out."

"I'm certainly not going to throw you out."

"Then hurry and take that shower, and be sure to scrub those naughty bits. I don't want to taste any funk on my tongue."

"With that kind of offer, I'd be happy to scrub the skin right off my privates. By the way, have you tried the immersion cap yet?"

"No, I don't even know what that is."

"This thing," said Calvin, holding his up to Dominique. "It was on the shelf next to my desk. You probably have one, too. Go get yours while I take a shower."

"Okay, I'm game for anything once. I'll be right back."

Calvin told the access system to let Dominique in when she returned. When he stepped out from the bathroom wearing his

Euclidian boxers, Dominique was lying on his bed with her silk robe open but still covering her sensitive areas.

"That instant-dry system after the pulsating shower is a clever idea," Calvin said nervously.

"Stop talking and get over here. I want to taste you," demanded Dominique.

Calvin gulped and walked to the bed. Dominique sat up, pulled away his boxers, flipped him onto the bed, and started nibbling and licking at the tops of his thighs. Calvin gasped and tried to sit up but was pushed back down by Dominique's hand on his chest.

"Stay put, big boy, I'm just getting started."

Dominique licked and nibbled Calvin's thigh up to his crotch, over to his other thigh, and back again until he was quivering all over. He watched her breasts sway as she worked him over.

"Let me tell you how this is going to go, Calvin." Dominique licked her lips and looked up at him sexily. "It's been a while since I've been with a man so I'm going to take my time with you. I'm going to kiss and lick every pore on your privates until you explode across my palate. I want you to just lay back and enjoy it. I expect you to do the same for me when I'm done. Once I have had my fill, you can have your way with me. How do you like that plan?"

"I think I'm going to explode right now."

"If you do I'll get my gun and shoot you in the foot."

"Okay, I'll hold it."

The next couple of hours were a dream come true for Calvin. He had often thought of Dominique and wondered what it would take to attract a woman as beautiful and fiery as her. When she was near he could hardly breathe or speak. It wasn't a lust, but a real attraction. She was his Cleopatra and Joan of Arc.

They both wore their immersion helmets. Calvin was floating in space again, but this time it was different. His entire being drifted away as their bodies intertwined. It was as if he was part of the universe and she was a constellation about which he revolved. Her scent, her touch, the sight of her eyes on him made him weak all over. The deeper they went into the Ryan Nebula, the deeper he wanted to go. Not just into the nebula, but into her heart. His body melted into hers until he no longer had a sense of himself. An hour later he came to, lying next to her.

"That was just heavenly, Calvin. The helmets were a great idea. I guess I'm going to have to make frequent visits to see the rest of space with you."

Dominique hugged him and Calvin kissed her tenderly on her lips. She gasped and pushed him away. "That was nice, Calvin, but we're still just friends, so don't get it twisted. And if you tell anyone about our little tryst I'll cut off your balls. See you tomorrow." She blew him a kiss and walked out the door. Calvin collapsed on his bed with a smile.

CHAPTER 25

Medical Exams aboard the Andrea

"Okay, I admit it, this is great," said Dominique. "It just took me a while to believe this crazy contraption wouldn't fall to the ground and kill us. How fast do you think these things can go?"

"Who knows?" said Calvin. "I know they can go faster than I can stand. It gets to the point where I can't breathe and I have to back off."

"Do you want me to ask one of these guys?" said Betty. "I get to going as fast as I can stand it and one of these guys zips past me."

"Is your Euclidian that good?" said Dominique. "I'm still learning basic stuff."

"I spend as much time as possible in the language rooms. I don't want to be killed or thrown into the captive cells for not picking up the language quickly enough."

Betty waved at a passerby and asked in Euclidian, "How fast can these things go?"

"The chair has no top speed," the person responded. "The top speed is whatever you can stand. As you lean forward the chair's speed will keep increasing until you pass out and then the chair will set you down."

"Thanks!"

"You don't say thanks when someone does you a favor. You just say *got it*, or *righteous*, or *brotherhood*." With that he sped off.

"Hey, you two," shouted Betty. "Shouldn't we be getting to the medic?"

"You are such a party pooper," said Dominique. "But you're probably right."

The three made a U-turn and headed for the medical center to get their checkup.

"Hello, I am Valera. I will be your medical technician today. I will tend to your medical needs. I speak some English and will be able to communicate with you."

"Hello, I'm Calvin and this is Betty and Dominique. I love your name."

"Yes, Valera is nice to hear and easy to say, but try spelling it. My name is spelled with eight letters and two numbers, Vao2le4roa. Somehow it is pronounced Valera and my mother was fine with that."

"Is the examination going to be painful?" asked Dominique.

"Not at all. Not only will you enjoy it, but you will love how you look and feel once I am done with you. I'm very experienced in genetics, and my procedures are effective no matter what your species. I work at the cellular level and can address most of your ailments using cellular regeneration. While I can't make you live forever, I can give you a healthy life as long as you are alive."

"Should we make separate appointments?" asked Dominique. "Or can you treat us all at the same time?"

"Not to worry. I am assigning an assistant to each of you. Take off your clothes and walk through this opening." Valera pointed to what looked like a disco doorway. "It will cleanse your skin and perform an initial scan of your skin surface. Once you are in the center, stop and spread your legs for a few moments. Calvin, you will also need to hold your penis up momentarily."

"I'd be happy to. Do you think you can get rid of the extra hair down there?"

"Yes, but not during this procedure."

Calvin said, "Since I'm the man, I guess I'll go first." He started to strip down. "Don't you ladies get any ideas."

"This is not a one-at-a-time exercise," insisted Valera. "Everybody get naked now! If it makes you feel any better, your assistants and I will be naked as well."

"As if that helps," complained Dominique. "We wouldn't even know what to get excited about on your bodies."

"You will in time," said Valera with a smile.

Betty and Dominique removed their clothing along with the assistants who snickered in the process. The women followed Calvin through the device, where they discussed the experience.

"What did you think? I felt all tingly across my skin and somehow I just feel clean. Look at my nails even," said Calvin, holding them up to be seen.

"I might be more into your cheerfulness if I wasn't standing here naked," Dominique sneered.

"Why are you bothered, Dominique? You have a gorgeous body."

"Thanks. Now stop staring at it."

"Calm down, Dominique," urged Betty. "They said we had to be available at a moment's notice even if we're naked. Plus, we don't want to anger anyone who may be following us."

"This way," their assistants said in Euclidian.

Dominique turned back toward Calvin. "Sorry for snapping. I like your body too."

"Thanks. Until this recent captivity, I've been working out." Calvin flexed his muscles. Dominique just smiled.

They each were led to a padded table and requested to lie on their back.

"Your assistants only speak Euclidian," said Valera, "so please respond in kind. They will start by removing moles, warts, scars, bumps, tattoos, wrinkles, and anything else that is not a normal part of healthy skin. Your assistant will touch a spot and ask if you want the spot addressed then, if you do, use a skin mender pen to address it. Say *ahs* if you do not want an area modified. You can watch the progress of the treatment on the monitors above you. Reposition the monitor as needed when the assistant moves you to work on other areas. I suggest that you get your tattoos removed. We can redo them later if you want, using a safer method."

The assistants probed, cleared, and mended the skin of their patients, returning them to their youthful form. For the most part the Earthlings enjoyed the treatment.

"This is better than any spa treatment I ever had," said Dominique. "I just wish it included a massage."

"You're right about that," said Betty. "*Ahs!* Valera, how do you say 'wait'?"

"*Ema.*"

"*Ema!*" said Betty to her assistant. "He pointed at my areola. He's just going to remove the mole and not my areola or nipple, right?"

"*Sah*, he will only remove the mole."

"What about the hair around it?"

"That's normal, so that will stay."

"What if I want it removed?"

"Yeah, I like that idea myself," said Dominique.

"Permanently or just this one time?" asked Valera.

"Permanently," Betty and Dominique said in unison, both laughing.

"Just point where you want the hair removed permanently and say '*unda tepa sita*.'"

"I like that idea," said Calvin. "Now I can finally have smooth balls and butt crack."

"Shut up, Calvin," yelled Dominique. "We don't want to hear that."

"Oh, you can have smooth breasts, but I can't have smooth balls."

"Stop it, you two," said Betty. "Valera, how do you say please and thank you?"

"You do not say those things in the Euclidian language. You tell people what you want, they do it or not. If someone does a good job you just say that instead of saying thank you."

"That sounds a little cold."

"In our culture it is not."

"Goodness, do they have to be all up in my butt crack?" said Dominique angrily.

"They have to check everywhere, Dominique," said Valera. "They are not interested in you sexually."

"Fine, then *unda tepa sita* while you're in there."

Calvin and Betty both laughed. Dominique smiled and shrugged.

"Can they adjust our breasts?" Betty asked shyly.

"They can tighten the skin around them to make them perkier. If you want to decrease or increase their size, you can have that done on your own time."

"What about adjusting my penis size?" asked Calvin.

"Yes, that can be done, but on your own time. However, you should be careful how large you make it, because that will limit your interspecies options."

"Wow, I never thought of that. What kind of options do I have?"

"This is not an anatomy class or dating service. You will have to figure that out on your own. Your assistants are going to process your eyes now, removing calcium deposits, floaters, and any corneal abrasions. We will also adjust your eyesight so you have perfect vision for your species."

"What about changing our eye color?" asked Betty.

"On your own time," said Valera.

"Of course."

"Next we will adjust your hearing, then your joints, and check your internal organs. During those tests we will remove any malevolent organisms and boost your immune system. This is what permits us to visit planets without worrying about getting sick. The last thing we will do is your teeth. Any fillings, crowns, and dentures will be removed and your teeth will be restored to normal health. Since you won't be able to talk during the procedure, we will do that last."

"Can you straighten and whiten our teeth?" asked Calvin.

"On your own time," Valera, Betty, and Dominique recited in unison.

Calvin chuckled. "We're going to be busy on our own time."

An hour later the three emerged from their medical treatments and stood in front of mirrors to examine their refurbished bodies.

"So how do you feel?" asked Valera.

"Great!" they responded.

"I am glad to hear that you are happy with the procedures. You can get any of the cosmetic work you want done at any time. We do not do it here, though. Use your UCD to find a *zuni fabur* or look for a blue light of this color by a door," said Valera, showing them the display on her UCD.

"The assistants did an amazing job, Valera," said Betty.

"I totally agree," said Dominique.

"Ditto," said Calvin.

"Okay, time for you all to go. Come back any time you have medical issues. Remember, a brilliant smile is the perfect start to a brilliant day."

CHAPTER 26

Going to the Ball

"*Uan mat blani*," said a voice in Betty's cabin.

"*Sah*," replied Betty, not knowing what else to say.

The door to her cabin opened and there stood Uan, dressed for the ball.

Betty smiled. "Uan, you look simply resplendent."

"You look quite ravishing yourself. This is going to be a great evening."

"Yes it is. Let's go get the others."

Uan and Betty entered the corridor to find Calvin and Dominique nervously waiting for them.

"*Stowtan bitar*, everyone," said Uan.

"*Stowtan bitar*, Uan," they responded.

"You all look lovely. I am sure you will have a wonderful time. I will take you to the camp on the surface and introduce you to the captain. After that you will be on your own. I urge you to stay as long as the ball lasts, and to meet as many people as you can. Use your UCD to connect with people. You can speak English into it and it will translate your statements into the local language of the listener and vice versa. It is a little crude though, as you will have to hold it to your ear as people talk to you. And of course the translations are not always perfect. I hope you are inspired by this opportunity to embrace the adventure of your new lives. When you are ready to return to the ship just say *trey* into your UCD and you will be transported to your cabins. Now, everyone say *jestala* into your UCDs to arrive at the entrance to the ball."

They did as Uan requested and were transported to the camp at Key West.

"What do you think of the place?" asked Uan.

"This place is swank," said Calvin.

Dominique was shaking with anticipation. "I really love it."

"I think we're going to have fun tonight," said Betty. "Can we meet the captain right away so we can get to the fun part?"

"Sure," said Uan. "The receiving line is over here. Just remember what I taught you and you will be fine."

There's that smell of ginger again, thought Dominique.

The three waited nervously for their turn to meet Captain Shisal and hoped that they wouldn't say anything to get them killed.

"Look at the elaborate tapestry all over the place," said Betty. "Someone went to a lot of work to make it look like a Euclidian event."

"How do they make them sparkle the way they do?" asked Calvin. "And look at the ceiling, with that elaborate scene of space that keeps changing. Look! One of those floating disks just took that guy's empty plate and napkin. How cool is that? Floating bussers."

"Speaking of floating, look at those floating chandeliers," said Dominique. "They are just divine. And all the people! This is like the Chalmun's Cantina on steroids. Is that the captain, with the gold collar on his coat?" asked Dominique with a quiver in her voice.

"Yes, that is him," said Uan.

"Wow, he is huge. I don't think I can do this."

"Look at him, Dominique. You see how he smiles as he greets everyone?"

"*Sah.*"

"Well, he is excited to meet everyone and he is especially looking forward to meeting the new crewmembers from Earth. Remember, he personally approved your request to join his crew."

"Okay, I'll try to relax."

"Trust me, you will enjoy meeting him and you are going to have tremendous fun tonight."

When they finally reached the captain, Uan greeted him first.

"*Stowtan char. It's good to see you, captain. This looks to be a wonderful ball.*"

"*Stowtan bitar, Uan. I hope you are doing well.*"

"*Yes, captain, I am. I would like to introduce you to three new crewmembers from this planet.*"

"*Stowtan char,*" said Calvin, "*sheeman Calvin.*"

"*Stowtan bitar, Calvin,*" said the captain.

"*Stowtan char, sheeman Betty. I'm excited to be your new crewmember.*"

"*Stowtan bitar Betty,*" replied the captain. "*I am glad to hear you are taking time to learn our language.*"

"*My pleasure, captain. I hope to be a diplomat for you some day.*"

"*If you keep learning the way you are, I'm sure you will do just fine.*"

"*I will, captain.*"

"*Stowtan char, sheeman Dominique.*"

"*Stowtan bitar Dominique. You are quite lovely. I'm glad you joined us tonight.*"

Dominique panicked and looked wide-eyed at Uan, not knowing how to respond. Uan started to come to her rescue, but Shisal waved him off. He raised his UCD to his head and motioned for Dominique to do the same.

"*You are quite lovely. I'm glad you joined us tonight,*" Shisal repeated into his UCD. This time Dominique heard it in English from her UCD.

"I am honored to be here, captain," said Dominique, smiling and wiping away tears. "I really love your outfit. Maybe we could dance later."

Captain Shisal let out a hearty laugh. "Why wait?" He took her hand, led her to a nearby dance floor, and waltzed her around for a few moments. A crowd gathered around, but Dominique could only see the captain and for now she was the belle of the ball. The captain soon ended the dance and bowed to Dominique before returning to the receiving line.

"Dominique!" gushed Betty. "What did you say to get a dance, you lucky thing, you?"

"I just said we should dance later and he dragged me out here. I have no idea why I said that. It just sort of blurted out."

"It seems like you said the right thing. I don't think he's going to be killing you anytime soon. I guess you feel like an idiot now for being so nervous."

"I'm just glad we're finished with the introductions. Let's get some drinks and have some fun. I'm going to do a lot of dancing tonight."

Uan joined them. "It looks like you three are going to be just fine."

"So what should we do first?" asked Calvin excitedly. "After all the tension of the indoctrination, I'm ready to have some fun."

"How about some drinks?" said Betty. "I want to try that Tammarian grog I keep hearing about."

"Make that two," said Calvin.

"Make it three," chimed in Dominique. "I can't wait to try my UCD again with the bartender."

"Why not make it four? I quite enjoy Tammarian grog," said Uan.

They walked up to the nearest bar and ordered their drinks.

"I can't believe it worked that easily," said Calvin. "Cheers, everyone. To our new adventure."

"To our new adventure," said the others. They clinked glasses and sipped their grog.

"Wow, now that's a drink," said Calvin.

"No kidding," agreed Dominique.

"Is it okay if I take Betty away from you two and show her around?" asked Uan.

"Of course."

Uan and Betty disappeared into the crowd while Calvin and Dominique went to look for food.

***

Cobalt and Li Xiao arrived at the ball in matching outfits that drew the attention of the crowd. Everyone wanted to know the identity of the masked woman except, of course, Uan. He had a good idea and he was not happy to see her again.

"Betty, excuse me for a moment. I need to say hello to an old friend," said Uan.

Uan greeted Li Xiao angrily. "*Stowtan bitar.*"

"*Stowtan bitar. So good to see you again,*" Li Xiao replied happily in perfect Euclidian.

"*I wish I could say the same. At least you had the character to not pretend you don't recognize me. I'm surprised that you speak Euclidian.*"

"*I'm a crewmember on the Andrea. I'm expected to speak Euclidian.*"

"*Cobalt, this traitor interrupted me when I was attempting to kill an escapee for the captain. She could have jeopardized the entire mission.*"

Li Xiao broke in, "*He is not my handler. If you have a problem with me, then talk to me!*"

"*Maybe I should talk to the captain. I'm sure he would love to hear your story.*"

"*Uan, what is this I hear?*" said Captain Shisal as he walked up to them. "*From what I can tell, the mission has been a success.*"

"*Stowtan char, sheeman Li Xiao, a new crewmember. Forgive the disturbance, my captain. It's a personal matter that we can handle in the arena.*"

"*Stowtan bitar, Li Xiao. You have made quite a brave challenge. An Earthling challenging an Ossie in the arena. That should draw quite a crowd.*"

"*I'll make quick work of this feeble Earthling,*" boasted Uan.

"*I agree that I am hardly a match for someone with your powers,*" said Li Xiao. "*So we should make it more of a fair fight. You can't use your cloaking ability and you must take a shot of beer before the fight.*"

Uan smirked. "*You've been tracking me, haven't you?*"

"*Is that a yes or no?*"

"*It's a yes, and when you lose you must leave the ship.*"

"*You go too far, Uan!*" said Cobalt. "*She has a right to be on the ship.*"

"*She should be killed for her behavior, so banishment will be letting her off lightly.*"

"*You will beat her and then throw her off? I don't see that as letting her off lightly.*"

"*Quiet, you two!*" Shisal ordered. "*Li Xiao made the challenge. It is up to her to accept or reject the conditions.*"

"*I accept the conditions. And if I win, you stop your attacks against Pico and Morgan and I get your pulse rifle.*"

Uan looked at the captain for his approval to accept and Shisal nodded. "*I accept your offer, but there is little risk to me. It will be good to see you off our ship.*"

"*Then it is settled,*" said Captain Shisal. "*We'll set up an arena here in a day or two. Until then I don't want to hear any more acrimony at my ball. Is that understood?*"

"*Sah char,*" they responded.

"Cobalt, thanks for bringing me to the ball," said Xiao. "I apologize for the disruption, but I needed to do something to protect the Earthlings. I'm certain I can defeat him. Plus, I wanted to meet the captain."

"I was happy to bring you to the ball," said Cobalt. "But I don't understand why you would risk your position on the ship to help strangers. What are you doing with your device?"

"I'm placing a waypoint on the captain."

"Have you lost your mind?"

"I want to be able to find him to make a deal for my family."

"Why do you think he would agree to a deal for your family?"

"I believe I can find him something valuable enough that he will free my family in exchange for it."

"You are taking a big risk, Xiao. The captain is not one to be bargained with. He may feel if a crewmember finds something, it belongs to him in the first place."

"Then it will have to be something so unusual that he will make an exception."

"Well, if anyone can do it, you can."

"Thanks for your confidence in me. This means that I will have to spend some time on Earth."

"Do what you need to, Xiao, just stay safe."

"I will, darling."

***

"Uan, who is that woman you were speaking to?" asked Betty. "And what were you talking about? You looked angry."

"She prevented me from killing the alien that escaped from the ship. Somehow she has become a crewmember."

"So what were you discussing?"

"To save the alien and his friends, she challenged me to a fight in the arena. When I win I will have her thrown off the ship."

"Why would you do that?"

"Because she betrayed our trust and does not deserve to be part of the crew."

"That sounds cruel even for you."

"It is the right thing to do. Now, instead of discussing that interloper, let us enjoy the ball. Can I get you another Tammarian grog?"

"You're right. But I want to try something different. Just surprise me."

"I would love to."

***

Xiao thought long and hard about what she could offer Captain Shisal in exchange for her family's freedom. Finally it came to her: the twelve zodiac statues originally created for the fountain at Haiyantang in the Yuanming Yuan Garden. Four of the statues were in China's Poly Art Museum, one was in the Capital Museum in Beijing, and two others were in a Christie's warehouse, all of which Xiao easily retrieved after the ball. The whereabouts of the other five were unknown. Xiao searched several museums and known collector's houses to no avail. Eventually she gave up the search, stored the seven statues she had found in her apartment, and returned to the *Andrea.*

***

Goron had Pura beamed to the *Andrea* and got her a temporary room to use to prepare for the ball. She was given an intricately woven dress that felt as light as a feather. It had a blue and red pattern that sparkled as she held it. At first glance she felt it would be too big for her, but when she put in on it seemed to caress her body. It held in her tummy, lifted her breasts and hugged her buttocks ever so firmly. A personal assistant arrived at her room to help Pura complete her preparations for the ball.

"*Stowtan bitar, Pura.* I am Inxa, your assistant. I help you ready for ball. My English not so good."

"Hello, Inxa. Thanks for helping me."

"You must greet people with *stowtan bitar.*"

"Oh, forgive me. *Stowtan bitar, Inxa.*"

"Good." Inxa sat Pura in front of a mirror. "I change face, you tell me when you like."

Inxa pressed some buttons on the mirror and Pura's reflection became shaded as if by makeup, with pink cheeks and red lipstick.

"Is this my face," Pura asked. "or just the image that changed?"

"Just image. Your face will change later."

"Less pink," said Pura, pointing at her cheeks. Inxa responded by making her cheeks less and less pink until Pura asked her to stop.

"Now smooth out." Pura made a rubbing motion over her face. Inxa responded by blending the color more into her natural skin.

"Perfect!" Pura pointed to her lips. "More red. Stop. Now darker. There, that's it."

"Now we do hair," said Inxa. "Look at self." Pura watched her image as different hairstyles appeared.

"That's it," she said when she saw a circled design that looked both elegant and futuristic.

"Maybe highlights?" Inxa asked.

"Sure." Pura's hair began to sparkle. "Oh my goodness!"

"You no like?"

"I like very much. When you said highlights I didn't think you meant this."

"No understand, but long as you happy. We done now."

A knock at the door signaled that Goron had arrived and it was time to go to the ball. Pura opened the door not knowing what to expect. There was Goron, with a smile that displayed his shiny green teeth. He was still an alien, but somehow Pura was comfortable in his presence. He was wearing a tight fitting, long-sleeved shirt that glittered in the light from the hallway. It looked silky and soft to the touch. The sleeves clung to his muscular arms and flared at the wrists to reveal a bracelet apparently made from diamonds. *But those large stones couldn't possibly be diamonds, could they?*

Goron's pants were made of the same material as his shirt, but slightly darker. They were snug around the waist, loose on his legs, and flared at the bottom around shiny maroon shoes.

"*Stowtan bitar, Goron,*"

"*Stowtan bitar, Pura,*" Goron responded, nodding in approval at her Euclidian greeting.

Dexin appeared from behind Goran. "*Stowtan bitar, Pura.* You look stunning. I hope you don't mind me joining you as your translator."

"Thank you for the compliment. I don't mind you being here at all."

"Goron wishes to give you this flower from his planet in tribute to your great beauty."

Goron handed the flower to Pura and Inxa attached it to her hair.

Goron held out his arm and spoke slowly in English, "I would be honored if you would join me at our ball."

"I would be delighted," Pura said gleefully.

Pura took Goron's arm and they proceeded down the corridor. It felt to her like *Beauty and the Beast*. Though Goron had a handsomeness to him, he certainly wasn't a typical human. His hand was a little cool to the touch, and hard, as if she was holding a stone. His skin was smooth and firm, but not soft like human skin. She detected a scent of ginger, which could have been his cologne.

They transported to the surface and entered the ballroom. Pura was mesmerized by the sight of so many Euclidians and other aliens. The scene was otherworldly, yet somehow it seemed normal. She was surprised to see other humans. And now there was a stronger scent of ginger in the air. *I wonder if that is natural for the Euclidians?*

A female Euclidian approached Goron and smiled. "*Stowtan bitar, brother.*"

Goron hugged her. "*Stowtan bitar, sister. This is my new Earthling friend, Pura.*"

"*Stowtan bitar, Pura. Sheeman Vagina,*" said Vagina, holding out her arm.

Dexin said, "She said her name is Vagina. Grasp her arm to return the greeting."

Pura took Vagina's arm with her hand, suppressing a smile. "What did you say her name was?"

"Vagina," replied Dexin who smiled in understanding of the question. He explained Pura's reaction and Vagina laughed.

"Maybe we could call you Gina," said Pura, "at least while we're on Earth."

Dexin translated and Vagina nodded in assent.

Goron placed his arm on his sister's shoulder. *"I think you just made a new friend."* They all laughed.

At the end of the ball, Goron took Pura back to her room aboard the *Andrea*, with Dexin nearby as always.

"Pura," Dexin said, "Goron says he would still like to spend the rest of the evening with you, but you are under no obligation."

"Tell him I'm having a great evening and I don't want it to end now. I'll take a shower and meet him my bedroom."

"Goron says that he will see you back here in fifteen minutes. The computer will announce him. Just say *sah* and the door will open for him."

"*Sah*, okay. Hey, I'm learning Euclidian!"

Pura took a shower, put on the robe that had been provided for her, and sat on the bed to wait.

"*Mat blani Goron*," the computer announced.

"*Sah*," replied Pura.

Goron entered and kneeled before her. Pura took a deep breath and pulled him into the bed with her. She found him passionate and patient. *I don't know what I was afraid of. This is just wonderful.*

The next morning Goron was still holding Pura. *I hope he enjoyed the evening as much as I did.*

Goron stirred and looked down at Pura. "Please   stay."

"Sah," Pura said, smiling up at him. Goron smiled and kissed her on the forehead, sighing heavily. She decided to greet the morning the way the evening had ended, and climbed on top of him.

CHAPTER 27

Chaell and Phoebe Take a Swim

"Phoebe, now that the ball is over," Chaell said. "Are you ready to relax? I picked out a nice beach on an island near our camp."

"You know how I love to swim. Where is this place?"

"It's across the bay from our camp. They call it Sunset Key. I am assured that it is deserted, so we should be safe from any of the indigenous population."

"So what are we waiting for?"

"Guard, have the ship transport us to the beach on Sunset Key."

"Aye, aye, captain."

Chaell, Phoebe, and the guards arrived on a pristine beach at a vacant resort.

"What do you think?" asked Chaell.

"I love it," said Phoebe.

"So let's dive in."

Chaell stripped off his clothes and leapt into the water. Phoebe admired his muscular body as he dove. *It's hard to believe that a man with such huge responsibilities can just turn it off and enjoy himself like that. All I can think about is those damned Alphas on Delta and how to get rid of them.*

CHAPTER 28

The XO Gets a Backup Plan

"Gafar, this is the XO."

"Yes, XO, how may I be of service?"

"You've been setting aside some special items for the captain and tagging them with his seal?"

"Yes, I have."

"I need you to send a copy of that seal to Malcolm, to use for our special project."

"Will do, XO."

"Did you find a large supply of refined gold, packaged for easy movement?"

"Yes, XO. There is an establishment called Bullion Vault in a city called London, in a country called England. It has several tons of gold."

"I didn't really need all those details. Just send the coordinates of the place to Malcolm."

"No problem, XO. I'll take care of that right away."

***

"Malcolm," said the XO to his Ossie assassin, "Gafar will be sending you the captain's seal and the coordinates for a large stockpile of gold," said the XO. "Place a couple of tons of the gold in an out of the way place in the basement of the resort where the ball was held. Apply the captain's seal to it. Make sure the gold is hard to find. It has to look like it was intentionally hidden."

"No problem, XO. When will he be in position for me?"

"He's going swimming later today. I'll let you know as soon as that happens and where."

"I'll be ready for him."

CHAPTER 29

The XO Takes Over

"Attention on the ship! Attention on the ship! This is the XO speaking. It has been discovered that Captain Shisal hoarded several tons of gold for himself and he has disappeared on the planet below. I am assuming the role of captain. The first officer will become the XO, and the first officer's role will remain vacant until we return to Euclidia. We will not waste resources searching for Shisal, but if he is seen he should be captured or killed on the spot. That is all."

"Logistics, this is the captain speaking. Have Shisal's property placed under my ID. I will be moving to his cabin. Have it cleared out within the hour."

***

"Xiao, did you hear that?" asked Cobalt.

"Yes, but what does it mean?"

"The XO is executing his own private mutiny."

"Why should that affect us?"

"He might decide to have you imprisoned, or to perform another sweep of the planet to remove more people. It's hard to say what his intentions are. Do you mind getting your friends to safety and staying with them for a while? I'll update you as soon as I have more information."

"If you say so. If there is any trouble, please join me."

"I will, Xiao." Cobalt kissed her. "Now go."

***

"Uan, this is Cobalt. Can you meet me on the planet? It's important."

"Sure," replied Uan. "I'll see you in front of our camp."

A few minutes later they were standing in the warm sun of southern Florida.

"Uan, could you turn off your UCD? We need to chat about something privately."

"This is out of the ordinary, but I will comply for now. Okay, what do you want?"

"The XO claims that Shisal was caught trying to hide several tons of gold for himself, and has taken over as captain."

"I heard the announcement, but it didn't make sense to me. The described actions were out of character for Captain Shisal. I'm sure that the XO is framing him in order to take his share of the profits. But what can we do about it?"

"I'm not sure, but how can you feel safe with the XO in charge? He might refuse to accept the Earthlings onboard the ship. We should try to find Shisal and if we can't, get our friends off the ship."

"So how do we find him?"

"My friend Li Xiao placed a tracking beacon on him at the ball. She wanted to find him later to convince him to return her family."

"And how was she able to do that?"

"I gave her one of our Beam Machines."

"I can't believe that you could be that irresponsible! Were you deliberately trying to sabotage the mission?"

"What can I say? I fell for her. Anyway, if I hadn't, we would have no hope of finding Shisal now."

"We don't even know if he is still alive."

"True, but it's the only hope we have. I need you to meet with her to see if she can help us."

"What? After she publicly humiliated me with that stupid challenge. I don't want to be anywhere near her again until I am thrashing her in the arena!"

"If you want to help get Shisal back as captain of the *Andrea*, you need to do this. I have to get back to the ship for a project. You know the XO is vengeful enough to throw our friends in the holding cells just because we were associates of Shisal."

"Now you are simply being manipulative."

"Is that a yes or no?"

"It's a reluctant yes."

"Great! Reactivate your UCD. Here are her coordinates." Cobalt transmitted the information. "Now there is one teensy weensy little thing you need to know before you go."

"What now?"

"Li Xiao is with the alien that escaped from the ship. You have to promise me you won't harm him or his Earthling friends."

"You can't be serious! Do you know what that little creature did to me? You might as well ask me to cut off my hand."

"You want to find the captain, right?"

"I'll spare them, but I won't like it. And I'm not promising I won't kill them later."

"I guess that's the best I can hope for. I'm off. Good luck with Xiao."

"I'll grab Calvin off the ship and go right away."

"Send me an update when you can. I'll be free in a few hours."

"Certainly," replied Uan as they both transported to the ship.

***

"Calvin, I need to go to Earth briefly and I want you with me."

"Great! Another 007 mission?"

"Not exactly, but it could be dangerous. Show me your UCD. I'm sending you the coordinates now. Press this command here, like I'm doing. Select the coordinates. When you are ready, press this command to transport."

"I'm ready.

"Then press the command and we should arrive together."

CHAPTER 30

Water

Water is the key to all life in the universe. In places where it is plentiful it is worth very little. And in places where it is scarce it is the most valuable possession a person can have. Ask anyone stranded in the desert what they would give for a glass of water, even dirty water. A thunderstorm after years of drought can be a godsend.

It's not just that water produces life, sustains life, and shelters life. It is great for cleaning, farming, extinguishing fires, manufacturing, waste removal, ceremonies, and countless other things. On many planets, fresh water is in short supply. Its scarcity causes wars, deaths, and even extinction. The inhabitants of these planets would give up anything else to have access to fresh water.

The Euclidians were well aware of the necessity of water for the planets in their system. Since these planets were members of the Intergalactic Alliance of Planets, the Euclidians were not permitted to invade them without provocation. But they could trade with them for the precious cargo.

***

A group of people started to congregate on the State Route 520 floating bridge in Bellevue, Washington. They watched the enormous vehicle draining Lake Washington of its water, of its vitality. The vehicle would periodically shoot a spray of unneeded water onto the shore, covering the shoreline houses in polluted water, undesirable vegetation, and dead aquatic life.

Angry onlookers on the Medina shore watched as the aliens drained their planet of water. They felt helpless and desperate. How long did they have to live? A small boat took off from shore with three men in it. They were heavily armed and determined to take out the giant vehicle. They approached the vehicle, which was hovering mere inches above the water surface. When the men were just a few meters away, they fired their weapons: a shotgun, an automatic rifle, and even a grenade launcher. None made even a dent in the vehicle.

The unmanned vehicle ignored the attackers and continued draining the lake. The attackers were undeterred and continued firing on the vessel until their ammunition was depleted.

"That's a horrible mess, isn't it?" said a man to a woman as they stood on a dock overlooking Lake Washington.

"You're telling me. I just opened a new barbershop and thought I was finally going to realize the American dream. Now the only hair I can cut is my own and only using scissors. You know Rudy's on Bellevue Way?"

"I really never spent much time on my hair. I know you have it bad, but I used to be the richest man in the world and was close to extinguishing polio. Now I wonder if it was all a waste."

"Wow, I guess my barbershop wasn't such a big loss."

"Losing a dream is always a big loss. By the way, I'm Bill."

"Glad to meet you, Bill. I'm Deb."

***

Morgan got bored sitting around the house and decided to take Pico down to the Potomac to see if there was any sign of life. They walked through the neighborhood enjoying the quiet but hoping to see others walking around. Unfortunately the streets were deserted.

Memories flooded through Morgan's mind: the children always playing in the yard in front of the blue house, the old lady sitting at the upstairs window at the house across the street, the sprinkler running in the yard at the house on the corner, and the little beagle barking at everybody behind the chain-link fence.

"Pico, this isn't the neighborhood I remember. It's different without the people. Let's walk to the water."

From the bank of the Potomac, they saw a large alien ship hovering overhead, pulling water from the river. There were a few people in small boats attacking the ship, but they were just wasting their time.

"Pico, I have an idea. Let's go find a garage."

Morgan took Pico a couple of blocks away and found some cars in the lower level of a garage.

"Pico, can you use your shaman ball to move those cars? I'd like to try something."

"Sure," said Pico.

"Place them on the street near the water."

Pico pulled out his shaman ball and slowly levitated each car. He put a few scratches on them trying to navigate the ramps in the garage.

"Don't worry about the scratches and dents. They're going to be a lot more banged up once we're done with them," said Morgan.

Pico lowered the last car to the ground. The Euclidian mining ship was still soaking up river water.

"Okay, Pico, this is what I want you to do. As fast as you can, send the cars into the sky, as high as you can. Then let them drop on the ship."

"Okay, but this is going to take a while."

Pico pulled out his shaman stone and focused on it until he was covered in a bright blue glow. He then focused on the cars, which slowly lifted into the air. "You're doing it, Pico!"

Pico loved to hear the words of encouragement. Morgan watched as the cars disappeared into the clouds. He was tingling with anticipation about what was about to happen.

"How high up do you think they are?" asked Morgan.

"I think they are a little over two miles up. That is as far as I can lift them." Pico was shaking with the effort of concentration.

"Okay, let them drop on the ship and let's see what happens."

One after the other Pico let the cars drop. With blinding speed, the first one hit on the top of the Euclidian mining ship near one end with a big explosion. A cheer came up from the people in the boats, who thought it was an attack by the U.S. military.

The ship stopped what it was doing and appeared to be trying to repair itself. Then the second and third cars hit the middle and other end of the ship, causing bigger explosions than the first. Giant fireballs erupted from where the cars hit. Sparks flew high into the air from holes in the hull. The ship shuddered and then fell into the river. An even louder cheer came from the onlookers.

"You did it!" said Morgan, hugging Pico tightly. "You destroyed their ship. We need to figure out how to destroy more of them. Do you think you can teach me how to do what you do with your shaman stone?"

"I can try. Look, the ship is sinking."

"Yeah, and the people in the boats are starting to throw things at it. Wow, it just disappeared. And look, there's another one, plus some sort of escort ship. I bet it's there to protect the mining ship. Now that we know they can be hurt let's build a plan around it. I don't think we'll have any more success today."

"That sounds like a smart decision."

***

Morgan and Pico arrived back at his foster parents' place excited and anxious. Morgan waved at his houseguests and went to the basement to have some private time with Pico.

"Pico, we made great progress today. You did an amazing job taking out that alien ship. I feel we could make better progress if I could be of more assistance somehow. I feel so powerless letting you do everything. I don't want to sit on the sidelines anymore, watching you make all the effort. I want to be in the game. Teach me to do what you do."

"I'm not sure I can, but I will teach you how I connect to my shaman stone. Since we are still connected, you will be able to see what I see. The rest is up to you."

"I will make this happen, Pico. The world depends on it. Please teach me what you know."

"Okay, focus on what I am doing. I relax my mind and feel the vibrations from my stone. I pull those vibrations in and direct them back out at the stone. You can see the blue glow of the stone intensify as I connect with it. Now I pull in the magnified vibration and focus on what I want to accomplish, for example, lifting that chair. I don't try to lift the chair with my mind. I see the chair rising and it does. Now you try to connect with my stone."

Morgan took the stone from Pico and tried to focus on its vibration the way Pico had. He worked on breathing in as a way to feel the vibration and soon felt a connection to the stone.

"Morgan, you are doing great. The stone is starting to glow. Now try to lift the chair."

Morgan focused his energy on the chair. The chair vibrated, but did not rise. Morgan tried harder, but eventually lost his connection with the stone.

"Morgan, keep my stone and continue to practice. I feel that eventually you will perfect your connection with it.

CHAPTER 31

Phoebe

Phoebe's species had evolved in the northern hemisphere of the planet Delta. The area had an arid climate and was covered by thick jungle. For a quarter of the Delta year, the place where Phoebe lived was engulfed in total darkness. The jungle was full of life that had adapted to the low light conditions. These species typically had acute sight and hearing and a heightened ability to sense the presence of other nearby creatures. It was as if they could feel the electrons radiated from a body in their direction.

In the darkness of the jungle, men from the island of Arubia would wait in silence next to trees, looking and listening for their prey. Knives, staffs, and bows and arrows were their weapons. They would kill animals large and small to take back to their village for food. The Arubians of Delta mostly cooked their food, accompanying the meat with fruit and vegetables gathered by the women.

The island of Arubia was isolated from Delta's other inhabited lands by vast amounts of water. The southern edge of the island consisted of a huge desert, which further isolated the jungle inhabitants and prevented discovery by early explorers. As the Delta civilizations advanced, they eventually found the lost tribes of Arubia, which had descended from the same humanoid species thousands of years before. The Arubians were taller, smarter, stronger, and faster than their civilized counterparts; the slower, weaker, and less bright Arubians had long ago been eaten by predators or killed in tribal disputes. Furthermore, Arubians did not tolerate those who were unable or unwilling to give back to the tribe, and such individuals did not survive. It was a brutal practice, but the Arubians felt that culling nonproductive members of their tribes was important to their long-term sustainability.

The Arubians eventually assimilated into the larger Delta cities, many becoming soldiers, athletes, and park rangers.

Phoebe grew up in the jungles of Arubia, but moved to one of the older cities on the island when her parents decided she needed an education. Phoebe and her brothers enjoyed going back to the jungle during their time off.

In the jungle, Phoebe enjoyed going out at night, to strip naked, close her eyes, and walk with her arms outstretched so she could get in touch with everything around her, the trees, plants, insects, and animals. Every pore on her body would tingle as she reached out with her senses, pushing herself to not miss anything. She would pause on occasion, lift her head, and catch a drop of water as it fell from the forest canopy. She respected life, but was not afraid to snuff it out when warranted. Her pet peeve was mosquitoes, which took her blood and gave nothing in return. In moments of weakness, her pet peeve drove her to take out her sword and slice through the pesky *bêtes noir* blindfolded. That way she felt she was at least giving them a fair chance.

After graduating from college, Phoebe and her three brothers joined the military for the opportunity to fight. But except for small skirmishes, there wasn't much fighting on her planet until the Alphas showed up.

The Deltas first met the Alphas when they received a distress call from the Euclidians, an advanced species that had showed up in orbit around Delta. They set up formal relations with the Euclidians, who seemed to be a friendly species. The Euclidians were the only alien species the Deltas had come into contact with until they engaged the Alphas in battle above Euclidia. The Euclidians were near defeat when the Deltas came to their aid.

"This is going to be the first test of our alliance," the Delta air wing commander had said. "The Euclidians are under attack by a race called the Alphas. They had an alliance but the Alphas just launched an unprovoked attack against the Euclidians. The Euclidians don't really have a space-based military. They've been using their resource extraction vessels to hold off the Alpha fleet. They only have one left and they're sending it here to open a space portal for us to fly through to Euclidia to assist them. I need everybody to be patient and on the alert as we wait for the portal to open. Once the portal opens, I want all birds launched. Attack anything smaller than their resource vessel."

"Lieutenant Phoebe Asten, ready to deploy. Armament is activated and all systems are go."

"Hey, little sis, be patient," said Phoebe's brother through her headset. "You'll get more action than you can stand in just a few moments."

"Have you ever seen an Alpha or their ships?" Phoebe asked.

"Yes, I was on a detachment with our brothers and saw a few while on leave. They were pretty puny and didn't seem that tough. They only had diplomatic vessels in the area when I was there so I don't know what their military capabilities are."

"How are our brothers doing?"

"They're fine. Their squadron is assigned to Battleship 5. We may not even see any action if that portal never opens."

"Trust me, if they conquer the Euclidians, the Alphas will be coming for us next."

"Why would they want to attack us?"

"Why would they want to attack the Euclidians?" Phoebe asked.

"Listen up, squadrons," said the air wing commander. "The portal is open and some of the Alpha ships came through with the Euclidian resource ship. Battleship 6 is going to launch its squadrons to take care of the Alpha ships. The rest of us are going to Euclidia. As soon as our battleship gets through the portal, all squadrons will launch. We will be joining Battleships 1 and 3 to clear the area above Euclidia of enemy vessels. Battleships 4 and 5 will go after the Alpha ground troops."

"Commander, this is Lieutenant Phoebe Asten. Is our mission to disable or destroy the Alpha ships? Also, should we go after their escape pods?"

"We don't know what disablement means when it comes to Alpha ships. Our mission is to destroy as many as we can and that is what I expect you to do to the best of your ability. Ignore the escape pods. They'll have to land on the planet and squadrons from Battleships 4 and 5 will address them as needed."

***

"Squadron commanders," said the battle group commander. "We are exiting the portal into Euclidian space. You have your battle plans. Stay focused and take out the Alpha vessels with impunity. Euclidian freedom is at stake, and quite possibly our own if we fail here. Do not fail! That is all."

"Okay, Squadron 176, this is your commander speaking. Remember what you learned in training. Stick close to your wingman and don't leave our designated area of engagement. We are fourth in line to deploy. Follow my lead and stay focused. Deployment has started. Start your engines. Prepare to engage the enemy. Here we go! Fight with honor, pilots!"

One by one the pilots rolled their fighters into the chutes and launched into space. Phoebe, being one of the junior pilots, took her vessel to the starboard side of the formation, just to the rear of her lead pilot, Joss.

"Phoebe, let's clear the three Alpha fighters to our starboard side. I'll lock onto the first one and you grab the second one. We'll regroup on the third."

"Got it, Joss. I have a lock on the second vessel and am firing."

"The first one is down and I'm going after the third."

"Joss, I've taken out my target and now there are two Alphas approaching from above. I'll break away and engage them."

You Alphas have lots of vessels, but they don't maneuver very well, thought Phoebe. *Oh no!*

"Joss, I was hit from my blind side. I took out the first of the new vessels. The third has a lock on me."

"Not anymore. I just took it out. Now you get that last one."

"One second…wait for it…and kaplooey."

"Great shot, Phoebe. It appears so far that their shields are no match for our weapon systems. Let's rejoin our squadron and continue the cleanup of our sector."

"I'm with you, Joss."

Within two hours of entering Euclidian space, the Alpha ships were all taken out. The invading ground troops were still fighting back from reinforced bunkers that were impenetrable by the Delta and Euclidian forces. Despite several attacks they were not able to stop the Alphas from sending plasma blasts into Euclidian cities.

"General," reported a Euclidian field commander, "our artillery and the Delta ships are having very little impact on the Alpha bunkers. Unless we can take them out, millions more people will be killed."

"Commander," replied the general, "focus your efforts on getting civilian populations to shelters, and try to neutralize the Alpha blasts before they strike. Request that the Deltas do the same. Communications, connect me with resource ship *Waldwick*."

"On screen, general."

"Commander, this is General Lapsik. I'm leading the military effort against the Alphas. Great job on holding off the Alphas and getting the Delta fighters here. But now if we don't do something quick we are going to be forced to surrender or watch most of our citizens be obliterated. I want you to launch all of your mining vessels and start creating trenches deep below the enemy bunkers. There are ten enemy bunkers deployed at the coordinates I'm sending you now."

"Coordinates received, general. I'm sending four vessels to each site. Plus, I have an idea that our Delta friends can help us with."

"Roger that, commander. Keep me posted."

"Ambassador Parlo," said the *Waldwick*'s commander, "I need you to speak to your squadron commanders. I need your vessels to fire on the bunkers at these ten locations when I give the command."

"I would be happy to," said the Delta ambassador, "but we haven't had much success penetrating their bunkers."

"I understand, but I want them to try something different. On my command, I want them to attack the bases using heat-generating weapons, if that is possible."

"Our vessels can be configured in that manner as needed. Let me contact our fleet admiral and get the message to him."

"Much respect, ambassador."

"Fleet admiral, this is Ambassador Parlo. Could you have your fleet break off their attack on the Alpha bunkers to have their weapons systems configured to fire heat blasts?"

"Certainly ambassador, but I don't see how that will have an effect."

"The Euclidians are executing a plan that needs heat generating weapons. I will send you the coordinates of the ten bases that they want attacked and let you know when to commence."

"Very good, ambassador. I'll contact the fleet and let them know what they need to do. Battle Groups 4 and 5, break off your land based attacks. Have your squadrons equip their vessels for heat blasts. Battle Group 4, here are the coordinates for the five Alpha bases you will be attacking. Battle Group 5, here are your attack coordinates. I will alert you when I need the attack to begin."

Five minutes later, Battle Group 4 responded. "Fleet admiral, this is Battle Group 4. Our squadrons are configured and standing by for your orders."

"Battle Group 5 is ready as well, admiral."

"Status received. Stand by for the attack order," replied the admiral.

"General Lapsik, this is resource vessel *Waldwick*. Our mining vessels have been deployed and are digging below the bunkers. The tactic seems to be working. The Alpha bunkers have sunk at least fifty meters into the ground and are sinking deeper."

A loud cheer went up in the command center.

"No time for cheers yet," said the general. "They can still fire on our cities. We need to execute part two of our plan. Have all your mining ships expel metallic minerals into the holes above those enemy bunkers. I want those holes filled to the top, right away. Let's get this job done!"

Three minutes later, the mining vessels had completed with their task.

"Ambassador, have your ships attack now," requested the general.

"Fleet admiral, this is Ambassador Parlo. Attack now."

"Battle Groups 4 and 5, attack now," ordered the admiral.

The squadron vessels attacked the ten enemy bunkers that were now covered in deep piles of metallic minerals and unable to fire their weapons. Under the heat from the blasts, the piles became molten metal that engulfed the Alpha bunkers and cooked their inhabitants. The bunkers finally fell silent.

"Joss, you see that?" said Phoebe. "By working together we were able to defeat those bastards"

"You can say that again, Phoebe. Time to head back"

"I'm with you, Joss."

"General Lapsik, it's over," said the ambassador. "The Alphas have been cooked by the molten metal. Once it cools those bunkers will be nothing but large blocks of metal. What should we do with them?"

"I'm sure the Alphas will want their men returned for proper burial, so have them beamed to Alpha and release them a couple of dozen kilometers above their capital city. Let's make an event of it: four days from now at high noon. And I want it televised!"

Phoebe returned home with her squadron, a decorated war hero. Soon after, the Delta military was expanded and practice maneuvers increased in preparation for a war with the Alphas that might come. And come it did.

***

"Joss, tell me what you heard."

"It's not good, Phoebe. A swarm of Alpha fighters came out of nowhere and destroyed Battleships 1, 3, and 4 before they could fire a shot. They were sitting ducks. The Alphas have obviously upgraded their weapons systems."

"The crew was able to escape, right?"

"No, Phoebe, none of them made it off the ships."

"My brothers? Nothing from my brothers?" Phoebe demanded as tears welled in her eyes.

"Nothing. Some of the crew was off the ship on leave, but your brothers were not among them. Get your head together, Phoebe. We have the battle of our lives ahead of us. Their ships are faster than ours and can penetrate our shields. We're just lucky we were out on maneuvers or our battleship might have been destroyed, too. Get to your fighter, we need to take off soon."

"You don't have to tell me twice. I'm ready to kill those bastards."

They took off with their squadron to no avail. One by one the battleships and squadrons were taken out by the Alpha's more advanced firepower. Phoebe took out three Alpha ships before her fighter was disabled. She beamed to safety before it was totally destroyed. There were too many Alpha ships and troops for the Deltas to repel them. By the time the Euclidian ships showed up to assist, it was too late to save the Deltas from annihilation.

The Deltas surrendered and the Euclidians agreed to a truce with the Alphas to end their attack on the Deltas. In less than two days the Alphas had beaten the Deltas into submission.

"What do you mean, we surrendered?" screamed Phoebe at her squadron commander.

"Phoebe, there is no one left to put up a fight. Our battleships have been destroyed, our space stations are gone, and the entire population of our moon has been killed. The few fighters we have left across this sector cannot successfully engage the hundreds of fighters they have in the air above us. Remember the ten bunkers that killed millions of Euclidians? There are twenty-five bunkers on our planet, waiting for the order to exterminate us."

"What about the Euclidians?"

"We would all be dead before they got here. They signed a truce with the Alphas agreeing not to attack them if they agreed to end their violence against us."

"You know my last brother and Joss were killed when we went to fight them."

"Phoebe, you should be checking on the rest of your family. Forget about trying to attack the Alphas."

"Communications are down. I can't get through to my family."

"You'll have to wait until you can. For now you are restricted to your barracks. Any military personnel caught off base will be killed on sight."

"So we save the Euclidians from extinction and they turn their backs on us. And all we can do is cower before those bastard Alphas."

"Phoebe, go to your quarters and cool off. There is nothing more you can do here."

"You mean there is nothing more you will let me do."

"Dismissed, Lieutenant Asten."

"As you wish, commander." Phoebe saluted the commander and went to her quarters. *I will make them pay. My brothers' deaths will be avenged.*

Phoebe would have to wait to seek revenge against the Alphas. Soon after the surrender, all Delta military personnel were imprisoned as war criminals. During Phoebe's five-year imprisonment, life on Delta changed drastically. The Alphas took control of all government and law enforcement activities. Delta citizens were relegated to subservient roles. Though business owners were allowed to keep their businesses, they were heavily taxed.

The Euclidian attack on the Alphas that destroyed their home planet pushed a lot of refugees to move to Delta. Deltas were imprisoned and killed in order to make room for the immigrating Alphas. Phoebe was happy to hear about the attack. Unfortunately, it did not make life any better for the Deltas.

When Phoebe was released, the only job she could get that suited her experience was as a bodyguard for wealthy businessmen. She attempted to join a resistance movement, but the Alpha's surveillance mechanisms made that all but impossible. She saved her money and quietly told people to wait for the revolution to come. "So many people cannot continue to bend to the will of so few."

One fateful day, Phoebe and a couple of colleagues were protecting a client when they were ambushed by hoodlums looking to make some quick dough. Everyone else in her group was killed and she found herself looking down the barrel of a gun held by the only surviving attacker. Before the assailant could pull the trigger, he was killed by a Euclidian resource ship captain who happened upon the scene.

It was Chaell Shisal. Phoebe owed him her life and now was unemployed, so she decided to become his bodyguard. It would get her off her occupied planet and hopefully make her some money that she could use toward the revolution she often thought of.

"Phoebe!" Chaell shouted. "Are you coming in the water or are you going to just stare into space?"

"Coming, Chaell." She pushed her thoughts of revolution to the back of her mind, stripped off her clothes, and jumped into the water.

CHAPTER 32

Yoyo Foils the Attack

"That command initiates a self-destruct mechanism," said Commander Filo.

Yoyo was frightened. She said, "Set it to destroy the shuttle in six minutes."

"This will kill us and destroy the Alpha ship," said Filo as he entered the command.

"It is a small price to pay to save the lives of millions of people."

Command accepted, said the computer. *The ship will self-destruct in six minutes.*

"Commander," said Yoyo, "is there anything you want to talk about for the last six minutes of your life?"

Filo's face was filled by fear. "I want you to stop this foolishness and let me finish my mission."

"I'm afraid I can't do that, Kenyon. We can be on a first name basis now that we are dying together, right?"

"I don't want to die. At least not now. Not like this."

"Trust me, this isn't the way I planned to go either. I was just starting to enjoy my job on the *Adele.* I thought my ambassador position was real. You just used me and my people to get back at the Euclidians."

The ship will self-destruct in five minutes.

"Please stop this madness. There is no reason to destroy the shuttle. You can just take us back to the ship and have me arrested."

"No one would believe me. As a high-ranking officer, you could have me killed for treason or some other made up offense then hatch your plan with some other unsuspecting Magi. Maybe you have a backup plan in place already, in case you were unable to get this shuttle."

"Then why bother blowing us up? Just have me land us on Euclidia or take you back to Tammaria."

"Because at least I will have two Alpha ships and a mastermind out of the way and unusable."

"Yoyo, listen to reason…"

The ship will self-destruct in four minutes.

"…I can make you very rich. I can make your people wealthy beyond your wildest dreams."

"That's the whole point, Kenyon. We don't dream of being rich or taking over the world or ever hurting anyone for personal gain."

"But won't your family miss you? What about the new team you're in charge of as ambassador?"

"Except for Jesmino, I don't know them very well. Jesmino is a bit odd but I will miss her. I wish I could say goodbye to her, but there are more important things to focus on right now."

"Why do you want to say goodbye to me?" asked Jesmino as she appeared on the shuttle out of nowhere.

The ship will self-destruct in three minutes.

"Why are you destroying the ship?" said Jesmino. "Won't that kill you?"

"Who are you and where did you come from?" asked Filo.

"I'm Jesmino. Don't you remember me?"

"You sound like her, but you look like a Euclidian," said Yoyo.

"Oh, I forgot," said Jesmino, and she changed back to her Magi form.

"Oh my goodness," said Yoyo. "How did you do that? And how did you get here?"

"How I change is hard to explain, but I told you I would keep in touch, so I monitored you via a few atoms that I placed in your brain. I heard my name mentioned so I came to see what you needed."

"But how did you get here?"

"At the subatomic level, one can be everywhere at once and I decided to be here."

"What is she talking about?" said Filo.

"I still don't know. She was babbling about that stuff the last time I saw her."

"Jesmino, can you disable the self-destruct mechanism?" asked Filo.

"I guess so, but I don't like to interfere."

"Jesmino, he's trying to use this ship to harm Euclidia, possibly killing millions of people, including Tammarians like my new friend Belo."

The ship will self-destruct in two minutes.

"That doesn't sound very nice."

A voice came from the communications console. "Commander Filo, this is Alpha ship *Lansing,* come in."

"Don't answer, Kenyon!" ordered Yoyo.

"Yoyo, don't do this," Filo begged, his face contorting. "Do you want to kill your friend and colleague Jesmino as well? I thought you liked her."

"Oh, don't worry about me. I will be a long way away from here before the blast occurs."

"Jesmino, can you take me with you?"

"Yes, but it's not an easy process."

"Commander Filo, this is Alpha ship *Lansing*. We are going to extend our cloaking mechanism to hide your ship. Please respond."

"What do you mean it's not easy?" said Yoyo. "Will it take more than two minutes?"

"No, it would be almost instantaneous. However, it will require me to compress the empty space between your atoms, making your body smaller that the width of an eyelash. Do you know how much empty space there is in an object? It's really amazing, considering how dense an object feels when you touch it. Even metal objects can be shrunk down to a fraction of their size."

The ship will self-destruct in one minute.

"Jesmino, there really isn't much time left. Do you think you could hurry this up?"

"Sure, but I should tell you about the side effects."

"Will I survive?" said Yoyo impatiently.

"Yes, of course. I wouldn't attempt it otherwise."

"What do you meant by attempt?"

"I've never really done it before. Theoretically, it should work."

"So do it now!"

"Okay, where do you want to go?"

The ship will self-destruct in ten seconds.

"Anywhere on my ship, now!"

"What about me?" said Filo.

"Leave him! Go! Now!"

"Okay!"

CHAPTER 33

Instant Molecular Redistribution

One of the most important advances of Euclidian scientific research resulted in the instant molecule redistribution (IMR) device. It impacted every aspect of daily life: sports, entertainment, construction, and military. Before its creation, people had to have multiple sizes of an object for various uses. Now they could have one item and resize it as needed.

The IMR device rearranged the molecules in an object in a way that changed its size. For example, Phoebe had one in her staff that permitted her to lengthen it for fighting or shrink it down to make it easier to carry around. The mass of the staff did not change, only its size.

Early versions of the device were impractical for most uses because of the heat generated by the process of molecular redistribution. Researchers later found that bombarding molecules with uni-polarized strings caused the bonds between molecules to dissipate without an appreciable increase in heat.

Once the process was perfected, tiny IMR devices were applied to a wealth of objects where dynamic expansion and retraction was desired. Dining room tables could be resized to accommodate various numbers of guests. Likewise plates could be resized to hold large or small amounts of food. The ability to modify the size of devices had a powerful impact on their utility, for example, a viewer could be used as a personal handheld device or stretched out and placed on a wall for viewing by many people.

The IMR device made doors, drawbridges, and lifts easier to deploy and use. A person who had trouble going up stairs could stand on an expanding platform to go to different levels in a house without using the space required for a ramp or elevator.

The application where the IMR device exhibited the greatest benefit was in repairing the hull of space vehicles. Space vehicles were often damaged by space debris. While a ship's shields helped to protect it from space debris, they were not perfect. Large objects or an attack by an enemy vessel could penetrate the shields and produce gaping holes in the hull.

The IMR device could seal hull breaches almost instantaneously by expanding the molecules in the metal to fill the breach. For that reason, hulls were manufactured at double the ordinary thickness in order to have extra material when needed. The hulls also contained several redundant IMR devices in case some were damaged during a breach.

Like many Euclidian products, IMR devices were protected by tamper proof construction methods and intelligent programming to prevent them from being used inappropriately. For example, only Phoebe could resize her staff. If it was already expanded and another person tried to use it, it would collapse and be unusable.

The IMR device was one example of how the Euclidian investment in research had made them a formidable military force. That investment also drove their exploitation of technology and the research being conducted on the planets that they invaded. The Alphas, to the contrary, focused on conquest and pillage, with very little thought of acquiring technology. Alphas often destroyed a planet just to chalk up another military victory and never investigate what new technology might be available.

CHAPTER 34

Yoyo Heads to Earth

"Jessmmmino, whyyyyy am I sooo coldddd? Where are we?"

"We are back on your ship as I promised you. I took you to your job, which is where I saw you most of the time. You are cold because of the decompression of your atoms back to their normal size. You are probably blind as well, but that will pass."

"Whattt isss the clapppping?"

"You are standing naked on the stage, shivering. The people here probably think you are performing."

"Why am I naked?"

"When I compressed your atoms each item was separated into distinct clumps. When you were reconstituted everything was expanded separately. You will be happy to know that your UCD survived the process as well."

"Can you put my clothes on me?"

"I don't have a way to do that mentally, and you are shivering too much for me to get you into your tight outfit. While you warm up I will take off my robe and do an exotic dance around you so people will think this is a real performance."

Jesmino removed her robe to expose a glittering costume like the one she had seen Yoyo wear. She began undulating around Yoyo to the cheers of the bar patrons.

"Jesmino, what's happening? There is more clapping and I can see blurs now."

"People are applauding our performance. I think I am doing quite well considering I have never done this before."

"I can see you now. Why aren't you naked and shivering?"

"Because I am not an organic being. Everything you see before you I generated from free atoms. I was created a millennium ago to serve a race of advanced beings. I became self-aware and learned to use the power of sub-atomic physics to travel the universe and experience different places. I traveled so much I lost my way back and decided to live amongst your people for a while."

"Wow, your story just gets more and more fascinating. Unfortunately, I don't have time to hear more right now, because we have a few problems to solve. First, what happened to the shuttle?"

"It was destroyed," said Jesmino as she danced around Yoyo, "along with the commander and his ship."

"That thing you did to me. Can you do that to the cloaked Alpha ships that are waiting to attack Euclidia?"

"I guess, though it will take me a moment to find them all. Do you want me to bring them all here?"

"No, just compress them where they are."

"Okay, I can do that."

"How long will it take you?"

"I'm finished. They are all tiny objects now."

"Will they ever return to normal size?"

"No, they will more than likely be caught in the gravitational field of a nearby planet and be burned up in its atmosphere without anyone ever knowing what happened to them."

"That means that no one will ever know what happened to Commander Filo either. I think I can move well enough to get my clothes on. You can stop that goofy dance now."

"I don't think the audience thought it was goofy. We should probably take a bow, don't you think?"

"Sure!"

The two held hands and bowed while the clients in the bar erupted in applause and laughter. Yoyo put her clothes on and exited the bar with Jesmino close behind.

"Jesmino, I need you to find out where the XO of the *Andrea* is."

"I don't know how to do that."

"Can't you find him the way you found me?"

"No, I never connected with him the way I did with you."

"Can't you just search for his atomic pattern or something?"

"Not really. There are infinite places to look and therefore it might take infinite time to find him."

"Yoyo, I need you to step away from your friend," said a security guard pointing a weapon at Jesmino.

"She works for me," replied Yoyo.

"It doesn't matter. She shouldn't be on the ship without permission. We can't even figure out how she got here."

"Sorry about that, Yoyo. I'll see you back on Euclidia." Jesmino disappeared.

"I apologize," Yoyo said to the guard. "I don't know how she does that. I'll make sure she doesn't do it again."

"Fine, Yoyo, but we will have to write this up. We can't have people just popping on and off our ship at will. That shouldn't even be possible. Why don't you come with us and answer some questions. We should be able to let you go after that."

Yoyo went to the security office and was interrogated. Once she was alone with just one officer, she persuaded him to forget about all the charges. Yoyo decided that she needed to find out where the XO of the *Andrea* was and then save Captain Shisal from him.

"Hello, lieutenant. You run the transport room here, right?" she asked an officer in one of the secondary transport rooms.

"I'm one of the people that run this particular transport room, but you shouldn't be here," replied the officer.

"How could you deny my sparkling blue eyes a little light conversation?"

"I guess a little conversation would be all right."

"Can you tell me where the XO or the captain of the *Andrea* is?"

"That's not really something I track. It's a completely different ship."

"Please try to find out, if you don't mind."

The officer consulted the ship's computer. "Well, the *Andrea* is away on a mission right now in the newly charted planetary system XAB1123. Getting more specifics will take some time."

"Look at me!" commanded Yoyo. "Your life depends on you getting the answer. Do what you must to get the answer, but get it right away. Do you understand?"

"Yes, Yoyo. I will get the answer you need."

Yoyo paced back and forth until he finally responded to her.

"I found them. The XO is aboard their ship above the second planet in their solar system. The captain's whereabouts seem to be unknown. There are indications that he might be dead. I have his last known coordinates, if that helps."

"Yes, send me there right away."

"I don't have the authority…"

Yoyo cut him off. "Do it!"

"Right away, Yoyo."

"Arghhh, what the hell is this place?" Yoyo screamed, covering her face with her hands and squatting to protect her body from the rays of the Florida sun. She grabbed her UCD and screamed at the transport operator to beam her directly to her cabin.

Yoyo grabbed her robe and goggles and ordered the transport officer to send her back. She got there in time to see a battle unfolding. She saw several species fighting each other and no one was wearing a uniform. There was only one Euclidian and she assumed that must be the captain. Not being a trained fighter, she could do nothing except watch the fight and hope for the best outcome.

CHAPTER 35

The U.S. Military Prepares to Fight

In a bunker deep below the White House, the president was conferring with those members of the military and intelligence community that were still available for duty.

"Where do we stand, gentlemen? I know your reports will be limited due to the lack of personnel and loss of standard communications, but tell me what you can. Let's start with the navy."

"We had some limited communications with ships using onboard radios that were stored in internal lockers. When the invasion started the aliens went after big targets, our carriers, destroyers, cruisers, and submarines. They just disappeared from the water without a trace. Reports from foreign navies indicate the same thing."

"After the ships were taken, what we assume are aliens set up several lines of airships stretched along the planet's longitudinal axis. There were hundreds of them in staggered formation, moving pretty fast. The airships proceeded westerly and almost every human being vanished beneath them. We believe that almost everyone who was below ground or underwater at the time was protected. Several of our reports come from divers who saw the craft go by. Our smaller ships seem to be intact but the personnel are gone. No lights or beams of any kind seemed to be emanating from the crafts. However, it seems clear that they are responsible for the disappearance of human life.

"Approximately ninety-nine percent of our land-based personnel are gone. We have two fully equipped submarines, now hidden in underwater caves. Two others attempted to engage an alien vessel that appeared to be harvesting our water from the Atlantic Ocean off the coast of Bermuda. Their missiles, torpedoes, and the submarines themselves vanished. Our current force now consists of the two hidden submarines and a couple thousand sailors and marines spread out across the globe."

"Thank you, Admiral Bruckheimer. General Gannon, give us a report on the Air Force."

"Mr. President, I don't have much to report. All of our radar, missile, and satellite systems are basically dead. Our aircraft are gone. We are communicating with surviving airmen via battery-powered radios. We detected an anomaly beyond the moon just before our systems went out. It must have been the alien ship. Unfortunately it moved too quickly for us to respond. Soon afterward, our nuclear missiles vanished, then our aircraft and support equipment. We have about five hundred airmen left, most of them hiding out in bunkers. We lost seven stealth fighters, which had been stored in an underground bunker, during an attack on one of the alien ships over D.C. We never even got a shot off. We have three more in bunkers, but for now we don't dare use them. That's all I have to report, Mr. President."

"General Passman, what is the condition of the army?"

"Mr. President, I also have very little to report. Our armored vehicles have been taken. I'm only in contact with about eighty-five soldiers. We have tons of hand weapons, but no one to use them, and they probably wouldn't be effective against the aliens."

"Is anyone aware of any alien forces on the ground?"

"I have one bit of news, Mr. President," said Mathers, the CIA Director.

"Yes, Director Mathers."

"We have a field agent in Miami that has been working with a militia in south Florida. It appears that humanoid aliens have set up a base in Key West. It doesn't seem to be a military base, although armed personnel are patrolling the perimeter. The other aliens appear to be on vacation.

"It appears that humans are no longer disappearing. The aliens now seem to be focused on industrial goods and natural resources. I believe we have almost no chance of getting through their defenses. Our only viable option may be to try to end their mining of Earth's resources."

"What do we know about their mining vehicles?" asked the president.

"The ships are massive, they move pretty slowly, and they don't seem to have offensive or defensive capabilities. They ignore what have so far been futile attacks, mostly by civilians using hand weapons. The mining ships are protected by airships that eventually respond against attackers."

"Okay, gentlemen. I need more information if we are going to a successfully attack these aliens. Find out what you can about their camp in Key West. Talk to anyone that has survived an attempt to take out a mining vessel. I want updates from any foreign military you can contact. If underground vehicles have been left intact, let's find some and start scouring the country for intel. You have your orders. We need answers and we need them now! Let's move, gentlemen."

"Yes, Mr. President," they all responded.

CHAPTER 36

The Hunting of Chaell

Malcolm watched as Phoebe and Chaell glided into the warm waters of the gulf. The salty water was distasteful to Chaell as it stung his eyes. Still he enjoyed the quiet of the water. He floated on the surface and enjoyed the heat of the sun. Phoebe enjoyed the salty taste of the water as it reminded her of the waters around Arubia where she grew up. While Chaell remained on the surface, Phoebe dived to the seafloor to investigate the sea life and rock formations.

In a playful mood, Phoebe swam at Chaell and dragged him under. They wrestled and chased each other under water. Chaell forgot about the stinging salt and Phoebe forgot about the troubles on her home planet. She led him to the sea floor where Chaell pinned her to a rock outcropping. He nibbled on her neck and when she didn't resist he grabbed her hips and pulled her close. She let out a burst of bubbles from her open mouth, pushed him away, and swam for the surface.

Two guards watched over them and their belongings. Malcolm felt he could easily take them out. He had a metal bag that would block UCD signals, and a jammer for signals from UCDs not in his bag. Malcolm cloaked himself and turned on the jammer. He put his UCD in the bag then collected Phoebe's and Chaell's UCDs and put them in the bag. He took their weapons and then ran at his prey. He held a short sword, taken from a local museum, low behind him. He approached the first guard and swung his sword to decapitate him. He jumped at the second guard who was startled by his colleague's demise. Malcolm sliced diagonally through his body, leaving him in a bloody bifurcated heap. He put their UCDs in his bag and dragged the carcasses behind the nearby cabana and into a dumpster.

Still invisible, Malcolm returned to the beach and sat next to a tree to wait for Phoebe and Chaell to exit the water.

***

"Phoebe, where are the guards?" asked Chaell.

"They're dead, like you two are going to be real soon," said Malcolm as he came into view.

Phoebe grabbed her clothes and looked around for her UCD and weapon.

"They're gone, Phoebe. You won't be calling for reinforcements or blasting me. I did leave your staff so you won't be completely defenseless."

"Why don't you just shoot us?"

"I'm not a coward. I'm going to kill you the old fashioned way. I'm going to give you a good beat down and end it by chopping off your head." Malcolm vanished.

"Chaell, take cover in the trees. Duck!" screamed Phoebe as she blocked a blow from Malcolm's sword. She squeezed the center of her staff to extend it to full size.

Malcolm carried the medieval battle sword so that metal fragments left behind could not be traced to him or cause suspicion that the attack came from the *Andrea*. Malcolm was cloaked, but Phoebe could sense him. She fought him off as Chaell took refuge in the trees.

Phoebe and Malcolm locked weapons. He leaned into her and uncloaked. "You are going to pay for humiliating me in front of my people. I'm going to defeat you, decapitate you, and then kill your captain."

"Big plans for such a little man," Phoebe said, looking down sideways at Malcolm. "Now that you've lived a miserable life, I'm going to see to it that you die a horrible death."

They pushed away from each other and continued the fight. Malcolm leaped into the air and came down swinging his sword with great ferocity. Phoebe fended off the attack and countered. Malcolm blocked her and kicked her to the ground. As he went to take advantage of her fall, a small person in a tight pink outfit appeared in front of him.

"What is this?" Malcolm screamed angrily, annoyed that this person was blocking his attack on Phoebe. He swung his sword, but the person disappeared before he could land a blow.

"Die, Malcolm!" shouted Phoebe as she landed a blow to the side of his head and knocked him to the ground.

Malcolm was stunned, but that wasn't good enough for Phoebe. She lunged at him to crush his head. Malcolm managed to block her blow with his sword but Phoebe leaned down on him, exerting increased pressure on his sword.

"Malcolm, I should've killed you the first time we fought. I'm going to fix that mistake right now."

Phoebe leapt back and swung her staff. Malcolm blocked her blows and tried to get to his feet. He found an opening and swung his sword at her thigh, but Phoebe was too quick and she knocked his sword from his hand. She lifted her staff above her head and hesitated.

Malcolm didn't understand what happened, but took the opportunity to grab his sword and stab her in the abdomen. Phoebe looked at him in disbelief as she was impaled on his sword. He kicked her off his sword and to the ground.

Malcolm raised his sword over his head. "Now I take my prize by separating your head from your body,"

***

"Look!" screamed Morgan. "It's the assassin!"

Li Xiao jumped in front of Morgan and Pico to block them from Uan with her sword. "I thought we had a deal, Uan."

"Relax. I am not here for your friends. I am here to see you."

"You know him, Xiao?" asked Morgan in an accusatory tone.

"Yes, we met at the ship's ball and I challenged him to a battle in the arena to save you two."

"A battle you will lose. Then I will finish what I started by killing these annoying pests."

"And we'll be waiting to put you in your place like we always do," said Morgan, and Pico gave a silent thumbs up.

Denise stepped in front of Uan, angry and afraid. "Was it you that killed my brother?"

"I certainly may have. I have killed quite a few people since I have been here," said Uan without emotion.

"He was a patient in the hospital. He was no threat to you. You seem to feel comfortable killing for no good reason."

"Oh, him. It was unintentional. He just got in the way."

Denise raised her voice and leaned into Uan. "Got in the way? Well, I want an apology."

"Now you are getting in my way. I will not apologize, but I will give you a spear to the chest if you do not move. I will not apologize for that, either."

"Denise, we can't win this," said Li Xiao, pulling her away from Uan. "Getting killed is not going to bring your brother back or help us out of this situation."

"Okay, but this isn't over. Somehow I will find a way to get back at you."

"We shall see. For now I have important business to discuss with Li Xiao. Can we talk privately?" Uan motioned for Li Xiao to step to the side of the room.

Xiao left Denise's side and walked to the kitchen with Uan and Calvin.

"Who is that strange looking guy?" asked Norma.

"He's the assassin that came from the alien ship to kill Pico," said Morgan.

"What on Earth for?"

"They were afraid that Pico would warn Earth or use his powers to stop the invasion."

"So why didn't he warn Earth or stop the invasion?"

"He didn't know if they were really coming and had no evidence to prove their existence. Pico may be able to lift people off the ground or heal them of disease, but he can't destroy a spaceship."

***

"Cobalt tells me you might know where Captain Shisal is," said Uan.

"Sure, but why don't you just contact him on his UCD?" said Xiao.

"We have been unable to. It appears he has gone missing and now the XO has taken over the ship. Cobalt believes that the captain has been captured or killed by people helping the XO."

"I knew that the XO had taken over the ship, but I didn't know he was responsible for the captain's demise. I did place a waypoint on him. I wonder if it works if the person is dead."

"Let us hope that he is not dead. The XO might not stop at killing the captain."

Xiao pulled out her transport device and looked up the captain's waypoint. "Here he is." Xiao showed the device to Uan. "He's standing behind some trees, watching something."

Uan grabbed the device from her hands. "We need to see what he is looking at." Uan stretched the device to about 30 centimeters across.

"Oh my goodness. I totally didn't know you could do that," exclaimed Xiao.

Uan just looked at her and shrugged, then adjusted the view on the device.

"Look, Malcolm is fighting with Phoebe. The XO must have ordered this attack. I need to get down there to help her. Take me there and then bring the captain here."

Uan shrank the transport device to normal size and handed it to Xiao.

"Calvin," he said, "tell the others what we are planning. Help out as you can. The XO may have more people out to kill the captain."

Xiao grabbed Uan's hand and they disappeared.

Calvin returned from the kitchen and spoke to the others. "Listen up. The captain of the alien ship and his bodyguard are being attacked by some people sent by the ship's XO. Uan and Li Xiao have gone to save them. They should be back soon with the captain."

"You mean the alien captain of the ship that is attacking Earth is coming here?" Morgan asked excitedly.

"Yes, but he's not that bad a guy. I mean, he is big and scary looking, but he normally doesn't kill people without provocation."

"Oh, that makes me feel real comfortable," said Norma. "So what kinds of things provoke this guy?"

"Things like not following orders, failing at training, or not finishing your work."

"Almost anything then," said Denise with a look of concern. "Is this really the kind of person we want here?"

"I guess I understand your trepidation. At this point, though, I'm not sure how we could throw him out."

"Great," said Norma. "We've got an alien Attila the Hun coming to stay with us and no way to protect ourselves against him. I wonder who is going to get the master bedroom?"

***

Xiao and Uan arrived at the beach in the midst of Phoebe's battle with Malcolm. Xiao gasped as Phoebe leaned backward just in time to dodge Malcolm's sword.

"Captain," shouted Uan, "I'm here with Li Xiao, the Earth woman who just joined our crew. She is going to use her Beam Machine to take you to safety."

"I don't want to leave Phoebe."

"Captain, it's more important that we keep you safe. You've been betrayed. The XO has taken over the ship. I'll stay and help Phoebe. As soon as we take care of Malcolm we'll join you and figure out how to get you back in charge of the *Andrea*. Go with Li Xiao!"

"Phoebe's been stabbed! What the hell is going on here?"

"Li Xiao will explain once she takes you to safety. I need to go."
Uan leaped into battle. Li Xiao grabbed Shisal's arm and they
transported away.

***

"Is this what it's come to, brother?" said Uan, walking up to
Malcolm as he was about to decapitate Phoebe. "Where is the honor in
this?"

"Hello, brother," said Malcolm. "I'm about to get my honor back
after she took it during our last fight."

"What does that have to do with killing the captain?"

"He is no longer the captain. He has been declared a traitor. I'm
just here to pass justice on him. Don't you think that's the honorable
thing to do?"

"You know what I think, Malcolm. There is one too many Ossies
on this planet." Uan swung his sword.

***

Moments after Li Xiao had left, she returned with Chaell Shisal at
her side.

"Oh my goodness," exclaimed Norma, looking up at the imposing
figure of the extraterrestrial in front of her. The scent of ginger from
his skin filled her nostrils. Everyone in the room was wide-eyed, open-
mouthed, and panicked except for Calvin who had already met the
man.

"*Stowtan char,*" said Calvin, hoping to help break the tension in the
room.

"*Stowtan bitar, Calvin,*" responded Chaell, which did not do much
to ease the tension in the room. As a matter of fact, Denise fainted.

Wow, he remembered my name, thought Calvin.

"I mean you no harm," said Shisal in Euclidian, holding up his hand in a gesture of calm. *"I am Chaell."* He extended his hand to Norma.

Norma reluctantly shook his hand. "Did he just ask me to chill?"

"No," said Li Xiao, "he said 'I mean you no harm, my name is Chill'."

Norma pointed to herself and said, "I'm Norma."

Morgan held out his hand. "I'm Morgan. This is Pico." Pico waved.

"You are the one that got away. You will have to tell me that story one day," said Chaell.

"I would be happy to, as long as you don't kill me," Pico replied telepathically.

Chaell laughed out loud, which helped everyone relax.

"What's so funny?" said Denise as she came to.

Chaell held out his hand to her. *"Hi, I'm Chaell."*

Containing her fear, she shook his hand. "Denise."

"Li Xiao, we should monitor the battle to see how Phoebe is doing," said Chaell.

"Sah char." Xiao expanded her Beam Machine and set it on the coffee table.

Everyone gathered around the device, mesmerized by what they saw. Uan and Malcolm were in heavy battle while Phoebe lay on the ground in pain. No one knew how the outcome of the fight would impact them. The person responsible for attacking Earth was now seeking refuge with them, while the person who wanted to kill Morgan and Pico was fighting to protect another alien who had been stabbed. It was so much to take in. The Earthlings felt like they had been dragged into a weird science fiction movie.

"Morgan", whispered Denise, "do you think Pico could incapacitate that alien?"

"Why would we want to do that?"

"Maybe if we turned him in they would let some of our people go."

"Pico says they wouldn't care. He says it's more likely that the assassin would come back and kill us all. But if this guy gets his ship back, he might help us."

"I'll have to trust Pico."

"What are you two whispering about?" asked Norma.

"We're trying to figure out who we should be helping here. It appears this guy is our best hope."

"I'm sure if he wanted to kill us we would be dead already. Let's just hope he doesn't decide to take us with him if he ever gets his ship back."

The two Ossies battled to the death as Chaell looked on from Morgan's living room.

Calvin used his UCD to contract Betty and Dominique on the *Andrea*, "I need you to come and help me down here on Earth. I'll explain when you get here. I'm sending you my coordinates now."

"We don't quite know what's going on, but we are one hundred percent behind you," said Dominique.

"Ditto," said Betty. "See you soon."

Moments later, Dominique and Betty transported next to Calvin.

"Calvin, what's going on?" asked Dominique.

"The captain was framed as a traitor and the XO took over the ship."

"Yeah, we heard."

Chaell looked up from the monitor. *"Thanks for coming."*

"Oh my goodness," said Betty, startled by Chaell's presence. "*Stowtan char.*"

"*Stowtan char,*" added Dominique.

"*Stowtan bitar,*" replied Chaell. "*I appreciate your support.*"

Chaell turned his attention back to the screen to watch with the others as Uan and Malcolm continued to fight.

"Li Xiao," said Denise, "if you can bring Phoebe here, Pico and I might be able to save her."

"It's too dangerous right now. If they move away from her, I can get to her without being harmed myself."

"Look! Malcolm's down," shouted Morgan. "Maybe Uan will defeat him."

"What just happened?" asked Calvin excitedly. Uan had fallen to the ground for no apparent reason.

Chaell moved his fingers across the screen and zoomed out the view to reveal an Alpha with a rifle, hiding behind a rock formation.

"I'll get him," said Li Xiao.

"Then who will save Uan and Phoebe?" asked Calvin.

"I can't do both," said Li Xiao.

"Drop me off with the ugly guy," said Calvin, "and you save Uan and Phoebe. Let's move. We don't have time argue. Uan can't hold off Malcolm much longer, wounded the way he is."

Li Xiao gave Calvin her sword and they transported. She dropped him on top of the Alpha then popped over to help Uan.

"Hey, you!" Li Xiao ran at Malcolm, throwing darts at him as she came. A couple of them pierced his skin, which distracted him from Uan. He cloaked and went after Li Xiao but she also disappeared. She reappeared next to Phoebe and beamed her back to the house.

"Denise!" yelled Xiao. "Do what you can to save her. I'm going back for Uan."

"Morgan," said Denise, "help me get her into the guest room. Pico, come with us."

Li Xiao returned for Uan. As she stepped on top of him so that with the contact she could transport him to Morgan's place, Malcolm uncloaked next to them.

***

The Alpha was stunned by Calvin dropping on his head. He lost his rifle, but felt he could take out an Earthling. He jumped to his feet and came at Calvin.

"Come on, buddy," said Calvin. "I want to show you something the guy you shot taught me." He pulled Li Xiao's sword from behind his back and thrust it into the Alpha's chest. Calvin pulled it out, spun to the right, and sliced through his neck.

The Alpha staggered backward. Calvin said, "I guess you won't be shooting anybody else from behind rocks, will you?" The Alpha just looked at Calvin perplexed, not understanding what he was saying. Moments later he was dead, face down on the ground. Calvin looked back to see how Li Xiao was doing with Malcolm.

Where did everyone go? thought Calvin. He saw no one except Uan, who was lying on his back. "Yes!" exclaimed Calvin as Li Xiao appeared on top of Uan with her transport device in her hands. Then he watched in horror as Malcolm appeared above her. He drove his sword through her back and into Uan's chest as the pair disappeared.

Calvin covered his mouth and fell to his knees in despair. "No!"

***

Out of view from the others, another Alpha with a rifle appeared in the trees. As he trained the rifle on Uan he heard a noise behind him, and swung around to see what it was.

"Don't shoot," said Yoyo, lowering her goggles. "I'm a friend."

"Okay, friend. Why are you here?"

"I'm here to stop you from killing the captain of the Euclidian ship that's in space above this planet. Can you explain the fighting that's going on here?"

"Malcolm is the Ossie standing up. He's fighting Uan, the other Ossie. Malcolm is here to kill the captain." The Alpha pointed at Li Xiao. "I don't know who that person is."

"Where is the captain?"

"I don't know."

"I want you to kill Malcolm," said Yoyo. "Oh no! I think he just killed the two others. Okay. Use your weapon to kill Malcolm. Wait, the other two have disappeared. Find out their coordinates. Now Malcolm is gone."

"I'll try. Transporter room, can you send me Uan's coordinates?" The Alpha showed Yoyo his UCD. "Here they are."

"Thanks, I have them. Now I want you to kill yourself."

The Alpha fired his rifle just as Yoyo had her transport room officer beam her to Uan's coordinates.

***

Li Xiao and Uan returned to the house. "They're hurt!" said Betty. "Denise, we have two more casualties for you to look at."

"Put them in Xiao's room," said Denise. "We'll be finished with Phoebe in a minute."

"Who is that?" screamed Norma as a small hooded figure wearing goggles appeared in the room.

"*I'm a friend,*" Yoyo said in Euclidian "*You must be the captain. I have come to help save you from the Alphas who are killing all the ship captains that were responsible for attacking their planet.*"

"*Welcome,*" said Chaell.

Betty translated for the others as best she could. "I believe she said that she is a friend who came to help save the captain."

***

"Captain, this is Malcolm. Can you find the coordinates of Uan and beam me there? I have reason to believe he is with Shisal."

"Sure, Malcolm. I'll have the transport room take care of that. You should be there momentarily."

A few seconds later, Malcolm was standing in Morgan's house. Morgan, Pico, and Denise walked out of the guest room and stopped in their tracks at the sight of Malcolm. Pico gestured at Malcolm and began to raise his arms.

"No you don't!" said Malcolm. He rushed the group and knocked them to the floor then turned to face Chaell. "Now it's your turn to die." Malcolm lifted his sword above his head and cloaked as he ran at the captain.

ACKNOWLEDGEMENTS

Firstly, I would like to thank my wife Renee for her support and patience as I wrote this book. My son, Davon, who runs http://FamilyLobby.com, continues to prominently assist me in the creation of my book. A special thanks to Derek Canyon at http://derekjcanyon.blogspot.com/ who gave me a lot of guidance on how to publish and where to get additional assistance. I would also like to thank Qiaolin Mao for assisting me with the marketing of my book. Thanks to Chris Bennett and Evette Sharps Tripp for reviewing my book.

Lastly, I would like to thank my family, friends, and colleagues for their inspiration for the contents of this book.

www.ingramcontent.com/pod-product-compliance
Lightning Source LLC
Chambersburg PA
CBHW071253170626
46809CB00001B/205